ADVANCE PRAISE FOR *FACTOR MAN*

"*Factor Man* gives us a hero for our times: a tech genius with common sense and a commitment to social responsibility. An original, smart thriller that stretches your imagination and keeps you engaged to the end."
—AMY ROGERS, author of *Petroplague*

"Ben Stiller should play me in the movie!"
—ROBERT HASDAY, Partner, Duane Morris LLP

"A fantastic job of taking us on a ride featuring engaging characters, exciting action and deep-thinking heroes and villains of a type all too rare in the genre. I greatly enjoyed this book."
—BART MASSEY, Associate Professor of Computer Science, Portland State University

"A real page-turner, thanks to the characters, plot twists and humor. Even though I'm nicer than the guy in the book, I still loved it."
—BRIAN FINN, ex-president of Credit Suisse

"A classy and clever thriller best read with your phone off and your brain on."
—MARK BLACKABY, author of *You'll Never Be Here Again*

FACTOR MAN

MATT GINSBERG

FACTOR MAN. Copyright ©2017 by Matthew Ginsberg LLC. All rights reserved. First edition, 2018

Published by Zowie Press, 29585 Fox Hollow Road, Eugene, OR 97405

Library of Congress Control Number 2017918091

FIC028020 FICTION / Science Fiction / Hard Science Fiction
FIC036000 FICTION / Thrillers / Technological

ISBN 978-0-9997571-0-9 (hardcover)
ISBN 978-0-9997571-1-6 (trade paperback)
ISBN 978-0-9997571-2-3 (ebook)

Cover design by The Book Designers (www.BookDesigners.com)

To my wife, the computer scientist
And to my kids, who always liked stories like this one

Prologue

In the four years since appearing on the Internet, the individual known as Factor Man has reached out to exactly five human beings. In spite of this minimal contact, he (or she) is now one of the best known, richest and most powerful men (or women) on the planet.

Of those lucky five, all but one are now ridiculously famous. There is the New York lawyer, Robert Hasday. Concierge services for Factor Man are provided by the social organizer Jess MacMurray, known to the world as Pepper Potts. No one knows the name of the member of the hacking group Anonymous who has worked with Factor Man, but everyone knows what that hacker did. And there is the reporter William Burkett, who has very mixed feelings about all of it.

The fifth person is not so famous. He's a banker named Brian Finn. The fifty-something retired ex-president of Credit Suisse. Balding. Overweight in spite of his best efforts not to be. An extremely good guy, as far as I can tell.

Finn and I met over coffee about six months ago. I have no idea if I was followed or not. Sometimes I'm followed, sometimes I'm not followed. I don't really care either way any more.

Finn gave me an envelope, and then we talked about Finn's role in the leveraged buyout of RJR Nabisco in the 1980's. I wrote a story comparing the buyout frenzy of the 1980's to the Internet bubble of today, and no one seemed to realize that my meeting with Finn wasn't about the 1980's at all.

It was all about the envelope. Inside was the story of Finn's interaction with Factor Man. Brian told me it was okay to write about it, provided that no one learned of his involvement until the day before FCOP. Factor Man's instructions, he said. I agreed to not even look at it until a week before FCOP.

Finn isn't Factor Man. He doesn't have the background. I don't think Finn even knows who Factor Man is. He might, though.

But it doesn't matter. Tomorrow, we'll all know. FCOP. Pronounced Eff-COP. The Factor Man Coming Out Party. And Brian Finn is going to be one rich son of a bitch.

My name is William Burkett, and I'm the reporter. People claiming to be my friends call me Wilbur. Orville would be worse, I suppose.

This is the story of the last four years. And if we hadn't all lived through it together, no one would believe a word of it.

1

FACTOR MAN
MAY 12, 2017

Werner Heisenberg was a physicist born just as the nineteenth century ushered in the twentieth. He made such significant contributions to physics that he won the 1932 Nobel Prize for creating the field of quantum mechanics. He had an uncertainty principle named after him. He figured out how stars worked.

This last contribution has always struck a personal chord with me. Rumor has it that some time shortly after Heisenberg figured this out, a friend commented to him one evening how beautiful the stars were. "They are," Heisenberg is said to have replied. "And I'm the only person in the world who knows why they look that way."

I stared at my computer screen. This was my Heisenberg moment, I figured.

My computer had two windows open. In one, numbers streamed by slowly. In the other, an email waited to be sent. Twenty-one words that might change the world. All I had to do was click on send.

But once those twenty-one words were out there, I could never get them back. So before clicking send, I thought about it.

I thought about the science.

I thought about Denise, down at the barn working with the horses. Even after many years of marriage, they would always be her first love. If the email changed my life, it would change hers with it.

I thought about our kids, no longer living at home and beginning to make their own way in the world. If I sent the message, they would be making their ways in a different world than they had explored yesterday.

I thought about my plan. I wondered if my family and I would be safe. I wondered if I would indeed manage to deflect at least the worst of the disruption to which my technology might lead.

And I thought about Heisenberg. About knowing something that only you know, and that you know will change the world in ways you cannot predict. It took a generation for quantum mechanics to beget nuclear weapons, and longer still for the science to lead to a new and clean – albeit dangerous – energy source. My discovery, I suspected, would have as great and as unpredictable an impact, but far more quickly.

I thought about science, and the ethics of science. We scientists just do what we do, and somehow trust that the things we discover will be used more for good than otherwise. It's never been clear that such optimism is justified, and no one ever gave us the moral authority to unleash our personal progress on the rest of the world. But we're scientists. We do what we do.

I thought about Denise, and the kids, and the unknown consequences.

I thought about the plan.

I thought about Heisenberg.

I thought about science.

I hit send.

Burkett
May 12, 2017

I was relaxing, smoking a cigarette, and feeling pretty good about myself. Yeah, yeah, I know. Smoking is bad for you. Hopefully, I'll manage to quit before it kills me.

On this particular night, though, I wasn't worrying about it. An article I had written a few months previously with a statistical analysis of Donald Trump's tweets had gotten a ridiculous amount of traction. I'd heard that afternoon that it had been selected as a finalist for an annual prize regarding Best Use of Data in a Breaking News Story.

This is the kind of thing I do. From late 2016 until now, I've been a reporter for the *New York Times*. I owe my job to Nate Silver, who runs a website called fivethirtyeight.com. 538 presents news (and sometimes predictions) based on statistics. Nate started his life as a quantitative analyst doing sports statistics, and applied the same techniques to predict who would prevail in various political contests. For example, he called every state correctly in Barack Obama's presidential victories in 2008 and 2012. He's basically gotten everything right since then, too, except for the Donald Trump thing. No one saw that coming, although Nate was closer than most.

Anyway, Nate got famous and the website, which was owned by the *New York Times* during the 2012 election cycle, was responsible for something like a sixth of *all* the nytimes.com traffic. When Nate switched to ESPN before the 2016 election, the *Times* decided they needed to replace him with a statistics group of their own. They hired a bunch of young hotshots, and I was one of them.

On that night in May of 2017, I was twenty-eight years old, with a new Ph.D. in statistical economics from the University of Texas at Austin. I loved my job, which was to use statistics to figure out cool stuff. Predict who was going to win the world chess championship. (Yes, humans still played chess.) Analyze the words in Donald Trump's tweets and show that they bore more resemblance to the rhetoric of the alt-right than to any form of rational discourse. The *Times* gave me a great deal of slack on the writing side, allowing me to duplicate the informal style that Nate used at 538.com. Unusual for a major news outlet, but totally fine with me.

I lived in Brooklyn, in a two-bedroom apartment that's a third floor walkup. I don't have to tell you this; I still live there and you've seen the apartment on TV and the Internet. Reporting may be the best job in the world, but the pay is only modest. Maybe I'll try to negotiate a better deal for myself after FCOP – the Factor Man Coming Out Party – is over. Until then, though, I've got enough to worry about.

Nowadays, I miss my privacy. Smoking that cigarette and relaxing on a Friday night in May four years ago, I didn't even have a Wikipedia page. I was just getting started at the *Times*. A bunch of folks in ridiculously small circles knew who I was, and that was about it.

That was all just fine with me. As a kid, my heroes had been Batman and Robin, folks cool enough to appear in comic books and with attitude to boot. By 2017, I looked up to Carl Bernstein and Bob Woodward, the reporters who broke the Watergate story. Reporting can be quite a noble enterprise, and my interest in the truth dwarfed my interest in fame or fortune. It wasn't even clear to me that I had any real interest in fame or fortune.

I remember it was raining. An early summer thunderstorm in New York City, around midnight. I stubbed out my cigarette and went to check my email. Six messages.

```
From: tdalton@nytimes.com        you didn't win but great job
From: KBURKETTJR@aol.com         Mom had a great time
From: factorman0@gmail.com       returned favor
From: trindell@wisconsin.edu     rerunning those numbers
From: kate@bedandbreakfast.com   best deals of the year
From: emmabhardaway@gmail.com    can't make it - sorry!
```

You see it right away, of course. But all I saw was that it was Friday night, and Emma had just blown me off for Saturday. Well, sometimes life is like that.

So I went to bed.

* * *

Saturday mornings, I play basketball. I pretty much suck, but so do all the other guys. We meet at eight because that's when we can get the gym, play until around ten, and then have coffee.

Eight o'clock is pretty early, but coffee can go on for hours. I tell you all of this only so that you understand why it was a little after one on Saturday afternoon when I got back to my email.

Factor Man would eventually reach out to five of us, of whom four would become known to the public. Finn was the lucky one. The Favored Four, they call the rest of us, although it's not clear to me how favorable it is to live under this ridiculous microscope. For better or worse, I was the favored first.

```
From: factorman0@gmail.com
To: wburkett@nytimes.com
Subject: returned favor

Mr. Burkett:

You did me a kindness once, and I'm returning it.

factorman0.blogspot.com
```

The story is yours, and yours alone, for forty-eight hours.

FM

I checked the time at which the message had been sent. Fourteen of those hours were already gone.

Next, I did what you would have done. In fact, I did what pretty much everyone has already done. I visited the Factor Man web site.

I have a fast method for factoring large numbers. This is a problem, because it breaks public key encryption. And if I figured it out, so will someone else eventually. It's not really viable to simply keep it secret.

To make matters worse, or perhaps better, the method works by converting number factoring problems to Boolean satisfiability and then invoking what appears to be a polytime SAT solver on them.

At some level, this is good. A polytime SAT solver is, in the long term, only promise. We will cure more diseases, and be healthier. We will be more efficient, and better able to get resources to those of us who need them the most. We will be more able to cope with a huge range of problems, not the least of which is global warming.

In the short term, however, a polytime SAT solver is only peril. There will be no more unbreakable codes. And in a world that has become increasingly dependent on them, that means there will be no more secrets.

My hope in this blog is to deal with this issue, to help us collectively achieve the promise while avoiding at least some of the peril. To that end, I will be embarking on a program that involves two separate phases.

The first is demonstration. I need to show the world that I can indeed do what I say I can do.

The second is distribution. I need to make the technology available to everyone.

For the first phase, I will simply factor large numbers in public. The way this works is as follows. If you want a number factored, send that number in an email to factorman0@gmail.com. I will select five numbers each day and respond in this blog (factorman0.blogspot.com) with the factorizations.

But there are some rules.

1.   The numbers must be of a size I specify. Currently the numbers must all be at most 5 bits in size. Hardly a challenge! But every three days, I will permit the numbers to be one bit larger.

2.   When you request that a number be factored, you must include legitimate identifying information for yourself. Only one number per person per day, please.

3.   All of the numbers to be factored must be the product of two primes.

My hope here is that as time passes, recognizable public figures will ask for ever larger numbers to be factored, allowing folks to understand that I can indeed do what I say I can do.

I will be factoring 64-bit numbers on November 11, 2017.

I will be factoring 128-bit numbers on May 22, 2018.

I will be factoring 255-bit numbers on June 10, 2019.

By 2019, I expect that anyone relying on public key encryption will have found another way to protect their data. I encourage people relying on public key encryption to switch to at least a 256-bit encoding scheme as rapidly as possible. I will not factor 256-bit numbers in public.

After the demonstration phase is complete, I will move forward with distribution. This will work as follows:

On June 10, 2019, I will begin accepting bids for a license to use the technology. The license will be perpetual and will be exclusive for one year. Bids will not be accepted from entities whose goals conflict with the goals of the government or citizens of the United States of America.

On July 10, 2019, I will provide the technology to the highest bidder and announce that bidder's identity.

On July 10, 2020, I will provide the technology to the government of the United States.

On July 10, 2021, I will make the technology publicly available and will reveal my identity as well.

It is my intention to deal relatively harshly with any attempts to interfere with this overall plan by, for example, attempting to bring down this blog or my email address, or attempting to discover my identity before I choose to reveal it. I remind anyone considering doing these things that no corner of the Internet is beyond my reach.

If you would like a 5-bit number factored, please send me an email with both the number in question and your true identity.

And until July 10, 2021, I will simply paraphrase the immortal Tony Stark: I am Factor Man.

The now-famous counter was at the bottom, showing the number of visits the page had received. That counter, as is well known, now shows something in excess of 350 *billion* visits to the Factor Man web page. When I looked at it that morning, it said, "1".

Back then, of course, I didn't really know what most of that stuff meant. But I had a friend who did.

* * *

Every year in March, I go to the American Crossword Puzzle Tournament, or the ACPT as the participants call it.

This may strike you as a fate worse than death. But it isn't. Believe it or not, it's fun.

The tournament is run by Will Shortz, the crossword editor for the *Times*. Held in Stamford, Connecticut, it's attended by about six hundred of the best crossword solvers in America. The 2005 tournament was the subject of a documentary called *Wordplay*.

The event is fun in a couple of ways. First, it's exciting. After solving seven puzzles shared by all six hundred contestants, the top three finishers get up on stage and solve one last, brutal puzzle while everyone else watches. Whoever finishes that puzzle first wins, assuming they don't make a mistake. The finalists (wearing headphones and with their backs to the audience so that they can't hear the raucous commentary going on behind them) announce that they're finished by raising their hands.

In 2015 Dan Feyer, who had won the previous five contests, finished first. But rather than raise his hand, he decided to check his work. The next contestant to his right, Tyler Hinman, had won for the five years before Feyer started winning. In the five years Feyer had won, Hinman had generally been second.

Hinman was working frantically to finish. Knowing that Feyer was fast, Hinman had decided to raise his hand the moment his puzzle was done.

Feyer was checking. Hinman was writing. Feyer's puzzle was perfect, but he didn't know it. Hinman's was also perfect thus far.

Finally, one of them raised his hand.

Hinman's hand went up half a second later, and the audience exploded. Feyer's streak continued, although it would be broken by Howard Barkin the next year.

The real reason I look forward to the ACPT, though, is the people. Part of what I cover for the *Times* is high-level mental sporting events. The world's best chess players, or bridge players, or what have you, are generally not a lot of fun to be around. Their self-images are too wrapped up in the games at which they excel.

But crossword solvers are somehow different. They all have day jobs. (The ACPT grand prize is only $5000, so they have to.) Feyer is a musician; Hinman is a computer programmer. The contestants include lawyers, authors, reporters like me, and Hollywood directors like Patrick Creadon, who directed *Wordplay*. It's an amazingly eclectic group.

And everyone is there to have fun. With the self-images mostly out of it, everyone wants everyone else to do well. Everyone wants everyone else to improve on their scores from the previous year. The only perennial villain is "Dr.Fill", a crossword-solving computer program. Dr.Fill solves the puzzles in the back of the ballroom where the contest is held. When each puzzle is done, Shortz announces how Dr.Fill did on it; the worse the program did, the louder the applause.

I met Emma Hardaway at the 2017 tournament. I was a reporter, and she was a manuscript screener for a literary agency in New York City. Just a couple of word nerds at the same event. We introduced ourselves to each other while kibitzing a *Trivial Pursuit* game during the wine and cheese party that takes place the night before the tournament begins.

Emma was effervescent and charming. Tall, attractive, well-spoken and smart, but with a wicked glint in her eye that warned against taking her for granted. One of those interactions where you wish afterward you'd exchanged contact information. Well, there was always the next year's tournament.

In reality, though, I didn't need to wait that long. I bumped into Emma in a little coffee shop in SoHo, one of those impossible New York coincidences that make life in the city worth living. This time, I got an email address and – I thought – a tentative agreement to meet for dinner a few weeks later. But my email had said it was not to be.

* * *

A couple of years before I met Emma at the 2017 ACPT, I met Montgomery Grimes at the 2015 event. He wrote the software that handles the scoring for the tournament, although the puzzles themselves are graded by human judges. (Those judges collectively examine about a million filled-in squares over the course of the weekend.) More interestingly, Grimes is the author of the villainous Dr.Fill, which he steadfastly refers to as "it" instead of "he". Dr.Fill finished 55th in 2015. Grimes gave an entertaining talk about how the program worked, and I included it in the article I wrote for the *Times* about the event itself.

When not working on Dr.Fill, Grimes is in steadfast denial of the fact that he's in his early sixties. In addition to running three startups (Mark Cuban is an investor in two of them), he and I have exchanged email over the years about a variety of his – for lack of a better phrase – mad schemes. He thinks he can use a couple of high-definition cameras and computers to figure out which way a rebound is going in basketball – while the shot is still in the air. Grimes believes he can explain birds' flocking as a mechanism to make evolution more efficient. He raised his kids on a diet of stories about a guy named John Gizmo, who bails them out of all manner of trouble with gadgets like the *cat transporter*, which is the size and shape of a flashlight but can hold millions of cats, the *beginning end*, which turns back time in a small area, converting the most hardened criminal into a crying infant, and the *gezuntifier*, which disables anyone who sneezes. I figured Monty was a smart guy and could tell me what was up.

From: William Burkett (wburkett@nytimes.com)
To: Montgomery Grimes (montgomerygrimes@gmail.com)
Subject: take a look?

Hey Monty:

```
Can you take a look at factorman0.blogspot.com and tell
me what you think?

Thx

William
```

Grimes is a weird duck. When you send him an email, he generally responds within five minutes. Doesn't matter what time it is. I don't understand how he does it. I wonder if his wife does.

```
From: Montgomery Grimes (montgomerygrimes@gmail.com)
To: William Burkett (wburkett@nytimes.com)
Re: take a look?

Whoa. This guy is really smart.
```

Our email dialog continued.

```
Burkett:  You feel like being a bit more specific?
Grimes:   Is this real?
Burkett:  I was hoping you could tell me. What does it mean?
Grimes:   Too much for email. Telephone?
Burkett:  Sure. Give me a few; I'll call you.
```

When Grimes says telephone, he means telephone. Not Skype, not Face-Time. I don't know if this is because he's ridiculously old school, or because he lives out in the sticks and his Internet connection is terrible. Could be either one.

He picked up on the second ring. "Hey."

"So what am I looking at here?" I asked. He explained it to me, or at least attempted to.

"Okay," he began. "Lots of problems involve what computer scientists call 'search'. That's not search like Google; it's search like looking for a needle in a haystack."

I mumbled something generally encouraging, and he continued.

"Imagine you're trying to go to a movie on a Friday night. It's 8:17, the movie starts at 8:35, and you're the kind of person who really hates being late for a movie. Can you get to the theater in eighteen minutes?"

"Sure," I told him. "The movie is only five minutes away from my apartment."

Monty ignored me. "One way to figure it out is to consider every possible path you might take. You head out of your driveway, and can go either right or left. Let's say you go right. Thirty seconds later, you come to the end of your block; now you can go straight, right, or left. You can also turn around, but that's clearly dumb. Let's say you turn right again. After thirty more seconds, you get to another intersection. More choices." Telephone or not, I could see him, walking around and waving his hands as he got into the topic.

"In fact, there are a *lot* of choices. Say you can get to about thirty intersections in the eighteen minutes available, and there are three possibilities at each intersection. So there are three choices at the first intersection, and each of those has three successors at the next intersection. That's nine possibilities. And each of those nine has three successors; you're up to twenty-seven. By the time you deal with all thirty choices, you'll have considered about…" He paused for maybe five seconds while he figured it out. "200 trillion possibilities. By the time you think about them all, the movie will not only have started, it'll be over. It'll be over and so will the sequel – if you consider a million possibilities a second, it would take about seven years to check them all."

I told him that if I was in such a hurry, I would just pull up Google maps and let my phone figure it out. People did, after all, tend to make it to movies on time.

"But even Google maps can't look at 200 trillion possibilities on your behalf. So how do they do it? Is there any way for them to tell, with absolute certainty, that they're giving you the most efficient route?"

"Presumably. That's why they have the app."

"But how does the app *work*?" He paused again, doubtless waiting for me to add an explanation.

I disappointed him.

"Here's the trick," he told me. "Instead of labeling each possible path by the amount of time it takes, you label each *intersection* by the amount of time it takes to get there. You start with the intersections next to your house; they're easy. And since you can always tell how long it takes to get from one intersection to another, you can gradually label intersections further and further out until you know how long it takes to get to the movie theater.

Voilà! Organizing the calculation this way, it takes about 900 steps instead of trillions."

"Okay. I think I'm following. That's how my phone can tell me when I'll arrive."

"Exactly," Monty answered. "But now let's think about a different problem. One summer," he said, "you decide to go on a giant road trip with your family. The plan is to visit every state capital in the continental United States, starting and finishing at your house. But you have to do it in three months, because that's when your kids need to be back in school."

I told Monty I didn't have any kids.

"Pretend," he answered.

I pretended.

"Can't do it," I finally said. "It's a stupid trip and no one in their right mind would spend three months with their kids in the car."

"Suspend your disbelief."

I suspended. I told him I had no idea if it was possible or not.

Grimes paused, no doubt waiting for me to say something more insightful than, "I have no idea." I disappointed him again.

"Fine," he eventually continued. "Let's think about this together. Suppose we decide to start with Albany. We know we can figure out pretty easily how long it will take you to drive to Albany from your house."

"Apartment," I corrected him.

"Whatever. Apartment. And then if Trenton is next, we can figure out how long it will take to drive from Albany to Trenton. So once you decide in what *order* you're going to visit the cities, it's not too hard to figure out if a trip that uses that order can be completed in three months. With me?"

Given our earlier discussion about how long it would take to drive to the movie, this made sense. Yes, I said. I was with him. He continued.

"The problem is that there are a lot of possible orders. In fact, there are over 12 novemdecillion ways to do it, where novemdecillion is a word you don't hear terribly often and probably don't want to. It means 1 followed by sixty zeroes."

"So twelve novemwhatever possibilities are a lot," I told him.

"Novemdecillion. More than a lot. It's too many to consider in any reasonable amount of time," he concluded.

"I can see that," I answered. "But couldn't we just figure out some new clever trick that lets us solve this faster? The family-vacation problem doesn't seem that different from the get-me-to-the-movie-on-time problem."

"They are different," Monty told me. "The trick we used before, labeling intersections instead of paths, doesn't work here. The city orderings seem like the basic things that we're considering."

"Okay," I said, encouraging him to continue.

"It turns out that no one knows if the family vacation problem can be solved in a reasonable amount of time or not," Grimes told me. "It's actually called the 'traveling salesman' problem by computer scientists, since it started by trying to figure out how long a traveling salesman would need to visit all his customers. The movie-on-time problem is called the 'shortest path' problem."

He kept going. "And think about it."

"Stop," I said.

He stopped.

I mean, he just *stopped*. Silence on the other end of the phone line. Finally, he asked, "What?"

I told Monty my brain was full.

"I'm just summing up," he answered. "If you want to know how long it will take to get to the movie, your phone can tell you. But what if you have to run errands, and you have fifteen places to visit before coming home. What order should you run them in? *There's no app for that.* That's the traveling salesman problem. The shortest path problem is somehow easy, and the traveling salesman problem is somehow hard. That's the real reason that Google maps exists but the event sequencing app doesn't."

I was surprised. "So this stuff actually matters in real life."

"It does. And 'easy' here turns out to mean something specific called, 'solvable in polynomial time.'"

I interrupted again. "You call this summing up? Use words of one syllable that I've heard before."

Monty paused before continuing. "Fine. This. Guy. Says. He. Can. Solve all things fast. Like the trip thing. As fast as God can solve things."

I couldn't believe he was actually doing it. I told him not to be an asshole.

"This 'Factor Man' can make any problem easy," Monty told me. "Any problem at all. It's as if he can just guess the answer to anything, so that all he has to do is check that his answer is right. You want to guess the right order to visit the capitals? He can do that."

Grimes paused, and I said nothing while trying to figure out what all this had to do with factoring and prime numbers. "He can solve any problem?" I asked.

"Yes. Any problem. The consequences would be profound, and not just for traveling salesmen. You want to break a secret code? Factor Man can guess the key."

"So there could be an app for that," I answered.

"Exactly. There could be an app that would let you hack into any system, decrypt any secret message. But that's only the beginning. Drug design, for example. That typically involves finding a protein that takes a particular shape. Computing the shape of a specific protein is easy, but guessing what protein to use is hard. Factor Man can guess, and drug design just got easy.

"You can play a perfect game of chess by always guessing the best next move to make.

"Even mathematics is easy. Recognizing a valid proof of some hard result like Fermat's Last Theorem is easy; finding the proof is hard. Factor Man is claiming to be able to just guess the proof and be right every time."

"He could solve anything," I summarized.

"He could solve anything." Monty went on to tell me that the algorithm Factor Man claimed to have, one that would allow him to make omniscient guesses that solved any problem, was called "God's algorithm" by computer scientists. Of course, most people believe that God's algorithm is reserved for God, and that mere mortals can never be so inspired. Grimes quoted MIT's Scott Aaronson, who had said that if God's algorithm existed, then "the world would be a profoundly different place than we usually assume it to be. There would be no special value in 'creative leaps,' no fundamental gap between solving a problem and recognizing the solution once it's found."

But Grimes, the mad scientist, disagreed. His view, he said, was that God's algorithm existed after all.

"Why?" I asked him.

"Because I don't think God would keep the best algorithms to himself."

Geez. Only Grimes would turn code breaking into a question about God's personal attitude toward the rest of us.

"What about this Factor Man guy?" I continued. "You said you thought he was really smart. Do you think he's solved this?"

"Do I think he's found God's algorithm? I have no idea," he responded. Grimes paused, and I could almost hear him stop pacing as he decided what to say next. "I've always thought that if someone *did* find God's algorithm, it would be a race. Either the government would kill him, or he would take over the world. Factor Man's plan might actually be a way to thread that needle. It's either the breakthrough of the century, or the fraud of the decade."

He paused again. "What makes Factor Man's post so smart is that he's not springing it on us all at once. He says that he has God's algorithm, and he can factor really big numbers. He can break encryption."

"Wait, wait." I stopped him again. "What do big numbers have to do with encryption?"

"There's a problem called 'number factoring', where someone gives you a number x and your job is to come up with two other numbers y and z that can be multiplied together to produce x again. Number factoring is used to encrypt information on the Internet.

"When you send your credit card information to Amazon, for example, Amazon gives you an x that you use to encrypt that information. But you can only *decrypt* the information if you can find the y and z that factor x. So if you can solve number factoring problems as x gets bigger and bigger, you can break the codes that are used to keep information private on the Internet.

"Checking that x is the product of y and z is easy. But if x is really big, like a googol or a novemdecillion, then there are too many possible y and z values to consider. Unless you use God's algorithm to guess the factors, in which case you can decrypt the message and steal the credit card information. But right now, all this Factor Man guy is offering to do is to factor numbers that are so small you could factor them in your head. A bit is a single 0 or 1 in computer memory somewhere, so a 5-bit number has to be less than 32. Factoring something like $22 = 2 \times 11$ isn't that tough."

"So why should I be impressed?" I asked.

"Because he offers to keep factoring bigger numbers. Normal methods for factoring numbers, just dividing by primes until you find a factor, will run out of steam at maybe 64 bits. There are some specialized techniques that can do better, maybe up to 90 bits. But by the time you get to 128 bits, it'll be obvious he's onto something."

I scribbled "128 bits" on a scrap of paper and circled it. "Can he just be using a faster computer?" I asked.

"Only in the movies," Monty answered. He sounded like he thought I watched too many movies. "To factor a number with one more bit, you need either a computer that's twice as fast, or twice as many computers. There aren't enough computers in the world to factor a 128-bit number with existing techniques."

"So when will we know if he's on the level?"

"There's no real point. As the numbers get bigger, it will become gradually more likely that he's for real."

"So when will we know?"

"If he's still going a year from now, we'll know." I couldn't tell from his tone what Grimes expected, if he expected anything at all. "But before then, not for sure."

"Do I write it up?"

"No idea. If you choose to write it up and you're wrong, you'll look like an idiot. If you choose not to write it up and you're wrong, you'll miss out on your Pulitzer."

"What would you do?"

Grimes told me he wouldn't be a reporter, and we hung up.

* * *

By the time my call with Grimes finished, it was dinner time on Saturday. I still had no idea whether to write about "Factor Man" or not. So, against my better judgment, I decided to ask my editor.

Now, there are some things you need to understand about editors.

First, they are not your friends. All those movie portrayals of avuncular editors nurturing their reporters along? Fairy tales.

Second, their primary goal is not to get the story out quickly. It's to get the story *right*.

They don't get the Pulitzer Prize if you scoop the entire planet; the writer does. The most exciting thing that arguably ever happens to an editor is that a story comes out that's wrong, and it matters, and his job becomes a living hell until some other editor makes a comparable mistake.

So editors are conservative. They don't like being rushed by a 48-hour deadline that's half gone, especially when the deadline itself was arguably provided by an anonymous nut case. Editors are generally not thrilled about being disturbed on Saturday evening, either, but I figured he'd rather be bothered now than at midnight.

Don't get me wrong. I like my editor. He's a fifty-year-old jogging fanatic named Thomas Dalton who lives in Denver with the woman he's been married to for approximately a century. They still seem to be madly in love. Empty nesters, with two kids both in college in California somewhere. Tom shows up for Skype conferences wearing a bow tie, so at least some of the stereotypes are true. He's smart, he's careful, and he's saved my butt on more than one occasion.

Before I contacted him, though, I tried to buy us some time.

```
From: William Burkett (wburkett@nytimes.com)
To: Factor Man (factorman0@gmail.com)
Re: returned favor

Hey FM:

My department doesn't work on the weekends. Any chance
of my getting seventy-two hours instead of forty-eight?
Thanks.

William
```

No response. And still no response after I grabbed a couple slices at a local pizza shop, so I gave up and sent the text.

to Tom Dalton [8:27PM]: Might need to talk. Supporting info sent by email.

from Tom Dalton [8:42PM]: At a thing, didn't read all details. Phone best. Ten mins?

to Tom Dalton [8:44PM]: Living the dream on a Saturday night. Call when convenient.

* * *

Dalton finally called around 9:30, and we spoke for maybe an hour.

For starters, I told him I wanted to write the story. After all, if Factor Man was on the level, it was indeed the story of a lifetime and likely to get me awards (perhaps even the Big Award). If Factor Man was a fraud, people would point at Tom as much as anything else. You get it.

Tom got it, too.

But Tom is almost as good at his job as I am at mine. He came up with a plan that would let me write about Factor Man without running the risk of looking like an idiot. He promised to make time on Sunday night at 8 to read whatever I had written and said that if it was good enough, he'd get it out by 10. We'd beat Factor Man's deadline by four minutes.

So I went back to the blog, reread it, and realized I still didn't understand most of it. Somewhat reluctantly, I called Grimes back.

"Yeah?" he answered.

"If I'm going to write this," I told him, "I need to understand the blog. Explain the rest of it."

"I thought your brain was full."

"Well, I drank some coffee and that made room."

"Excellent."

I waited.

"You still there, Wilbur? That was a three syllable word. I want to make sure you didn't pass out or something."

"Cute, Monty."

"Actually," he reassured me, "you already understand most of it. All that's left are *P* and *NP*."

"Hit me," I said.

"P stands for 'polynomial'. A computer scientist will often say that an easy problem is 'in P.' A harder problem, like the traveling salesman problem – remember that? – is not known to be in P.

"But if you had God's algorithm, you could solve the traveling salesman problem by just guessing the best ordering of the state capitals. We talked about that. You could take that best ordering and check if you could do it in three months. The problem would be polynomial again, back in P. Problems like this are said to be 'in *NP*,' where the *P* still stands for polynomial and the N stands for, 'if only I were smart enough to make a fantastic guess.' So *NP* actually means, 'If I were smart enough to make a fantastic guess, the problem would be in P.' The N actually stands for *nondeterministic*, but to a computer scientist it's the same thing."

"Non-what?" I asked. "Too many syllables."

"You're almost done," Monty told me. "In practice, *P* means 'no cleverness required.' *NP* means 'no cleverness required, if you can make an omniscient guess.' That bit of omniscience is why it's called God's algorithm. If *P* and *NP* are the same, it means that for any problem requiring a divinely inspired guess, like the traveling salesman problem, there is a clever algorithm that can make a correct guess quickly. Breaking codes. Drug design. Playing chess. Mathematics. You get it."

Amazingly enough, I felt like I did.

Grimes explained that Factor Man was claiming that he had found God's algorithm. He was claiming that *P=NP* and that he had a computer program that actually demonstrated it. He could actually do all of the things we'd been talking about.

"One last thing," he told me. "There are lots of problems in *NP*. We've talked about some of them – drug design, and so on. But there are some problems that are special. They're so hard that if you can solve them, you can actually solve anything.

"One of those superhard problems is called 'Boolean satisfiability,' and that's the problem Factor Man is claiming to have solved. Boolean satis-fiability is called SAT for short. So when he says in his blog post that he has a 'polytime SAT solver,' he's saying that he has proven that SAT is in *P*. Because SAT is a superhard problem, it means that *P* and *NP* are the same and all of those other problems are in *P* as well."

I looked at my phone, which somehow seemed like it was smarter than I was. I asked Monty if he would explain it all again when I realized I didn't actually understand any of it, and he said sure.

* * *

How to Find a Crackpot
William Burkett, The *New York Times*

In 1818, Victor Frankenstein supposedly withdrew to his laboratory and created a monster that changed the world. Can something like this actually happen now, two centuries later?

Times have changed in at least two important ways. First, science is much more a team sport these days; the average number of authors of a *Nature* paper in 2015 was nearly 20. Gone – perhaps – are the romantic days of isolated geniuses moving the scientific needle in unprecedented fashion.

But there is another difference as well. If you include the amateurs, there are many more scientists today than ever before. The Internet alone makes the scientific literature available in an unprecedented manner. When Stanford's Andrew Ng offered an online course in machine learning, over *twenty-five thousand* students registered. Perhaps one of these folks will be the lone genius after all.

There are certainly plenty of folks claiming to be the next Victor Frankenstein. In 2015, for example, a Japanese mathematician named Shinichi Mochizuki quietly claimed to have solved the "*abc* conjecture." This is widely recognized as one of the most important open problems in mathematics, and Mochizuki simply posted a (purported) proof of the conjecture on his web site. He has refused interviews, but there are conferences about his work. The conferences are described as increasing the number of mathematicians who have thoroughly studied the work so that they can no longer be counted on one's fingers. No one knows if Mochizuki is right, or a crackpot.

A similar area appears to be the esoteric question of whether *P=NP*. This, too, is described as one of the most important open questions in mathematics, with the general consensus being that *P≠NP*. Roughly speaking, *P=NP* would mean that it's possible to play a perfect game of chess, and that composing a beautiful symphony would be no more difficult than appreciating one. It would also mean that the encryption techniques underlying e-commerce provide essentially no protection at all.

In August of 2010, Hewlett-Packard's Vinay Deolalikar claimed to have proven that *P≠NP*, so that Internet commerce was safe. Two senior researchers suggested that the proof had merit, although it subsequently turned out to be fatally flawed. But the commotion surrounding the supposed proof was such that this paper published an editorial about it: "Step 1: Post Elusive Proof. Step 2: Watch Fireworks." In the end, Deolalikar, an outsider to the field of computational complexity that is concerned with such matters, had simply made a mistake.

Given the enormous number of amateur scientists floating around these days, it seems almost inevitable that some of them will make what appear to be scientific breakthroughs. How do we tell when they have, and when they haven't? Somewhat more bluntly, how can we tell if a purported scientist is a crackpot?

Not surprisingly, scientists worry about this as well. In 2009, anthropologist Pascal Boyer suggested that scientific crackpots could be identified as follows:

1. Crackpottery is foundational.
2. All crackpots are male.
3. Physics crackpots tend to be engineers.
4. Crackpots ignore other crackpots.
5. Crackpot theories are intuitive.
6. Crackpot theories are mathematically simple.
7. Crackpot theories are based on textbooks, not journal papers.

Other authors have formed similar lists.

There are two theories that I would like to evaluate in this context. As always, your mileage may vary.

One is Montgomery Grimes' suggestion that birds flock because it makes evolution more efficient. His argument is that by clustering together, a species can ensure that the weakest members are the ones typically killed by predators. Grimes draws an analogy with the old joke about two people running away from a bear. "Why are we running?" asks one. "We can't outrun a bear."

"I don't have to outrun the bear," is the reply. "I just have to outrun you."

So is Grimes a crackpot? The major journals certainly seem to think so; both *Nature* and *Science* rejected his paper describing the theory without review. According to Boyer's table:

1. **Crackpottery is foundational**. Explaining flocking would be foundational from the perspective of evolutionary biology.

2. **All crackpots are male**. Too bad, Grimes.
3. **Physics crackpots tend to be engineers.** Grimes is a theoretical astrophysicist by training, but also has a fairly impressive string of engineering accomplishments. Let's call this one a tie.
4. **Crackpots ignore other crackpots.** Grimes' article does a reasonable job of quoting other literature. We can probably give him a pass on this one.
5. **Crackpot theories are intuitive.** Yup.
6. **Crackpot theories are mathematically simple.** Not in this case. Grimes' paper involves a reasonable amount of mathematics, intricate enough that he had to build a computer simulation of the species in question to figure out what actually happened.
7. **Crackpot theories are based on textbooks, not journal papers.** Grimes' theory is based on a fairly well-known evolutionary model developed by Alfred Lotka and Vito Volterra early in the 20th century. Not textbook material, but not cutting edge journal stuff, either.

So Grimes scores 4½ on the crackpot scale of 7. Is that enough to deny him serious consideration by real biologists? It's not clear.

My second example is outside the box completely. Remember our old friend $P=NP$? Now take a look at factorman0.blogspot. com. You'll find someone who claims to have shown that $P=NP$ and even claims to be on track to prove it to the world.

Foundational, for sure. The blogger also appears to be male; he calls himself "Factor Man." The post reads like a scientist wrote it. It's impossible to tell if Factor Man ignores everyone else, if his theory is intuitive, mathematically simple, or what it's based on. Let's say 2 out of 3 on the criteria that we can actually evaluate.

The guy is, after all, basically threatening to bring down the Internet. Should we pay attention?

Not bad for 21 hours' work.

* * *

The blog began a few days later.

May 16, 2017
The Factor Man blog

22=2×11 (requested by David Parker)
21=3×7 (requested by Matthew Livingston)
25=5×5 (requested by Dan Davidson)
26=2×13 (requested by Emily Pandu)
15=3×5 (requested by Sam Wiseman)
Six bit numbers will be factored in three days.
This web site has been visited 2,037 times.

The deadline comfortably behind me, I decided to do a little more poking around. Grimes had told me that MIT's Scott Aaronson was doubtful that $P=NP$, and I had met Scott once while I was a graduate student at UT Austin. My then girlfriend had been a computer science grad student and told me that Aaronson was beyond brilliant and we needed to attend his visiting lecture on quantum computing.

I kid you not. To make matters worse, we got dragged along for dinner and somehow even wound up giving Aaronson a lift to his hotel afterwards. The things we do for love.

I tried reaching Aaronson at MIT, but it turned out he had jumped ship (for UT Austin, of all places). So I sent him an email, including a pointer to my *Times* piece. We connected by phone a couple days later.

More than anything else, Scott's response struck me as carefully considered. He had been unaware of the Factor Man blog, he said, but was also completely unimpressed by it. Extravagant claims combined with a demonstrated ability to factor small numbers added up to exactly nothing, he pointed out.

People who study problems like whether $P=NP$ are called *complexity theorists*. In the strange and relatively small world of complexity theory, Aaronson has a fairly high profile.

For example, he curates the complexity "zoo". It turns out there are many more things of interest to these folks than just P and NP, and Scott has a list of all of them. Hundreds.

He also has a blog called Shtetl-Optimized. Aaronson will give you a fairly long explanation if you ask why he chose that name, but the bottom line appears to be that a shtetl is a community like Anatevka in *Fiddler on the Roof*, and Aaronson feels like he belongs there, studying the word of God all day. He would choose to study mathematics and theoretical physics, but Aaronson's view of math and Rev Tevya's view of God may not be that far apart.

Aaronson has discussed the P and NP question on his blog. His basic view (again, I'm compressing substantially here) is that there are many problems in P, and many in NP. In some cases, those problems are incredibly close to one another, but the problems in P always seem to be just a little bit easier than those in NP. Scott believes that there is an "invisible electric fence" separating the two domains, and that if they were somehow the same, we would have bridged the fence at some point along the line.

Returning to Factor Man, Aaronson appeared completely confident that his ability to factor large numbers would turn out to be limited. At some point, he would simply become unable to factor the numbers that were being submitted. He would either admit failure or, more likely, he would just stop posting, returning to the anonymous Internet murk from which he had emerged. Most likely of all, Aaronson thought, was that Factor Man would multiply some big prime numbers together and then "factor" the results on the blog site.

I pointed out that that wouldn't cut it. Let's say someone famous, like Mark Cuban, decided to get involved, sending Factor Man some giant number to factor some time down the road. Factor Man wouldn't be able to factor it, and would keep factoring numbers submitted by (now invented) nobodies. Cuban takes to the airwaves and announces that he's been slighted, and the charade is pretty much over.

What I didn't understand was why Factor Man – whom Aaronson agreed was at a minimum reasonably clever – would set himself up for failure in this way. Why embark on a deliberately public demonstration that you have to know is doomed?

Scott told me that for some folks, fifteen minutes of fame is enough, and they don't care how that fifteen minutes ends. Seven billion people, you're bound to find a few nutters.

2

FACTOR MAN
JULY 12, 2017

When the blog hit six digit numbers (24 bits), I reached out for the second time.

From: factorman0@gmail.com
To: rjhasday@duanemorris.com
Subject: new client?

Dear Mr. Hasday:

I find myself in need of legal representation, and you have been recommended to me by a mutual colleague. The work will be international in nature and is likely to consist of two quite separable parts. One of these will be the drafting of a contract that will need to be absolutely ironclad, and the other part will involve document transfers of the type often handled by private couriers. I assume you have access to such individuals. You have been recommended to me because of your expertise in contract law.

For reasons that I expect will eventually become clear, I would like to remain anonymous. I understand that attorney-client privilege should protect my identity, but would like to exercise an additional degree of caution in this case. Please rest assured that I will not ask you to do anything immoral or illegal and, should I ask you to do something illegal or immoral, I would fully expect you to decline.

If this is acceptable, please send me a retention agreement by email. I will sign it and return it to you by conventional post.

Thank you in advance for your attention, and I look forward to working together.

FM

Hasday responded promptly.

From: Robert Hasday (rjhasday@duanemorris.com)
To: Factor Man (factorman0@gmail.com)
Re: new client?

Dear Sir/Madam:

While your request is unusual, I don't see any harm in potentially honoring it. Before I can offer you representation, however, I need to run a conflict check to see if your interests are adverse to any of our current clients. I cannot see how to do that without knowing who you are.

Bob Hasday

From: Factor Man (factorman0@gmail.com)
To: Robert Hasday (rjhasday@duanemorris.com)
Re: new client?

Dear Mr. Hasday:

I do not believe that conflicts should be an issue. There are certainly no conflicts at the moment, because there are no legal matters in which I am involved. I understand that conflicts may arise in the future but I will not expect you to represent me without an explicit waiver from any conflicting party.

```
Is that sufficient?

From: Robert Hasday (rjhasday@duanemorris.com)
To: Factor Man (factorman0@gmail.com)
Re: new client?

Dear Sir/Madam:

A retention letter is attached.

Because of the unusual nature of the relationship that
you have requested, we would like to ask that you provide
us with some sort of retainer in advance. Perhaps $10,000
would be appropriate?

I am curious as to the nature of the work that you have
for us.

Bob Hasday
```

Bob Hasday
Duane Morris LLP
1540 Broadway
New York, NY 10036

Dear Bob:

Thank you for your email. A signed copy of your retention agreement is enclosed, along with $10,000 in cash.

I am also enclosing a key to a safe deposit box at Sparta Global Intelligence Group, Löwengasse 39, 1030 Vienna. The box number is 1739 and the password is I@mF@ctorm@n. I will use the box to transfer additional funds to you as needed.

If I send you a message mentioning a famous physicist, please check the safe deposit box. I recommend strongly that your contact in Vienna have an untraceable cell phone used only for this purpose. Please put the key somewhere safe, and tell no one of its location.

That's it for now, and probably for the next year or so. But you'll hear from me.

FM

My best guess was that I would need to get cash to Hasday twice. Of everything I had planned, those two transactions held the greatest risk of discovery. My fingerprints were on the $10,000 in cash, but that would presumably be deposited and untraceable long before anyone cared. I had been careful to ensure that there were no fingerprints on the letter or the package that contained it. The package itself had simply been sent through the US mail.

One transaction was presumably now complete. I knew that the second, when it came, would be much more difficult.

Burkett
September 6, 2017

Mystery Web Site Gets 2 Million Views; Scientists Still Skeptical
William Burkett, The *New York Times*

An anonymous blog posted by someone who claims to have solved one of the major open questions in computer science recorded its two millionth view last night, but scientists remain skeptical that the blogger has actually achieved what is claimed.

The blogger, known only as "Factor Man," purports to be able to solve problems of arbitrary difficulty. He is demonstrating this by factoring numbers provided by his readers, which means that they present Factor Man with large numbers and he responds with two prime numbers that, when multiplied together, reproduce the original queries. As time passes, the numbers involved get ever larger.

The blog is currently factoring numbers that are 42 bits in size, or around one trillion. Scientists say that while factoring numbers of this size is relatively straightforward using modern computers, the problem becomes much harder as the numbers get larger. Factoring numbers that are 60 bits in size (about 10^{18}, or 1 followed by 18 zeroes) represents the limit of what can easily be done with existing technology. The Factor Man blog increases the size by one bit every three days, so this particular threshold is still a couple of months out.

Factoring problems are important because they are used to encrypt information being sent over the Internet. Computer scientists have developed encoding schemes where you can *encode* a message using a large integer, but to *decode* the associated message, you need to factor the integer used in the encoding. If it is possible to factor large integers quickly, information sent over the Internet will no longer be secure.

Somewhat more specifically, when a customer sends credit card information to an online vendor like Amazon, the credit card number is encrypted using a large number that Amazon supplies. Amazon (and hopefully only Amazon) can then decode the message to retrieve the original credit card information, since Amazon (and hopefully only Amazon) knows how to write the large number as a product of two other numbers. If arbitrary individuals could factor Amazon's number, they could also obtain the credit card and other information that was intended only for Amazon.

The numbers used for encrypting information on the Internet are generally 128 bits or bigger (10^{36} or so), so there is no current risk to what Factor Man is doing. He claims to be able to factor numbers of 128 bits and larger size, however, and will supposedly be doing so in about eight months. If true, this has the potential to wreak havoc with Internet commerce generally, not to mention other secure information.

Scientists are not terribly concerned because they believe that the problem Factor Man has claimed to solve is insoluble. Roughly speaking, Factor Man claims to be able to convert extremely difficult problems into much simpler ones, and most scientists believe this is not possible. A 2002 poll of leading complexity theorists, for example, found that almost 90% of them believed conversions of this sort are impossible in general.

If the scientists are right, the Factor Man blog will eventually be revealed as a sham. Although the blog is seeing an increasing amount of web traffic, there are no ads or other mechanisms from which Factor Man himself might benefit. If he has not done what he claims, he surely knows that, and his purpose in starting the blog remains unclear.

Some time between two and eight months from now, we'll know.

* * *

Time passed, and the Factor Man blog kept clunking along. Very slowly, the world began to notice.

November 8, 2017
The Factor Man blog

7679242802718243149=4128135071×1860220819
(requested by Wil Wheaton)
4642207329833315777=3608657033×1286408569
(requested by Donald Harper)
5829354591263741267=3615644117×1612258951
(requested by Donald Bischoff)
6369235188560869753=3095117269×2057833237
(requested by Megan Farnsby)
5198239902527246893=3693259111×1407493963
(requested by Michael Kennedy)

64-bit numbers will be factored in three days.

I occasionally read that this blog will inevitably make a fool of me because my basic claim that P=NP is untrue. There appear to be three basic arguments for this.

1.   If P were equal to NP, someone would have figured it out a long time ago.

2.   P can't be equal to NP because (for example) it's obviously much harder to write a brilliant symphony than it is to appreciate one.

3.   P is probably not equal to NP because there seems to be a natural boundary between them that cannot be crossed.

Let me deal with each of these in turn.

1. Someone would already have figured this out. This almost doesn't merit a response. It's sort of like Charles Duell's famous 1899 quote, "Everything that can be invented has been invented." Duell was the US Commissioner of Patents at the time; the only problem is that the quote is completely apocryphal and he never said it.

2. Making cool stuff is harder than appreciating cool stuff. The basic argument here is that it takes a Mozart to compose a great symphony, but your average schmo can appreciate one.

I would argue that this is in fact one of the most compelling reasons to believe that P=NP, as opposed to the reverse. What, after all, is the real difference between Mozart and Joe Schmo?

It's surely not hardware. Same number of brain cells, give or take. Same basic architecture, etc.

No, the difference between Mozart and the rest of us is entirely software. The fact that geniuses exist (be they Mozart or Hawking) and that they are in reality so extraordinarily similar to the rest of us suggests to me that P=NP after all.

3. Aaronson's "magical boundary" argument. This is perhaps the most interesting argument of the three. Scott Aaronson has observed that problems in P always seem to be ever so slightly easier than problems in NP, even at the best of times. He suggests that this means that the two classes are likely different. Aaronson draws an analogy to two groups of frogs – small yellow ones and big green ones. Intermix them as you may, they never actually breed. That suggests that they can't breed.

But one can certainly imagine otherwise. Perhaps, long ago, a certain physical deformity appeared so that only frogs that both had (or both lacked) the deformity could naturally interbreed. Over time, the frog population split into two types, which only looked like two species. If we go on to postulate that the deformity disappears if the frogs get enough potassium in their diet, all we need do is give them some supplements and they'll be interbreeding like crazy.

Put somewhat differently, if it looks like a duck, and walks like a duck, and quacks like a duck, it's probably a duck. But even if something looks different, walks differently, and doesn't quack, it might still be a duck – just in disguise and a little hard to recognize.

This web site has been visited 58,836,211 times.

Check it out. Wil Wheaton, child star of *Star Trek: The Next Generation* and regular on *The Big Bang Theory*, had asked Factor Man to factor something. The tweet followed quickly:

```
@wilw (Wil Wheaton): yup, can confirm number on fac-
torman0.blogspot.com actually from me. Big Bang folks
provided number. something to this after all?
```

Factor Man
November 8, 2017

Wil Wheaton. How cool is that? But the fact that Wil had asked me to factor something meant that I was about to get a lot more attention. Time to reach out again. This was the third time of what I expected would be a total of four.

```
From: factor.man@yandex.com
To: finnbrian@gmail.com
Subject: hello

Dear Brian:

I suspect that the posers are about to come out in force,
and wanted to try to connect with you before that happens.

I have a business proposition for you. Are you willing
to listen?

FM
```

```
From: Brian D Finn (finnbrian@gmail.com)
To: Factor Man (factor.man@yandex.com)
Re: hello

Always willing to listen.

BDF
```

```
Factor Man: Thanks.
```

First, let me acknowledge that I'm using a different email address for this, not my usual factorman0@gmail.com. I am doing this to ensure an additional level of protection, in case the Gmail account gets hacked.

But I am Factor Man. One of the numbers I will be factoring in tomorrow's blog post is 7973748292415255209.

I would like to borrow some money, an amount of your choosing between $5M and $50M. For each $5M you lend me, I will repay you with 1% of the funds received from the license to my code next year, with payment to you at the Factor Man coming out party two years after that.

In the event that the license fee is less than $500M (which strikes me as incredibly unlikely), I will repay you double the original amount of the loan, but in no case will I repay you more than the total amount of the license fee.

While you mull this over, let me add that I am someone whom you know and trust. I will reveal my identity to you if you want, but recommend fairly strongly that you not take me up on that – for your well-being, not mine. I also point out that if I wanted to rip you off, I would simply hack into one of your accounts and rip you off. But everything I have done so far (and everything I plan on doing in the future) is both legal and fair. I have no intention of changing that.

Finn: Interesting. Some initial questions. What do you expect the license fee to eventually be? What can go wrong?

Factor Man: It's hard to judge on the license fee. If I had to guess, I would say something between $10B and $100B. So I'm offering you a return of 20×, perhaps 200×.

A lot can go wrong. Most likely is probably that my identity is discovered and things somehow unravel. I don't believe that it will be discovered (in all honesty, this email is one of the weakest links). If my identity is discovered after the licensing deal is done, everything should still be ok. If it's discovered before the licensing deal is done, it will be a mess.

Finn: How would I get you the money?

Factor Man: I would ask you to establish a numbered Swiss account and transfer the funds. You would get me credentials for the account over the phone.

Finn: The phone?

Factor Man: Works for the drug dealers.

Finn: What about a contract?

Factor Man: I'm happy to sign whatever reasonable documents you draw up. But I'll be signing as Factor Man, so your legal protections will be limited. Even if I signed as myself, with the money offshore, your protections would still be limited. As I've said, if I wanted to steal your money, I would just … steal your money. And there's no need to transfer the funds at the moment. I'll let you know.

Finn: When do you need an answer?

Factor Man: Soon. There are some specific things I need to do, and the blog is about to get a great deal of attention. The risk to me (to both of us, actually) goes up with each passing day. How long do you need?

Finn: A week would be good.

Factor Man: Done.

* * *

November 19, 2017
The Factor Man blog

5141777043983270623=3515691407×1462522289
  (requested by Suzanne Bonamici)
7973748292415255209=3922087657×2033036737
  (requested by Donald Knuth)
7354934760809584847=3529199239×2084023673
  (requested by Stephen Rudich)
5361298675999551319=4043265371×1325982389
  (requested by Josephine McCall)
4912824077198864347=2508420991×1958532517
  (requested by Douglas Heller)
    64-bit numbers will be factored in two days.
    This web site has been visited 63,917,708 times.

Things were definitely picking up. Bonamici was a member of the House Committee on Science, Space and Technology. In fact, she was a member of the subcommittee on Research and Technology. Knuth was a retired Stanford professor who was on record as believing that P=NP but also believing that the "fast" algorithms wouldn't be fast enough to be useful. Rudich was a complexity theorist at Carnegie Mellon, and had shown that a wide range of techniques that looked like they might prove that P≠NP were simply never going to work. The other two names were unknowns.

* * *

```
From: Brian D Finn (finnbrian@gmail.com)
To: Factor Man (factor.man@yandex.com)
Re: hello
```

OK. I will agree under the following conditions.

The amount of my loan will be $25M. I will lend you $5M at the point that you factor 128-bit numbers, and then $5M more at 148 bits, 168 bits, 188 bits and 208 bits.

Both of us will have access to the numbered account. If you at any point fail to factor the numbers in question, I will withdraw whatever funds remain and contribute no more. You agree that if you have reason to believe that such a withdrawal by me is imminent, you will not withdraw the funds yourself.

You agree not to withdraw funds from the account after bidding starts for the technology, and to only withdraw funds subsequently if the remaining funds, together with the eventual licensing fee, exceed $50M. If the licensing fee plus the remaining funds is less than $50M, I get both the remaining money and the licensing fee in its entirety.

You also agree that you will withdraw money from the numbered account only as needed.

As you point out, there is an element of trust in this for both of us.

I am taking some solace from the fact that I am only committing funds at the point that you have demonstrated an ability to remove them by stealth anyway.

BDF

From: Factor Man
To: Brian D Finn
Re: hello

Agreed on all counts, with one small modification. Please open the numbered account now. I would like to get the account information from you before the whole world is watching. Feel free to deposit the bank minimum, and I will not withdraw anything until you have contributed the balance of the first $5M.

Done?

Finn: Done.

There were, in some sense, two transactions here. Brian had agreed to lend me $25 million. And I would, I expected, eventually repay him somewhere between $500 million and $5 billion as a result.

Would I need Finn's money? I might. There would be Hasday's bill to pay. There might be expenses associated with the Factor Man Coming Out Party; if there were, they would doubtless be substantial. And I was certainly hoping to enjoy the $25 million between the time Brian delivered it and the time when I could access all of my expected funds after my identity was revealed at the coming out party later on.

But was this really worth somewhere in excess of half a billion? In all honesty, I expected not. The real reason I offered Brian the opportunity to profit so at my expense was that being Factor Man was pretty damn lonely.

Fundamentally, I could share it with no one except Denise.

Sure. I could post something on the blog and have it read by millions of people. (I didn't know it at the time, but my readership would eventually pass that of every other printed word except the Bible.) But I couldn't really talk to any of those unseen millions because it wasn't an actual dialog. The Factor Man journey was an absurdly private one.

But now Brian was in on it with me. He would share in the profit or loss, and he would share in the journey. You can argue that $500 million is an awful lot to pay for a companion, and I will answer that while looking at it that way makes it sound like a lot, looking at it as a 5% tax on the Factor Man enterprise makes it seem a bargain.

Brian fulfilled his commitment two days later.

Finn: The account is open. $1K minimum. How would you like me to get you the information?

Factor Man: I need a phone number.

Finn: 516-662-2457

Factor Man: You will receive a call from 218-367-9210. I will not say anything. Please simply provide me with the relevant information. Read it twice, just to make sure. Is now convenient?

Finn: Sure.

Three days later, Brian got a package in the mail. It was a cell phone (218-367-9210), $1000 in cash, and a handwritten note: "Didn't want you to worry unnecessarily."

The postmark was Denver. But beyond that, Finn never tried to trace it.

Burkett
December 2, 2017

As the blog gained in popularity, Americans far and wide tried to use it to get what they always wanted: fame and money.

Fame was as elusive as usual, as the spots on the blog were increasingly taken by reasonably well-known (and sometimes less well-known) celebrities. These folks knew that as soon as the blog appeared, they would receive hundreds of thousands of Google hits, with comparable numbers of views on their web sites, Twitter feeds, or what have you. In the Internet age, those views are very much the coin of the realm.

Of course, not every famous person had a number factored. An Internet celebrity (who has already gotten so much bad press that I needn't name her here) complained bitterly about her absence, and was eventually asked how she selected a number to submit. "It was easy," she answered, "I just stuck a really long number into an email."

Of course, not many "really long numbers" have exactly the requisite number of bits. Of those, only a relative handful are the product of two primes. And of those, many are unsuitable because the factoring problem is too easy. A number that is the product of 2 and another prime, for example, is obviously even (just look at the last digit), and Factor Man would hardly enhance his reputation by noticing (say) that **33330761460464216926 = 16665380730232108463×2**.

And so it turned out that the problem of *submitting* a number that met Factor Man's requirements was reasonably difficult, and would get more so as the required numbers grew larger. A couple of inventive mathematicians created a small cottage industry by creating submittofactorman.com where, for the modest sum of $150, you could get a number that was guaranteed to conform to Factor Man's requirements. Their clientele was pretty much exclusively the rich and famous, who cared little about the $150 but cared greatly about having their names in lights, however briefly.

The two mathematicians turned out, not surprisingly, to be high school students.

The British, meanwhile, had a much simpler way to make money.

Factor Man and the Political Markets
William Burkett, The *New York Times*

> The British will bet on anything, whether it's the outcome of US political races or the color of the hat the queen will wear at her birthday party. There are Internet sites such as betfair.com where you can place such bets.
>
> As of a couple of weeks ago, you could bet on Factor Man. Initially, the betting markets were simply about whether Factor Man would succeed or fail to reach his stated 255-bit goal. But that market became incredibly lopsided (the nays had it), so the betting shifted to the point at which Factor Man (who was then factoring 69-bit numbers) would go down in flames. You could bet on 70 bits or less (not so many takers on that one), 71-100 bits, 101-130 bits, etc.

Some mathematicians came along (not the kids running submittofactorman.com; some real mathematicians) and said that after a reasonable amount of work looking at all the latest techniques, they had concluded that a good-sized personal computer could factor a 78-bit number in 24 hours. Larger numbers were unlikely.

So unless Factor Man had invented some new mathematics, they predicted, he'd run out of steam around 78 bits. That was assuming that he was devoting one computer to each of the five factorizations he published daily.

They went on to point out that factorization was "parallelizable," meaning that if you have two computers, you can (almost) do half the work on each one. So doubling the number of computers Factor Man had would, roughly speaking, let him succeed for one more bit. Amazon could provide him with lots of computers in the cloud, although it would get expensive fairly quickly.

The mathematicians got a tremendous amount of publicity, and the obvious conclusion was that 100 bits was out of Factor Man's reach, since it would require about twenty million computers according to the above analysis. There was a huge spike in the 71-100 bit bets, and all of the others trailed off. The betting markets responded, splitting the 71-100 range and collapsing some of the others. As of the time of this writing, here are the odds for the various ranges:

First failure (bits)	Odds
80 or less	3.6
81–90	0.7
91–100	6.6
101–128	34
129-256	23

To read the table, if you bet $1 that Factor Man will fail before reaching 81 bits, the odds of 3.6:1 mean that you'll get paid $4.60 if you're right (your original $1 bet, plus the payoff of 3.6 times that bet). If you bet the dollar that he'll fail between 81 and 90, you'll be paid $1.70, and so on.

So the prevailing wisdom is that Factor Man will fail somewhere between 81 and 90 bits, with that particular bet paying off slightly less than even money.

Alternatively, we can use the odds to compute the implied probability that Factor Man can factor numbers of any particular size. The probability for 69-bit numbers is 1, since he's already doing it. But 128 bits (a common size for numbers used for Internet encryption) are viewed as having only a 6% chance, and 256 bits (the size of the numbers Factor Man is suggesting be used instead) are a bit less likely still.

Of course, public polling may not be the best way to find this out. All we've got to do is wait and see.

* * *

As ever more people started paying attention, questions started arising.

The Factor Man blog was now getting millions of hits every day. Assuming that (say) 5% of the visitors asked Factor Man to factor a number for them, Factor Man would still need to sift through hundreds of thousands of messages daily. How was he filtering for submissions that met the criteria of being products of two primes? It was clear he could factor five numbers daily, but could he factor (or attempt to factor) hundreds of thousands?

Once he filtered, how was he finding the submissions from famous people, who were now dominating the Factor Man blog each day?

A Facebook programmer named Alex Gunderson had an idea about this. What he suspected was that one part of the process was simply to get the names out of the emails, and look for them on Wikipedia.

So Gunderson created an actor named Bob Thwick and gave him a Wikipedia page. Thwick was your classic B-list character actor, lots of small parts in big films. He had pictures (that Gunderson pulled from a randomly selected Facebook account), a backstory, the whole deal. And he submitted a number to be factored on the web page.

December 7, 2017
The Factor Man blog

3108547364451513006637=66042197591×47069108507
(requested by Mark Ruffalo)
2543180303080618090831=47952916709×53034945059
(requested by Danica McKellar)
3786123199377133637119=55426745599×68308596481
(requested by John Malkovich)
2867803314766004593513=51147568463×56069201351
(requested by Jerry Moran)
3166843927185980711161=47315996341×66929668021
(requested by Michael Genesereth)
   73-bit numbers will be factored tomorrow.
   Robert Thwick is not a real person.
   This web site has been visited 163,337,480 times.

Thwick might not have been a real person, but his Wikipedia page certainly got a lot of action. The pictures turned out to be some guy named Austin Simons who lived in Kansas, and it took almost no time at all for them to be tracked to Simons' Facebook. The Thwick Wikipedia page itself had been created a few days prior from an IP address that belonged to Facebook.

At this point, Facebook got involved, and learned that the pictures had all been scraped using Gunderson's machine, and that the connection used to create the Wikipedia page was from Gunderson's machine as well.

Gunderson was fired, the first recorded time that the Factor Man blog caused someone to lose his or her job.

Meanwhile, the five names got the usual scrutiny as well. Ruffalo and Malkovich were well known. McKellar had starred in *The Wonder Years* and then gotten a Ph.D. in mathematics from UCLA. Moran was on the Senate committee on Commerce, Science, and Transportation. Genesereth was computer science faculty at Stanford.

Factor Man
March 16, 2018

The Factor Man blog address was factorman0.blogspot.com, so the blog was hosted by blogspot.com. Blogspot was owned by Google.

In March of 2018, Google changed its home page so that it included a copy of my current Factor Man blog posting along with the usual Google stuff, including ads. Two days later, Bing and Yahoo did the same thing. Sundar Pichai, the Google CEO, commented to the press that since Factor Man was hosted on a Google site, Yahoo and Bing had no rights to rebroadcast the page. Google demanded that both Yahoo and Bing change their home pages back to what they had been.

This sort of stuff ticks me off.

```
From: factorman0@gmail.com
To: sundar@google.com
Subject: Factor Man postings

Mr. Pichai:
```

I have no objection to your putting my content on your homepage, provided that you provide me with daily hit counts so that I can update the counter on the Factor Man blog. Please send daily hit counts to this address.

Meanwhile, I am making similar requests of Bing and Yahoo, and expect that they will comply. Please retract your comments to the press regarding rebroadcast rights of Factor Man content.

FM

From: Kris Stafford (kstafford@google.com)
To: Factor Man (factorman0@gmail.com)
Re: Factor Man postings

I am the General Counsel for Google, and your email to Mr. Pichai was forwarded to me.

If you look at the blogspot terms of service, you will see that they include the following:

When you upload or otherwise submit content to our Services, you give Google (and those we work with) a worldwide license to use, host, store, reproduce, modify, create derivative works (such as those resulting from translations, adaptations or other changes we make so that your content works better with our Services), communicate, publish, publicly perform, publicly display and distribute such content. The rights you grant in this license are for the limited purpose of operating, promoting, and improving our Services, and to develop new ones.

Google hit counts are proprietary and I am afraid we will not be able to share them with you.

From: Factor Man (factorman0@gmail.com)
To: Kris Stafford (kstafford@google.com)
Re: Factor Man postings

You are confusing the tail and the dog here. I urge you to reconsider your response, but will only give you three days to do so. At that time I will post the attached.

FM

Because of intransigent behavior on Google's part (the parent of blogspot), I have decided to move the Factor Man blog to a separately hosted domain. Bing and Yahoo will continue to be permitted to reproduce the Factor Man blog on their home pages, but Google will not.

I know, I know. Why kick sand in Google's face?

It's a character flaw. I was brought up in a Jewish household, and Jews are territorial. Someone takes your stuff, you take it back. Someone hits you, you hit them back. ("Twice as hard," my father often told me.)

It's a policy that's worked great for centuries in the Middle East.

But yes, kicking sand in the face of the biggest guy on the beach is generally a mistake. I wouldn't find out for a while just how big a mistake it had been.

From: John Thomas (jthomas@google.com)
To: Factor Man (factorman0@gmail.com)
CC: Kris Stafford (kstafford@google.com)
Re: Factor Man postings

The number of hits to the Google home page since we started including your blog were as follows:

day 1: 34,342,817 (this was a partial day)
day 2: 298,322,184
day 3: 287,219,350
day 4: 302,128,322

Day 5 is not yet complete. In the future, you will be receiving this data automatically from dataservices@google.com. Permission is granted for both Bing and Yahoo to repost your blog as well.

3

BURKETT
APRIL 3, 2018

Conspiracy theories began to spring up. The two most popular ones were that Factor Man was in fact a hoax perpetrated by the NSA, and that he was a hoax perpetrated by Amazon. Neither of these really made much sense, but conspiracy theorists have never been daunted by that.

The NSA theory was the lowest hanging fruit of the conspiracy world, which generally views pretty much everything as an NSA conspiracy. The notion was that scientists at the NSA, the branch of the US government that deals with cryptography and similar things, had actually cracked public key encryption long ago. They had been using the results to spy on the American people for years, if not decades. For one reason or another, the NSA had decided now was the time to let the world know that public key encryption was no longer secure, and Factor Man was their preferred (and incredibly imaginative) way of doing so.

The NSA's motivation for letting the world know was vague, although a typical suggestion was that a foreign country (probably North Korea) was *also* about to crack public key encryption and the NSA wanted everyone to move to a more secure system as briskly as possible. This would have made more sense if anyone in North Korea had known a damn thing about complexity theory, but they did not. In fact, the vast majority of the world's complexity theorists were Americans.

The Amazon theory had its roots in the idea that Factor Man was actually the guy behind submittofactorman.com. After all, the numbers he had been factoring before there was all the commercial interest didn't show any technological breakthroughs. Once he got celebrities interested, he could just feed them problems through submittofactorman.com and no one would be the wiser.

The folks who subscribed to this theory were unfazed when the two high school kids running submittofactorman.com showed up. They were just Factor Man dupes, they said.

A more serious problem was that many of the numbers being factored didn't come from submittofactorman.com. Members of House and Senate committees weren't using the site; nor were computer scientists. How could Factor Man be dealing with queries that he wasn't generating?

Enter Amazon. Amazon had a ton of computing resources available, and could be using those resources to find large numbers of factorizations. So they could put together a list of millions of 65-bit numbers and their factors, and then when all of the Factor Man queries appeared, they could carefully select ones for which the factorizations were already known. Amazon's motives remained a bit obscure, but they at least had the wherewithal to pull the whole thing off.

If you were willing to devote ten thousand computers to the task of factoring numbers in advance, it turned out that you would have a pretty good shot at having five answers available if a thousand famous people submitted 64-bit queries. But it got worse quickly; you would need half a million computers to deal with 70-bit numbers, and about seven million to deal with 74-bit numbers. By the time Google put the blog up on its home page, the Amazon theory was beginning to die out.

The federal government, of course, remained a suspect.

* * *

With the conspiracy theorists came the spammers and the phishers.

From: factorman1809@gmail.com
To: randybooker34@yahoo.com
Subject: Factor Man vulnerability

Dear Mr. Booker:

The Internet is abuzz with the fact that I can break into the bank account of anyone who uses their computer for banking. I can break into the credit card account of anyone who uses their computer for electronic commerce.

Developing this technology has been expensive, and I need to recover my costs. I will shortly be approaching the big banks and e-commerce businesses and, for a fee, offering to leave their account holders alone.

They will undoubtedly pay this fee and pass it along to you. But for the much smaller fee of $2.99/month, I will guarantee that whatever your bank decides, your accounts will stay safe. Hopefully you will realize that this is a small price to pay for security in this uncertain world.

To arrange payment, please visit factormanprotectsme.com.

There was also:

From: keep.you.safe.1287@yahoo.com
To: jtibalt@hotmail.com
Subject: Factor Man vulnerability

Dear JTibalt:

As I expect you know, an individual is claiming to be able to break the codes that keep the Internet -- and your personal information -- safe.

This is a serious concern. Our company has developed technology that can protect you, and Visa has hired us to incorporate this information into your account. Once this is done, you won't have to worry about Factor Man (or anyone else) hacking into your accounts and stealing your personal information or worse.

Although there is a fee for our service, it is being paid by Visa. To take advantage of this opportunity, please visit cybersecurityexperts345.com and provide us with the necessary information. You can also call 844-329-2170 and provide this information securely by telephone.

Most people following the blog were now viewing it at least once a day, often much more through the Google, Yahoo and Bing home pages. The response to the phishing was brisk.

The Factor Man blog
April 11, 2018

142268511712715340159364088425447 9 = 49079419489494001×28987407184628479 (requested by Robert Downey, Jr.)

204177676907058268105174172819524 7 = 63564318042197221×32121429631560707 (requested by Harrison Ford)

149902164235097065939474746229174 9 = 58907834462498419×25446897785816071 (requested by Douglas Hofstadter)

130515824322671947302416538250076 9 = 41058336573096571×31787898686619539 (requested by Olivia Munn)

142238863203428149448147257017780 1 = 43277705260893391×32866544643705511 (requested by David McAllester)

112-bit numbers will be factored in three days.

It has come to my attention that certain individuals are attempting to exploit this blog for their own financial gain. These attempts appear to generally be of two types: (1) Individuals claiming to be me and threatening to breach people's security unless some sort of ransom is paid, and (2) individuals offering protection against my technology in exchange for a fee or private information.

Let me disavow both of these as publicly as possible. First, I will never ask anyone for either money or personal information. I have asked someone to lend me money exactly once, and that was months ago. Second, the technology that I have in hand is not something against which you can protect yourself. I am encouraging banks and other businesses to change their encryption methods precisely because that is the only way in which you and your information can be safeguarded.

If people are being ripped off by these folks, I will hear about it. If you're the one doing the ripping off, I suggest you stop immediately

and return any funds or information that you have obtained. If you do
not, I will name you, change the password on your financial accounts,
and make the new password public. That includes you, John Farnsworth of 222 Steelers Blvd in Pittsburgh. Apartment 3B.

This web site has been visited 67,299,231,222 times.

The phishing stopped, Farnsworth's life deteriorated considerably, and the
hunt for the mysterious lender began.

* * *

Scientists Changing Views on so-called "Factor Man"
William Burkett, The *New York Times*

The blogger known only as "Factor Man" is winning over
some converts. He claims to be able to factor large numbers;
in other words, to produce two numbers that, when multiplied
together, produce some original number supplied to him. If true,
this would have profound implications across modern society,
since this technology would allow its holder to decrypt virtually
every secret message passing around the Internet.

What's more, the technique Factor Man claims to be using
is a stunningly general one. Not only is he able to factor large
numbers, he says, but he can solve virtually *any* problem where
the answer, once produced, can be recognized as correct. If you
can recognize a great symphony, he can produce one. Describe
the desired effect of a new drug, and he can produce that, as
well. Such technology would have ramifications even more
profound than simply breaking all of the codes.

When Factor Man first made these claims about a year ago,
scientists were skeptical. Now, however, he appears to be
providing a public demonstration of his purported abilities,
factoring numbers provided by relatively unassailable third
parties (such as members of the Senate Science Committee)
and of such a size that the best computer scientists have been
unable to duplicate his results.

Steven Rudich, a computer scientist at Carnegie Mellon who works in a similar area, has no good explanation for Factor Man's abilities. "It's difficult to explain," he says. "It's hard to imagine a reputable scientist taking the approach of such a showman, but it's also hard to imagine how else he might be doing this." Rudich, curiously enough, is an accomplished amateur magician.

The US Department of Homeland Security is taking Factor Man seriously as well. In a recent press conference, DHS Secretary William Fingold said, "In today's world, cyber warfare is just as dangerous as conventional warfare. An individual with the demonstrated capability to penetrate the computer systems essential for our national defense is obviously a significant threat and will be treated as such. That said, all of our critical defense systems have safeguards that could not be bypassed simply by factoring a few large numbers."

Judith Banyon is the program manager for Information Security at Amazon, responsible for a team of over 300 engineers who are required to hold top-secret security clearances before being considered for a job. "Amazon takes all cyber security threats seriously," she told us. "Whatever technology this Factor Man has at his disposal, I'm confident that the private information of our customers will remain private."

Factor Man has specifically recommended that companies like Amazon switch from 128-bit to 256-bit encryption. When asked about this, Banyon said that Amazon has used 256-bit encryption as its standard since 2014, and was working to ensure that no systems had been overlooked when the transition occurred.

Is Factor Man Impacting E-Commerce? A Little
William Burkett, The *New York Times*

Once again, Factor Man is all the news. His web site has been visited almost eighty billion times. Four months ago, I reported on the perceived likelihood that he be able to factor numbers of any particular size. As he is now factoring 114-bit numbers, most of this is irrelevant. But the perception from a couple of months back was that if Factor Man got this far, he would quite possibly be able to deliver on his claims. That perception remains. The British betting markets have gone back to simply "Factor Man yes" and "Factor Man no." The odds on both are currently quite close to even, with "no" having a slight edge.

People seem to be paying attention in more profound ways as well. As an example, the fraction of US commerce conducted over the Internet normally increases steadily over time. Since Factor Man's claims gained traction, that fraction has been unchanged. This is a small effect, but large enough to be noticeable.

On a similar note, the total volume of credit card transactions typically climbs each year, as we use our cards for more and more business. The increase is almost always around 7% annually. Things were very different in 2009, when the great recession caused a 10% *drop* in credit card use.

While the past quarter hasn't shown an actual drop, the increase has been much closer to 3% than the usual 7%. People appear to be using their credit cards just a little bit less than might have been expected.

How much of this is attributable to Factor Man? It's hard to say. Maybe none of it. But given the current uncertainty regarding the security of the Internet, it wouldn't be a surprise if people decided to shop at brick and mortar stores, and to use cash, just a tad more often.

4

LIU
MAY 3, 2018

The paths that lead us to our destinations are more often winding than they are short. My involvement in Factor Man's story was by a circuitous route indeed.

My name is Janet Liu. I spend my life in the service of my country.

I was born in 1992 in the Beijing suburb of Yongshun. Chinese families were then only allowed to have one child, and female children were hardly prized by their parents. Many mysteriously died in childbirth. Many were quietly adopted by Western foreigners. Relatively few were permitted to grow up in their homeland. I was one of them.

My parents chose to raise me not because they fell in love with the baby girl in their arms, but because they felt it was their patriotic duty to do so. I was taught from infancy that love of country is more important than love of family.

Singlemindedness of purpose, I have learned, is wonderfully freeing from an ethical perspective. What is good for China is good. What is not good for China is not good. It is that simple. I have been told that my intelligence is considerable, and I need only examine a mirror to know that my physical assets are considerable as well. All of these gifts are entirely at China's disposal.

Please do not imagine that I am some sort of automaton, following the orders of the regime with mindless devotion. Nothing could be further from the truth. I am simply a talented woman who loves her country deeply, and who has committed her life to providing what her country needs. Perhaps, on a good day, you would do the same.

From 2004 through 2009, most of my teenage years, my family was stationed with the Chinese embassy in London, and I lived there. For four years beginning in late 2009, I attended Harvard University. The result is that my English is excellent and unaccented.

Especially at first, I found my time in the West difficult. If I were to summarize the issue in a single word, I would say simply that Western society is disorganized.

Perhaps an example will help. I can go into my bank in Harvard Square and ask them to convert $150 to Chinese yuan. They will happily do so, and will give me approximately 1000 yuan in return. The transaction will take about five minutes.

I can go into my bank in Beijing and ask them to convert the 1000 yuan back into dollars. They will also happily do so, and I will receive close to the $150 with which I began. The transaction will take approximately an hour, and I will need to complete a variety of forms indicating the reason for the exchange.

This is as it should be. If I am requesting a conversion of local into foreign currency, it is appropriate for the government to take an interest in my intentions. It is reasonable for them to be concerned that I plan actions that are not in the interests of the Chinese people.

I had many occasions to discuss this with my fellow Harvard students, who seemed somehow to feel that the Chinese approach diminished my personal freedom. I would counter that it is the organization implicit in Chinese society that grants us our freedom. Compared to the United States, we are free from crime. We are free from international terrorism. A population living in fear is surely never free.

It is not as if China is a dictatorship. Our leaders are elected according to the tenets of our constitution, and following democratic practices. It is true that the Communist Party is the only participant in those elections, but if you wish to be involved, all you need do is join that party, as more than 82 million of my countrymen have done.

I spent much of my time at Harvard hoping to meet fellow students who felt about the United States the way I feel about China, but I was disappointed. The students seemed to be either idealists, out to save the entire world, or simply self-centered, hoping to get rich as doctors, lawyers, or Internet tycoons. The ones hoping to get rich struck me as more genuine, but no one was devoted to the United States itself. Given the fractured state of American politics, perhaps this should not have surprised me. If so, that is yet another argument in favor of a system such as China's.

* * *

Although I did not know it at the time, the first step of my journey into the Factor Man story was taken by Factor Man himself. He failed to respect Kris Stafford, the Google general counsel. And Mr. Stafford was a man who had come to expect respect.

Stafford's view was that he was the general counsel for one of the largest and most powerful firms on the planet. He had graduated from Harvard and was not one of the idealists. From there, he had attended Yale Law before becoming an assistant district attorney in New York. He had been general counsel for a host of high-tech companies. He wasn't about to be thought of as the tail on anyone's dog, let alone Factor Man's.

The first thing Stafford did was to have someone examine all of Factor Man's email. He was on shaky legal ground in doing this, but only shaky as opposed to outright quicksand.

The Google terms of service did indeed give Google the right to use Factor Man's emails, provided that doing so was for the purpose of improving Google technology. Keeping Google encryption technology safe would certainly count, Stafford could argue.

As Stafford well knew, Google had been challenged on its terms of service in this regard, with a variety of plaintiffs claiming that the terms violated US wiretap laws. A US District Court judge had denied Google's motion to have the lawsuit dismissed, but that meant only that it would take Google years to prevail in court as opposed to months. The judge had also denied recognition of the plaintiffs as a class, which meant that they would each have to sue Google individually. Not many individual plaintiffs had the wherewithal to challenge Google in court.

Looking through the Factor Man emails didn't tell Stafford much. There were only two names of interest: William Burkett, Factor Man's original contact in the outside world, and Bob Hasday, his attorney from Duane Morris.

Stafford made a mental note to check Hasday's legal background when he had the chance.

All told, though, he didn't find much.

Stafford was pondering this when his administrative assistant interrupted him. There was a member of Google's technical staff outside, he was told. An employee named Bob Kovacs who had gathered the Factor Man emails. Kovacs claimed to have a few ideas that Mr. Stafford might find interesting.

Stafford brought him in, taking the second step on my path into the Factor Man story. "I pulled the emails like you guys requested," Kovacs began. He explained that he (and, needless to say, most of the other staff) had been following the Factor Man story. Their collective view was that Factor Man was, in some poorly defined way, a threat to what Google did. Internet security mattered, and supporting it was in Google's interests. Kovacs explained that he had an idea, but wasn't sure it was legal.

Stafford smiled. "I'm Google's chief counsel. Let me assure you of two things. First, Google won't ever do anything illegal. Second, you *can't* do something illegal by sharing a thought with me. Keeping Google on the straight and narrow is my job, not yours."

Kovacs considered. "It's China," he finally said.

"China?"

"China. First off, Factor Man has to be just driving them nuts. I mean, they have way more secrets than anyone else. About once a month, they try to hack into Google," Kovacs explained. "Like, everybody knows it's them. The government knows it's them, the public knows it's them, we certainly know it's them. Everybody. It's generally not a big deal. We see the attack as it starts, and nothing is compromised." Kovacs, nervous, stopped again.

"And?" Stafford prodded.

"Well, what if we weren't quite so vigilant?"

"We can't give an outsider access to our inside information."

"We wouldn't have to. If someone were to compromise a single email account, they wouldn't have any more access to the rest of Google than the account holder did."

"Thank you, Bob. Let me think about it."

Kovacs left, and Stafford did indeed think about it.

Burkett
May 22, 2018

National Terrorism Advisory System Activated as 128-bit Encryption Fails

William Burkett, The *New York Times*

With the Factor Man blog providing factorizations of 128-bit numbers today, the NTAS was activated for the third time. A bulletin was issued to the effect that technology appears to exist that is capable of breaking the encryption schemes used to protect much of the secure data on which American commerce depends.

The NTAS was introduced in 2011, replacing the much-maligned "red-yellow-green" Homeland Security Advisory System. Under the NTAS, four types of alerts can be issued: elevated, intermediate, imminent, and bulletins. The first three correspond to situations where specific and credible evidence suggests that a terrorist attack may occur. The fourth "bulletin" class is used to "distribute information about trends and non-specific threats."

The Department of Homeland Security, in issuing the warning, made it clear that there was no reason to believe that the technology, should it even exist, was in the hands of agents whose interests ran counter to those of the United States. They said in a statement, "In fact, all of the information we have indicates that there are no plans to use this technology for illegal purposes. We encourage all citizens simply to continue business as usual."

Given the NTAS bulletin, it seems that the search for the Factor Man blogger is likely to intensify even further. At this point, the government continues to say that there has been no progress in finding him – or her, as the case may be.

Factor Man
May 23, 2018

```
From: Brian Finn (finnbrian@gmail.com)
To: Factor Man (factor.man@yandex.com)
Subject: First $5M deposited
```

Please acknowledge receipt, if possible

BDF

```
From: Factor Man (factor.man@yandex.com)
To: Brian Finn (finnbrian@gmail.com)
Re: First $5M deposited
```

Confirmed.

FM

I love puzzles. I just wasn't sure how much I loved this one.

There were two circles. One included Brian Finn, me, the numbered Swiss account, and the Yandex email address that I used to communicate with Brian but no one else. The other included Bob Hasday, the Gmail account, the safe deposit box and, for all I knew, the rest of the civilized world.

The Factor Man in the second circle was going to need money. I might need it to defend myself, or to make arrangements going forward. I would definitely need it to pay Hasday, and perhaps to organize the coming out party that was still a few years away. The Factor Man in the first circle had money, courtesy of Brian Finn. I just had to get it from one circle to the other.

I figured a million dollars would suffice. My plan was to assume that the entire second circle – Hasday, the Gmail account, and the safe deposit box – had been compromised. But I also was going to assume that the first circle – Finn, the Yandex email address, and the Swiss bank account – was safe.

Mostly, this was because if any element of the first circle became associated with me, they all would be. Finn himself and the Swiss bank account would naturally lead to one another. The Yandex email account would lead to Finn.

And the problem was that if Finn were known to have a relationship with Factor Man, my identity would likely be discovered. I had to assume that people knew I had reached out to William Burkett, and I suspected strongly that I was the only person on both Burkett's and Finn's contact lists.

So I had these two circles. In theory, both were secret. But in practice, only one probably was. I had to move a million bucks from one to the other without compromising anything.

The transfer would presumably have to be in cash, plain and simple. Banking transfers are simply too well monitored, even in places like Switzerland that supposedly guarantee anonymity. The Swiss account was numbered, but the Swiss still knew the identity of the owner and had shown themselves totally willing to release that information under government pressure. So cash it had to be.

I could use a courier, but there were multiple problems with that approach. First, I would have to find and contact the courier. Neither email account would work for that.

More important, though, it wasn't obvious to me that a first-time courier carrying a million bucks could be trusted. I could threaten him with the wrath of Factor Man, but a courier carrying a million in cash might choose to simply drop off the net and retire to the Caribbean.

So the courier was going to be me. I bought a plane ticket to Zurich, a round trip in my own name for a two-week stay. There were fewer security cameras in the States than there would be in Switzerland, so I walked into a high-end magic store and bought a good wig. And off I went.

From: Factor Man (factor.man@yandex.com)
To: Brian Finn (finnbrian@gmail.com)
Re: First $5M deposited

Please tell Zurich that a courier will be withdrawing $1M in cash (Euros) from the account in five days.

To answer your obvious questions: (1) I am the courier, and (2) I may need the funds for continued operations. If I do need them, I am likely to need them fairly quickly, so I am moving them to an account I can access a bit more easily.

FM

5

LIU
MAY 24, 2018

My immediate superior in the Chinese military is Lin Hu Yong (Ph.D., Stanford, 2003), who directs the Fourth Department of the Chinese People's Liberation Army, or PLA. The Fourth Department focuses on computer vulnerabilities and is generally known simply as the Information Warfare Group, or IWG. Lin himself reports directly to General Zhao Zhang of the Logistic Support Department, who is a member of the Central Military Commission, or CMC. The CMC controls the PLA and the remainder of China's military.

We do not trust the West. China has been a world power since prehistory, while the West is a relative newcomer to the world stage. Based on the events of the past century, we see little to reassure us that the West has an appropriately humble attitude toward the responsibilities that accompany a world presence. If this hubris causes the West to act irresponsibly, China needs to be prepared.

Lin's job is to prepare for – but hopefully never to conduct – a cyberattack on the West in general and on the United States in particular. He is also responsible for the day-to-day business of testing American and other Western defenses by penetrating military and commercial enterprises.

It seems to be relatively common knowledge that China is doing this. In September of 2015, your American President Obama explicitly described Chinese cyber activities as an act of aggression and told China that America was "prepared to take some countervailing actions" if the behavior continued. China responds poorly to bluster, and our behavior was unchanged.

On September 25, 2015, Obama met with his counterpart, Chinese President Xi Jingping. After the meeting, Obama announced that the two leaders had "agreed that neither the U.S. nor the Chinese government will conduct or knowingly support cyber related theft of intellectual property including trade secrets or other confidential business information for commercial advantage."

There is a great difference between activities taken to achieve a commercial advantage and activities essential to preserve Chinese sovereignty and independence. The cyber activities under Lin's direction continued without alteration.

Part of those activities involved the individual known as Factor Man. We view Factor Man as a threat to China for three distinct reasons.

First, China herself depends on the ability to compartmentalize information. There are many things that our population at large need not know. In actuality, they are often better off not knowing these things. The supposed Factor Man technology could significantly impact our ability to provide our populace with only the information that is most important to them.

Second, Factor Man appears to be an individual, with no overarching responsibilities to a state or to the world in general. We do not believe that the power implicit in the technology he claims to control should be in the hands of a single man.

Finally, it is clear that this technology, should it exist, should be available equally to all nations. We cannot accept Factor Man's apparent plan of making the information available first to a commercial entity, then to the government of the United States, and to the rest of the world only two years after the initial release. This sort of bias is simply intolerable.

Unfortunately, Factor Man himself has an extremely small profile, and it has been challenging for us to interact with him in any way. The only public footprint of his activities is the factorman0 Gmail account. General Zhao himself has instructed us to obtain access to that account, but until recently, we had not succeeded in doing so.

When you log into a computer account, you enter your password. That password is encrypted and sent out over the Internet to the computer that you are trying to access.

The encryption algorithm is public, and the encrypted password itself is also vulnerable. If I can guess your password, I can encrypt it using the same algorithm, and then confirm that I have indeed reproduced what you yourself were sending. Doing this requires that I guess your password at the outset, which is why everyone is always told to make their passwords more complicated than "password", or their dog's name, or something along those lines.

Under Lin's direction, the IWG has built a huge database of guesses, along with their encrypted versions. Every English word is in the database, with every possible pattern of capitalization. So are the modifications that have become popular, like "p@$$w0rd" instead of simply "password." If your password is in the IWG database, we can figure it out as we see you using it.

That second part can be somewhat challenging as well. When you send a message to Google, it doesn't go directly there. It first goes to your Internet Service Provider, or ISP. The message itself is labeled: "Please deliver this to Google." Of course, it doesn't say that exactly; Google has what is called an IP address which, in Google's case, is 172.217.3.174. Your ISP has its own IP address; for example, AT&T's is 144.160.36.42.

The way to think of these addresses is that they are like normal addresses, but read backwards. Google's headquarters (not where they process email, but appropriate as an example) are located at 1600 Amphitheatre Parkway, Mountain View, California, USA. The 174 at the end of the Google IP address corresponds to the 1600 Amphitheatre Parkway street address; the 172 at the beginning of the IP address corresponds to "USA". It is as if the Google IP address of 172.217.3.174 actually reads, "USA, California, Mountain View, 1600 Amphitheatre Parkway."

Consider what happens when your ISP, at 144.160.36.42, gets your email message destined for Google. It looks at the destination address (in this case, 172.217.3.174) and the first thing it asks is, "Is this the same as the originating address?" (144.160.36.42) If it is, the message can be dealt with immediately, since you're trying to send a message that doesn't actually need to travel anywhere.

In this case, however, that is insufficient. Your ISP next sends your message to what is called a *router*. The router it goes to first knows about all of the computers whose addresses look like 144.160.36.x for some value of x. If your message had only been going to one of those addresses, the first router could have handled it.

But it wasn't; it was going to Google, which is further away than that. The router therefore sends your message to a second router. This one is like a fairly large post office; it can handle mail going to anywhere in 144.160.x.y, now for arbitrary x and y. That does not work, either, so the second router sends your letter to the "national" clearinghouse, which knows about everything in the 144 domain, which is to say any address of the form 144.x.y.z.

That still does not work. So your message finally goes to a global clearinghouse, where the process is reversed. The global clearinghouse sends the message to the computer responsible for 172.x.y.z, and that computer looks at the destination address to decide to send it to the post office responsible for 172.217.x.y. Then it goes to 172.217.3.x and finally (although this entire process typically takes less than a second) it finds its way to the original intended destination of 172.217.3.174. Google has the message, and delivers it to the intended recipient.

Even though the messages are encrypted, we at the Fourth Department want to watch them as they are transmitted from one machine to another. In order to do that, we need to intercept them somewhere, and there are a variety of ways to do this.

We could, for example, make our way into one of the moderate-sized post offices and simply tell that post office to make a copy of every message that the post office handled. That is generally unacceptably risky, however, because the post office would then start sending a great number of messages to mainland China, and the traffic would be awkward to explain. This is therefore an approach that we take only rarely. But the closer the routing machine gets to mainland China, the easier (and easier to explain) the process becomes. We are therefore much more likely to intercept a message sent to Google from Egypt than one sent from San Francisco.

A few hours before Factor Man first factored 128-bit numbers, we were fortunate. We intercepted a message to Google that both included login credentials and appeared in our database of possible passwords. And we were exceptionally fortunate in that the password was to an account that had the privileges needed to access other Google information.

Accounts such as this have a limited shelf life. First, there is always the chance that the user will simply change his or her password. Primarily, however, once we log into the account, the user is informed both that the account is in use elsewhere and that a login has occurred from an unusual location. We log in from a location in a randomly selected country, so there is little chance of the activity being traced back to China, but we still tend to have a limited window in which to download as much information as possible.

After a brief discussion with my team, we decided to download three things. First, we would get the entire factorman0 file. After that, we would get all of the Internet addresses from which Factor Man had logged into his Google account. And finally, we would download information for as many other Google users as possible. That information would be encrypted (of course), but it still might be possible to find a password or two in our ever-growing password database. We got the Factor Man data and a few hundred thousand passwords before the connection was cut.

After all of the data was analyzed, I found myself with three things:
- The names William Burkett and Robert Hasday,
- The addresses from which Factor Man had accessed his account, and
- A phone number.

The phone number was the easiest to trace. When you open a Google account, you have to provide a cell phone number. Google then texts you a message that you need in order to activate the account. While there are some free cell "numbers" on the Internet, all of them have been used many times to open Google accounts, and Google now rejects them. The net result is that it's tough to open a Gmail account without giving Google the number of a cell phone that you actually have in your possession. Factor Man appeared to have done just that, and now I had the number of the phone he had used.

Unfortunately, the number turned out to be a burner phone bought with cash at a Wal-Mart in San Jose, California. It had been used exactly once, to activate Factor Man's Gmail account. I got an approximate location by seeing which cell towers were pinged by the phone, which served to reduce the radius to San Jose airport, give or take. None of this was worth the favors I had to redeem from operatives with access to Verizon's and Wal-Mart's records.

The addresses Factor Man had used to access his Google account were better in that I could find them on a map, but equally useless.

When someone sends an email, their computer has to send it to Google. It'll go from a computer in Texas, say, to one in St. Louis, then one in Portland, then to The Dalles, Oregon, and then to a Google server there.

All of these addresses are recorded, so it is possible to take the incoming email and trace it back to its origin in Texas. Depending on the nature of the sender's computer connection, you can trace it back to a specific machine, or to a fairly small network of machines.

Unfortunately, Factor Man had connected from everywhere: Greece, Germany, Russia, and many other countries. He had been using machines associated with a computer browser called TOR. TOR stands for "The Onion Ring" browser. When you look at a web page using TOR, you get directed from one TOR machine to another before finally "landing" at the web site in which you are really interested. It is impossible to unwind these machine-to-machine hops to figure out where the original user had been physically located.

That left Burkett and Hasday. Burkett proved to be useless, a reporter that Factor Man had contacted before any of this really began. Hasday was much more valuable.

```
From: Robert Hasday (rjhasday@duanemorris.com)
To: Factor Man (factorman0@gmail.com)
Re: new client?

Dear Sir/Madam:

A retention letter is attached.

Because of the unusual nature of the relationship that
you have requested, we would like to ask that you provide
us with some sort of retainer in advance. Perhaps $10,000
would be appropriate?

I am very curious as to the nature of the work that you
have for us.

Bob Hasday
```

Factor Man hadn't reached out to any other lawyers, so he had presumably paid the $10,000 fee and retained Hasday.

Given the absurdly litigious nature of American society, your lawyers never discard anything. The cover letter for the retainer, and perhaps a copy of the check, would be somewhere in the Duane Morris offices. Electronic copies might exist on the Duane Morris servers.

But the cover letter would be far more valuable. Even the envelope might help, if nothing else were available. Both were physical evidence. They might carry fingerprints, or traces of DNA.

Most of the interactions I have with the West involve the acquisition of technology: patent applications, software, algorithms, and similar. Obtaining a specific file in the possession of a specific attorney would be far more difficult. But China needed to know who Factor Man was, so I needed to find Duane Morris' Factor Man file.

Factor Man
May 27, 2018

I had no idea that the Chinese had learned Bob Hasday's identity when I landed in Zurich. I had with me two weeks' worth of summer/fall clothes in a small suitcase, and an oversized but otherwise nondescript duffel bag. Inside the duffel bag were the wig and a large, bright blue, attention-grabbing backpack.

I was staying at the Belvoir Swiss Quality Hotel, in a room I had booked in my own name and with my own credit card. I passed through customs easily and made my way to the hotel, a delightful 4½-star property with a beautiful view of Lake Zurich. I was booked into the Belvoir Suite, an absurdly appointed room with hardwood floors, glass walls, and a price tag of about $800/night.

Please understand that I don't normally travel like this. But I figured that I was about to withdraw $1 million in cash from the bank, and I could afford to splurge a little. In all honesty, I'd earned it. If the overall Factor Man plan worked, I wouldn't care about the money. And if it didn't work, I probably wouldn't care about the money, either. I was all in, so I might as well act that way.

The food was excellent and the bed comfortable. The next morning, I got up, showered, shaved, dressed, had breakfast, and made my way to the bank that Finn had selected. (Credit Suisse; no surprise there.) While there, I learned how amazingly easy it is to withdraw a million dollars in cash (Euros, actually) from an account that holds five times that amount. I put the money in the duffel bag and returned to the Belvoir.

It had all seemed incredibly simple. Looking back on it, though, I realized that I must have revealed my identity fifty times over the course of that single day. I had paid for the meals and the hotel room. I had needed to show ID at the bank. Even though it was not part of the credentials Finn had given me, the bank itself wanted it as a part of the transaction. And I had surely been photographed many times, both in the bank and on the streets of security-conscious Switzerland.

It had been simple because it was *supposed* to be simple. This was the easy circle, the one that included Brian Finn. In this circle, I was just another tourist, just another bank customer.

The bed in the Belvoir Suite was just as comfortable the second night, but I slept badly. The next morning, I settled my account with the hotel and took a taxi to the train station. There, I bought a slightly unusual round trip train ticket toward Vienna.

Vienna. The safe deposit box. The second circle, where anonymity would change from being an impossible luxury to an absolute essential. The camera behind the ticket agent never blinked as I paid for my train ticket with cash. It was just after 8 in the morning.

Burkett
May 28, 2018

I, of course, didn't know a damn thing about any of this. Not about the five million dollars, or the trip to Zurich, or the Chinese, or the fact that Factor Man had managed to tick off Google. I just checked the blog every day, as we all did, and watched the numbers get bigger.

It was a lot like watching grass grow. The numbers being factored got bigger, on average, by a factor of two every three days. It took about a week and a half for them to add another digit. And trust me, the difference between a 40-digit number and a 41-digit number isn't all that impressive to behold.

Grass growing.

Meanwhile, the speculation continued unabated. The betting markets were now leaning pretty heavily in Factor Man's favor, with odds of about 4:1 that he would actually pull this off. The conspiracy theorists remained conspiracy theorists, and were joined by some even wackier folks, who maintained that Factor Man was a space alien, or a visitor from our own future.

Mostly, of course, people did what they always did. They watched, they were entertained, and they figured it would never really affect them.

And when I say people, I mean people including me.

* * *

It was a Friday morning around nine. Emma and I were just finishing breakfast.

In case you don't remember Emma, she's the one who stood me up the evening after my first (actually, my only) email from Factor Man. I have long since forgiven her, for which I have been richly rewarded.

You may be wondering what we were doing at home at nine on a Friday morning. The answer is that being a reporter (my job), and being a manuscript screener for a literary agent (Emma's job) both have their perks. There aren't many, but staring into someone else's eyes over Cheerios on a slightly lazy Friday morning is certainly one of them. We were dressed for work, mind you. We just hadn't gotten around to leaving yet.

On this particular Friday, our Cheerios were interrupted by a knock on the door. I answered it to find a couple of guys in suits.

"Good morning, Mr. Burkett," the taller one said. "I'm Special Agent John Hudson of the FBI." He showed me some ID and then gestured toward the shorter one. "This is Special Agent Ron Livingstone. May we come in?"

There are a couple things to point out here. First, "shorter" is only a relative term. Livingstone still had me by a good three inches. And Hudson, the other guy, wasn't just way taller than I was, he was broader as well. A looming physical presence. That's what comes from being the long arm of the federal government, I guess.

When someone like John Hudson shows up in the movies, the doofus who just opened the door generally does something clever. In response to Hudson identifying himself as a federal agent and asking if he can come in, maybe he whips out his trusty Walther PPK and shoots everyone. Maybe he's got a witty retort like, "Sure, but I'm on my way out. Please check that the dog has water." And maybe he just says, "No," and shuts the door.

I did none of these things. I didn't do the first two because I owned neither a pistol nor a dog. And I didn't do the third because I was too busy just standing there with my mouth open.

Hudson appeared to be waiting for me to close my mouth, which didn't happen. Eventually, he just asked again. "Mr. Burkett?" I stepped aside and let them in.

"Good morning, Ms. Hardaway," he said. "We're sorry to interrupt your breakfast." Nobody had told them Emma's name, first or last. I hate it when people know stuff about my personal life and I have no idea how they know it. I hated it so much that I closed my mouth.

This led to another staring contest, which I lost. "What can I do for you?" I eventually asked.

"We're trying to find Factor Man," Hudson said.

Interesting. It hadn't dawned on me yet why they were asking me. "You and the rest of the civilized world. Maybe you should take a number." I really need to think more before talking.

Hudson pulled up a chair and sat down. He did that thing where you turn the chair around and sit on it backwards, maybe leaning forward and resting your arms on the backrest. Livingstone just stood there. Do what you're good at, I guess.

"The first mention of Factor Man – anywhere, as far as we can tell – is in an article you wrote. Remember it? 'How to Find a Crackpot,' I think it was called.

"Blogspot has shared some of the records with us. Your article came out the day *before* the Factor Man blog was visible to the public. We'd love to understand how that happened."

Suddenly, this looked a good bit more complicated. "I'm a reporter. I report things. I'm good at it."

"We understand, Mr. Burkett. But reporting this particular thing, when you did, seems a bit, shall we say, prescient. As far as we can figure, there are only two possibilities. Either you're Factor Man, or you know Factor Man. So tell me: Are you Factor Man?"

"Absolutely." *Think first, William. Think first.*

Hudson seemed unfazed. "I see. In one of the first papers on NP-complete-ness, Karp listed twenty-one problems that turned out to be NP-complete. Can you tell me, say, three of them?"

I said nothing. Perhaps I was learning.

"Ah," Hudson continued. "So let's say you aren't Factor Man. That means you probably *know* Factor Man. Yes?"

Saying nothing seemed to be working for me. I kept it up.

"Let me cut to the chase here. We believe that Factor Man is someone you've had contact with. Maybe he sent you a text, or maybe an email at some point.

"We can get your contacts and cell phone records from Verizon, and your email records from your employer. But those things will take time. The FBI's view is that Factor Man, whoever he is, is potentially an imminent terrorist threat. So we came over here hoping to save that time."

I thought about this. I'm a reporter. I had no idea if they actually could get all that stuff through a court order or the like. On the other hand, there was nothing in any of my contact lists that would do them a damn bit of good. On the *other* hand, there was all the "never give up your sources" crap that journalists are supposed to believe in.

"I can't save you the time. I'm a reporter. I won't give up my sources."

I can't believe I actually said that. It was like a comic, where the words were hanging in some kind of balloon in front of my face.

Hudson considered. "Final answer?" he asked me.

"Final answer."

"I'm sorry." He reached into his jacket and pulled out a piece of paper. "Here's a warrant for your computer and your cell phone. Please provide them to us, and we'll let you get on with your morning."

Hudson's card was stapled to the top of the warrant. The whole thing totally sucked.

Liu
May 28, 2018

I did my research on Robert Hasday, generally known as Bob. He was a typical contract attorney in many ways. He stayed out of the courtroom, per-haps because he hated it, and had an extraordinary reputation as a draftsman, producing virtually flawless contracts that accurately reflected his clients' wishes. He tended not to meet with the clients in person, rather finding out what they wanted and making it happen.

Hasday's ability to "make it happen" was legendary. He could take a client's convoluted desires, untangle them, and prepare a legal document that was both rock solid and an accurate reflection of what the client had originally requested. He could also take material produced by another attorney, untangle it, and accurately advise his client of both the pitfalls and loopholes that a potential agreement contained.

For doing this, Hasday charged something upwards of $1000 an hour. He loved his work, and Duane Morris loved how well he did it. He'd been doing it for well over thirty years, and his clients all swore by him. The fact that Hasday cost so much meant that they typically used him only for their most complicated arrangements, which appeared to be to Hasday's liking. He had plenty of work, and the more complicated it was, the more he enjoyed doing it.

I assumed he would be surprised when I called to ask for an appointment in person. I informed Nancy, his legal assistant, that I was a prospective client on a sensitive matter and hoped that Mr. Hasday could make the time to meet with me. He had agreed, and the meeting was now.

Hasday's office was predictably impressive, just east of Times Square in New York City. Hasday himself was a bit shorter than my 175cm (5'9"), clearly smart, suit and tie, and looked to be about sixty.

The business card I gave him said that I was a principal with Zedong Enterprises, located in Beijing. The card was lightly perfumed, in English on one side and Mandarin on the other. I presented it in the formal Chinese way, using two hands, a custom stemming from an age-old requirement to demonstrate that one is not holding a weapon. I ensured that my English was slightly accented when I spoke.

Hasday invited me to sit, and we both did; Nancy offered us coffee before leaving, and we both declined.

"Tell me, Ms. Liu, what can we do for you?"

"Janet, please. My firm needs some assistance with a contract with a potential American partner."

I went on to explain that Zedong was a software development firm specializing in the development of user interfaces for the Chinese market.

I told Hasday that we were, for the first time, attempting to do business with an American firm, developing the user interface for a patient database system. The American firm had drafted a consulting agreement to manage the relationship, and Zedong was finding it difficult to understand.

"It is perplexing," I explained. "It is as if they have drafted the agreement with only their own interests in mind."

Hasday looked puzzled.

"I'm sure I have misunderstood," I explained. "It would be foolish of them to do that, as it would place our relationship on an adversarial footing from the outset."

Hasday smiled, and then told me that Duane Morris would be unable to represent me without doing a conflict check to ensure that they did not represent the American medical firm as well. "Assuming that there are no conflicts," he said, "We'll ask you to pay us a retainer. Then you can email me a copy of the proposed agreement and I'll take a look at it."

I feigned confusion. "We have many competitors in China," I explained. "It would be unfair to them to email the draft agreement to you."

A few moments passed, and I realized that I needed to clarify once again. "It might encourage them to try to break into your email servers. We would not wish to do that."

"I see," Hasday responded.

"May I provide you with a copy of the agreement now, with the understanding that you only examine it if you are able to represent us?" I asked.

Hasday responded that that would be fine. "Is it okay if I make a copy of this agreement and leave the original with you?" he asked.

I continued to look somewhat uneasy. "Yes, of course. Where will the copy be kept?"

"My files stay in this office, across the hall. When our case is completed, we keep them in offsite storage for twenty years."

"I see. That will be fine. Thank you for your consideration, Mr. Hasday."

"Bob. Please. But do understand that if the conflict check reveals an issue, we will have to destroy the copy of the agreement and ask that you find other counsel."

"Yes, of course," I told him.

"Excellent," Hasday said. "It should take a day or two, and I'll be in touch soon." He shook my hand and returned me to Nancy.

* * *

We broke in three nights later.

On the first night, one of my operatives identified the people who cleaned the building each evening. He offered to help them clean when they came back, and their initial reluctance was rapidly overcome by the fact that he was willing to pay a reasonably large sum of money for the privilege of providing such assistance.

Once inside the building, it was relatively easy. I had recorded my initial visit to Hasday's office using a camera hidden in one of the buttons on my dress, and that allowed the operative to locate both Hasday's office and the file room opposite. The locks were predictably not a concern at all.

The filing cabinet labeled "Hasday – Active," did not contain a Factor Man file, so the operative quickly scanned through all of the files. In the one labeled "pending," he found the letter.

> Thank you for your email. A signed copy of your retention agreement is enclosed, along with $10,000 in cash.
>
> I am also enclosing a key to a safe deposit box at Sparta Global Intelligence Group, Löwengasse 39, 1030 Vienna. The box number is 1739 and the password is I@mF@ctorm@n. I will use the box to transfer additional funds to you as needed.
>
> If I send you a message mentioning a famous physicist, please check the safe deposit box …

Using a small portable printer that he had brought with him, the operative scanned the letter and made a copy. Wearing gloves, he kept the original letter and replaced it with the copy in the file folder. He took the original envelope, placing both it and the letter in a clear polyurethane envelope in his pocket.

He then began a careful but ultimately fruitless search for the key to the safe deposit box.

* * *

Invaluable though it was, the letter unfortunately provided neither fingerprints nor traces of DNA. The lack of a key was perhaps regrettable, but also perhaps not. It would have been impossible to either use or duplicate it without Factor Man learning that we had it. The key itself was presumably in

Hasday's possession or in his house, and neither would have been difficult to deal with. But the risks in doing so were hardly negligible, and the advantages modest. We would do without the key, although we would take the obvious precaution of hacking into the Duane Morris email server and ensuring that if Factor Man contacted Hasday by email, we would be informed.

Factor Man apparently anticipated getting some money to Hasday at a point in the future. We had no interest in the money itself, but great interest in Factor Man.

It was difficult to know if he would bring the money to Sparta Global Intelligence Group, or trust that to a surrogate of some sort. I suspected that he would do it himself, as getting the money to a surrogate would be no easier in principle than giving it to Hasday directly, and would only introduce an additional complexity to the operation.

Assuming that I was correct, Factor Man would at some point be paying a visit to the address in Vienna. He would presumably send Hasday the message only after that visit was complete, however. Given that our goal was to find Factor Man, we would need to be at the safe deposit box beforehand.

There seemed to be no way to accomplish this other than simply by staffing it. Thankfully, Sparta Global was only open during fairly normal business hours, from 10AM until 8PM Monday through Friday. That would make things far simpler. We would watch the address when it was open, capturing video of every customer. We would also need to find a way to match the video to the person owning the box. I arranged with my superiors to have five additional agents meet me in Vienna.

* * *

"Sparta Global Intelligence Group" was better known simply as "Sparta Safes," one of a group of shops in downtown Vienna. There was open air seating across the street, which would make surveillance straightforward. The most significant problem was likely to be simple drudgery, especially if we needed to remain for an extended period.

The second most significant problem was that we had no way of knowing when Factor Man had left something in the box for Hasday. I had an idea about that, and entered Sparta Safes as a customer.

I rented a small box, taking surreptitious images of both the facility layout and of the single staffer who helped me. I was told about the four private areas in which customers could conduct business, although I was warned that Sparta was a small facility and the rooms were not electronically secure.

Once outside, I enjoyed a coffee and waited until the staffer himself left shortly after 4PM. He was presumably replaced by another staffer, and a second agent entered the facility to rent a second box and deal with that staffer.

Over the course of a week, there were a total of four employees, and we rented a box from each. Each staffer was followed to a relatively private location, where he or she was offered the sum of 25,000 Euros in exchange for a discreet but immediate phone call if anyone attempted to access box 1739. The staffers were told (correctly, not that it mattered) that since no attempt was being made to identify the owner of the box, nothing illegal was being suggested. All four of the staffers accepted without negotiation, and the wait began.

6

FACTOR MAN
MAY 28, 2018

I was booked on the RailJet 165 train to Vienna. RJ 165 left Zurich at 10:40AM; I used the time before departure to visit an electronics shop that opened at nine. I bought a pair of high-end night vision goggles with cash, and slipped them into the duffel along with the money. Back to the railway station in plenty of time, I boarded the RJ 165, even though I had no intention – yet – of going to Vienna.

Let me be clear here. I'm not a spy. I'm a computer scientist. In the world of Internet security, if you want to keep a company's internal network private, you put it behind a firewall. Between the firewall and the outside world, there is generally something called the DMZ, or demilitarized zone. If someone from the outside wants to access the company's network, they have to go through the DMZ. From there, they can use a limited number of tools to get through the firewall and access the network itself.

DMZ really is an appropriate acronym. You can get into it, but then you have to remove your weapons before going further. The DMZ keeps the network itself reasonably safe.

My view of the two circles was similar. The circle with Brian Finn needed to be kept safe; the circle with Bob Hasday was in the outside world and inherently unsafe. I had to go between the two circles – exactly once, if my overall plan held up – and to do that, I introduced a real-world equivalent of the network DMZ. When I eventually returned from the safe deposit box in

Vienna, I would use the DMZ as a waypoint to ensure my anonymity before reentering the world of the first circle.

At least, that was the plan.

In this case, the DMZ was a small town on the RJ 165 route called Ötztal.

Ötztal is a spectacularly beautiful town in the Tyrolean Alps. The Ötztal Glacier Road is the highest paved road in the Alps, over 9200 feet high. The valley itself was briefly famous in 1991 when a natural mummy from about 3300 BC was discovered there. Nicknamed The Iceman (also simply Ötzi), the amazingly preserved body provided a wealth of information about Europeans of the Chalcolithic age. Ötzi is currently on display in the South Tyrol Museum of Archaeology in Bolzano, Italy.

My plans were quite mundane. The round trip train ticket I had bought actually involved two trips, one from Zurich to Ötztal and one from Ötztal to Vienna some time later. I detrained in Ötztal, and walked to the Ferienschlössl, a luxury hotel that I had already confirmed had three crucial properties. They took cash, they had good quality Wi-Fi in the rooms, and they had covered parking.

I did not have a reservation at the Ferienschlössl, but they had space, and were more than happy to accept cash for a twelve-night stay, along with a significant security deposit. Living only on cash – but with plenty of it – definitely has things to recommend it. I made myself at home.

The next eleven nights were wonderful. I did, of course, have my daily number factoring responsibilities, but that process was nearly entirely automated by now, and most of what I did involved sending emails (through TOR, of course) to one notable or another in order to confirm that the numbers that supposedly came from them in fact did. I would post to the blog, close my laptop, and go hiking.

The Alps were extraordinary. Stunning scenery on all sides. It was early summer, and the altitude meant that the weather was brisk, almost fall-like. The days were clear and the mountain air so fresh you could taste it. Between the altitude and my general lack of exercise, hiking began as a struggle, but got easier every day. The first day, I had bought a cane to use as a walking stick. I rarely needed it any more, but brought it with me anyway.

As much as I appreciated the hiking and the scenery, though, I appreciated what I didn't do just as much.

I didn't talk to colleagues. I didn't talk with my family (whom, truth be told, I missed terribly). I didn't work. (Fancy that!) I didn't watch movies. I didn't see any ads. Amazingly enough, I didn't even worry.

And there was one other thing I didn't do.

I didn't shave.

I had gone without shaving for a week once thirty years previously, spent on a small yacht in the Caribbean. The week was great, but when I saw pictures from the end of the trip, I was mortified. Mostly, I looked so Jewish as to be unrecognizable; the photos showed a rabbi as opposed to a scientist. There had been other weeks in the Caribbean, but I had always brought a razor.

The day before I checked out of the Ferienschlössl, I rose early. I put the night vision goggles, the wig, the briefcase and backpack, and about $950,000 in cash in the duffel bag. About $40,000 was, amazingly enough, in my pockets. I had breakfast, walked to the train station, and boarded the RJ 161 at 9:51AM, as planned.

As I did so, I slipped on the wig. I had actually practiced this, and I think I had gotten pretty good at it. Once on the train, I entered a bathroom and trimmed my beard. I also transferred everything from the duffel bag to the backpack, and discarded the duffel bag itself.

Between the beard and the wig, I would not be recognized as either the rabbi or the clean cut American tourist by the folks at the Ferienschlössl. No one in Europe had even seen the backpack, until now. I put on a cheap pair of sunglasses that I had bought in the train station, and sent an email.

```
From: Factor Man (factorman0@gmail.com)
To: Bob Hasday (rjhasday@duanemorris.com)
Subject: physicists

Albert Einstein, perhaps?
```

I figured the money would be in the box before Hasday could possibly arrange a pickup, and the less time it spent there, the better.

And then I waited, hoping to allow the train to rock me to sleep. I would be in Vienna at 2:30, and would have a busy afternoon.

Liu
June 8, 2018

We almost surely saw the message before Hasday did. It was distressing, to say the least. It seemed unlikely that after a week of constant surveillance, we had somehow missed the drop-off.

Given that our goal was simply to identify Factor Man as opposed to interfering with him, we had only poor options. The broader goal was to ensure that China had access to the technology that Factor Man had apparently developed; as things stood, the technology might give the West unacceptable advantages in a variety of areas. The fact that China no longer refers to you as Western imperialists reflects more a change in language than one in attitude.

None of the more dramatic options would further this goal. We could break into the box, but that would serve to inconvenience Factor Man as opposed to identifying him. It would presumably alert him to our presence as well. We could destroy Sparta Safes in its entirety, making it appear to have been a terrorist attack. That would have the same effect. What we needed was a photograph, an address, or a fingerprint. An email address that actually meant something would be similarly valuable.

We decided to wait for the pickup. Maybe, just maybe, Factor Man would watch for the pickup as well and we could pick him up then. In the meantime, I had the unpleasant responsibility of contacting General Zhao and informing him that we had probably failed.

* * *

I would realize later that Factor Man was probably waiting as well. He had presumably arrived in Vienna, traveled to Sparta Safes (on foot from the train depot was as easy as any other option), and waited. Traffic at the small business was slow that afternoon; there was rarely even a single customer. Factor Man's preference was likely to have been to drop off the money in as crowded a facility as possible. I could imagine him, getting an espresso from a local café and waiting quietly for Sparta to see some business. Perhaps he was reading. Perhaps he was only pretending to be reading a book that he had purchased from a local shop in a foreign language. But there was no way to know. The park across from the safe deposit box had the same traffic as ever.

Shortly before four, three customers entered Sparta in relatively rapid succession. I got a call a few minutes later to inform me that box 1739 had been accessed.

I entered Sparta Safes briskly, removing my safe deposit box and noticing that three others did indeed appear to be missing. This was confirmed when the safe agent showed me to a private area, telling me that they were busy today and that I had been lucky to get the last remaining space.

The attendant had been correct when he told me that the booth was not electronically secure, and I placed a call to the agent who had been on watch with me. I told him that there were three possibilities. It was difficult to predict what a Duane Morris courier would look like; perhaps a businessman or woman of some sort, but it was hard to tell. I called in the four remaining members of the team; we would need to follow everyone, and still leave enough people in place to follow anyone else who appeared to be watching. My staff of five was distressingly thin.

We watched the traffic in and out of Sparta Safes. There was one new arrival, and four departures. Not counting the arrival, the departures were a man and woman dressed professionally, and a bearded man with a blue backpack, a cane and a slight limp. The professionally dressed man somehow struck me as the best prospect, and I decided to follow him myself; individual agents were assigned to the other two departures. As I left, I told the three remaining agents to follow the next three people to leave the square, provided that they had been there when the call about box 1739 had come in.

Following someone solo involves a nearly impossible level of tradecraft. If you can see the subject, the subject can see you. And eventually, he or she will wonder why it is that the same person keeps appearing, be it in restaurants, on the subway, or in a movie theater.

Of the six targets, three would eventually be lost because it was simply too difficult for one agent to track them. The professional woman seemed to notice what was up, boarded a crowded U-Bahn train and got off at the last moment. One of the three people leaving the square was short, and simply disappeared into a crowd. Another of them appeared to have noticed the pursuit and approached a police officer.

The three agents involved backed off and reported back to me. They were reassigned, so that each of the remaining targets now had two followers. I did not know at the time if we were still following the target of interest, but the following itself had gotten substantially easier.

Factor Man
June 8, 2018

Two circles. One public, one anonymous. Getting the money into the safe deposit in the public circle had, not surprisingly, been easy. Getting myself back into the private circle was potentially significantly harder.

I had no idea if I was being followed or not. But the plan I had produced so long ago assumed that I was, that I had somehow been picked up at Sparta Safes and now needed to make my way through the DMZ in Ötztal and back into the safety of the private circle in Zurich.

The first stop was Ötztal. But if the DMZ were to serve its purpose, I had to be clean when I got there. If I had a tail, I needed to lose it between Vienna and the Tyrolean Alps.

As I've said, I'm not a spy. If people were following me, it was a safe bet that they would be better at following than I was at looking. Probably much better. So I needed some way to become effectively invisible between Vienna and Ötztal. After a reasonable amount of deliberation – undoubtedly informed by too many spy movies – I had come up with a plan. The first step was to buy a disposable cell phone with cash.

At an Internet café, I used the cell phone as authentication to create a new email account and then pulled up craigslist. Google was kind enough to translate the page, and I found a handful of late model vehicles for sale privately. I sent messages to each of the sellers, and waited to hear back. I had an early dinner, since I didn't know when I would be able to eat again. Probably not any time soon.

The first response was within ten minutes and came before I had finished my meal. Yes, the car, a dark blue Toyota, was still available. The address was on the Erdbrustgasse, in the outskirts of Vienna.

I took a taxi to the location, and bought the little Toyota without negotiating, surprising the seller by – again – paying cash. The purchase consumed most of what I had held back from Finn's million dollars, but that was fine.

Liu
June 8, 2018

The two agents following the man with the beard and cane saw all of this and called me. "It's the one with the backpack," they told me. "He knows, and he's running."

This was excellent news for multiple reasons. First, we would be able to focus all of our assets on following a single man. Six trained agents can follow anyone with essentially no risk of detection. I redirected the remaining agents – myself included – toward the Erdbrustgasse.

Better still, though, it was not unreasonable to assume that we were following Factor Man himself. The courier wouldn't run. We must have gotten the timing wrong somehow. Perhaps I would be spared my call to General Zhao after all.

Factor Man
June 8, 2018

I drove the Toyota to the Ringstrassen-Galerien, a shopping mall between where I had bought the car and central Vienna. I parked at the shaded outer edge of the mall parking lot but did not get out.

I could only come up with three ways for people to tail me. They could drive along behind me, put a GPS on the car somehow, or use a satellite. I had plans for dealing with all of those.

Burkett
June 8, 2018

I, of course, knew nothing about any of this. I had no cell phone and no computer, so I pretty much knew nothing about anything.

The FBI heavies left, and Emma let me use her cell phone. I called my editor, who called the legal folks at the *Times*. They told me to go buy a new phone and a new computer, and expense them both. They also got a bunch of other lawyers involved, all of whom asked me the same questions about whether the FBI guys had mistreated me, and then went off to do lawyerly things.

I went to a Verizon kiosk and got a new phone. I told them that my old phone was lost, which seemed true enough. They asked me if I wanted them to remotely wipe my old phone.

Good question. I called one of the lawyers and asked him. He called me back ten minutes later and said that there was legal precedent that remotely wiping a phone in police custody counted as destruction of evidence. So I shouldn't do it.

The phone was locked, of course; I'm not a complete moron. I wondered if the FBI would manage to hack into my phone like they had the phone of those terrorists in California.

I went to a local Apple store and got a new computer. I restored it from a backup of my old computer, said backup being about two months old. Embarrassing in one sense, but totally irrelevant in another, since all that really mattered was my email, which was in the cloud anyway. I had been writing a story about the likely economic impact if Factor Man turned out to be able to do what he said he could do, and that was gone, but it would probably be better if I started over in any case.

So far, so good. But things were about to get a whole lot worse. I was about to learn that writing about the news is a lot more pleasant than actually *being* the news.

The *Times* lawyers (there were more of them than I could have imagined) filed about thirty court actions on Monday morning. They filed to get my computer and cell phone back. They filed to ensure that the FBI didn't hack their way into either one, on the grounds that it was an invasion of privacy and I hadn't been accused of committing a crime. They filed to ensure that the FBI didn't hack their way into either one on the grounds that since I was a reporter, my contacts were protected by the First Amendment. They said that the warrant itself had been improperly executed. And they filed a whole bunch of motions that were even less comprehensible than that.

The only real result of all of the legal wrangling was to make my life worse.

Yes, an emergency court order was issued on Monday telling the FBI to leave my phone alone. In actuality, though, it had taken them about five minutes to hack into it over the weekend. They got the phone numbers of a bunch of friends and business contacts, and that was about it. They did get into my email account from my phone, and they found out that Factor Man had used factorman0@gmail.com to contact me originally. My laptop got treated about the same.

The legal arguments in many of the *Times* cases were somewhat bizarre. It turns out that all the protections offered by US law are rooted in the US Constitution, and the courts have ruled that those protections don't apply to non-citizens outside the geographic borders of the United States. No one had a clue if Factor Man was a citizen or not. No one had a clue where he was, geographically speaking. So it wasn't clear if he was entitled to the same legal protections guaranteed the rest of us.

But the fact that the *Times* had filed all these cases became public knowledge. And that, unfortunately, made me something of a cause célèbre. People had sort of forgotten that I had introduced Factor Man to the world way back when, in my old "How to Find a Crackpot" article. Now, with some of the briefs filed by the government including mentions of my email communication with the "likely terrorist known as Factor Man," I became the one guy that the whole world figured knew him personally. And suddenly the whole world wanted to know me personally.

Since Factor Man had mentioned in his initial message that I had (apparently) done him a favor at some point, things became even worse. Maybe I *did* know him personally. At a minimum, it was reasonable that we had met some time. Whether I was on TV (which happened a lot), accosted in the street (which also happened a lot), or simply interrupted somewhere while trying to mind my own business (which also ... you get the point), everyone, it seemed, wanted to know what I thought.

What would Factor Man do next? Was he a fraud? Was there anyone from my past who stuck out as a likely candidate? Just thinking about all the people I had ever known, did they seem reasonable? Was there anyone odd or creepy? Any criminals?

It was all the same question, of course. And as often as I told people I had absolutely no idea about the answer, they just kept asking anyway.

7

HUDSON
JUNE 8, 2018

I've been an FBI agent for twenty-seven years. That's most of my life, and virtually all of my professional life. In all that time, I've gotten reasonable cooperation from exactly two journalists.

William Burkett wasn't one of them.

Mostly, he was just a kid. He hadn't learned that it's in everyone's interests to stop terrorists before they start, and he hadn't learned that favors to the FBI generally come back in spades. You treat us well, and we remember. Treat us badly, and we remember that, too.

Burkett would presumably learn both of these things at some point. But right now, he was just a kid. A kid with attitude, true, but they all have attitude.

We were surprised to learn that the Factor Man individual was using the same Gmail account both for his public persona and to conduct business. If he'd made that mistake once, he'd probably made it more than once. So I reached out to Google and asked to see all of Factor Man's email.

Google said no.

I always find this amazing. Google has zero concern for your privacy, and I mean zero. They keep track of every Internet search you've ever done. Getting your wife some jewelry for her birthday? Google knows. Checking out the hookers in Vegas? Google knows that as well. Its basic view is that your private information belongs to you and to Google. Just not to anyone else.

I next asked to see a list of Factor Man's contacts, arguing that the contacts themselves were not necessarily private, and that since Factor Man had not established himself as either a US citizen or resident, all of the contacts were potential co-conspirators in whatever it was that Factor Man was actually up to, and so on.

Google, ever obliging, sent me a list of the over one hundred million email addresses that had been used to send email to Factor Man.

It is always a mistake to believe that you can bury the United States government with data.

* * *

The National Security Agency, or NSA, used to be a relatively obscure branch of the United States government. Their job, roughly speaking, was to gather and analyze all data or other information that might be of interest to the government.

As data gathering became more common in society generally, the NSA was forced out of the shadows and into the public eye. When Edward Snowden showed that (again, roughly speaking) all of our cell phone conversations were considered "data or other information that might be of interest to the government," the NSA became a household word.

The NSA didn't like Gmail. The reason was that Gmail is encrypted: When you send a message using Gmail, it's encrypted before it even leaves your computer and heads out over the Internet. The recipient (assuming that he's also using Gmail) decrypts it only after it arrives on his machine. The large (and supposedly therefore unfactorable) numbers used for the encryption are part of your Google account.

The fact that the NSA can't *read* the emails annoys them greatly. But even though they can't read the emails, they are undaunted. Send a message over Gmail, and the NSA will quietly record where it's coming from. Read a message over Gmail, and they'll record where you are when you get it.

None of this worked with Factor Man, incidentally, since he used TOR. Much as the NSA disliked Gmail, they disliked TOR more.

But the list of email addresses provided to the government by Google was a treasure trove. Each email address included both a name (supposedly, the name of a contact in Factor Man's database) and an IP address, which was the Internet location that the contact tended to use when his Google account was active. It also included a timestamp, giving the date at which the contact last was in touch with Factor Man.

Much as the NSA didn't like Google and TOR, they liked Factor Man even less. Their relationship with Factor Man was fundamentally asymmetric: Factor Man could potentially learn the NSA's secrets, but not the other way around.

The NSA was generally in favor of asymmetric relationships. Just not when the asymmetry went in this particular direction. So they were eager to learn whatever they could from the contact list that Google had supplied.

For each contact, they began by finding all of the times that the IP address in question had been used to send or receive email from Google. That was straightforward, since they knew all the times that *anyone* had sent or received such email.

Then they found the message whose timestamp matched the most recent contact with Factor Man, and looked to see if the message was incoming or outgoing. They found, not surprisingly, that while a hundred million people had sent email to Factor Man, Factor Man had responded to far fewer. And it was rare indeed that the last email went from Factor Man to the contact, as opposed to the other way around.

If Factor Man was uninterested in factoring your number, the email would be inbound (to Factor Man) only. If he checked your identity, there would be an outbound message asking for confirmation, and then an inbound message providing it.

Burkett's exchange with Factor Man didn't show up, which meant that the last message was from Burkett to Factor Man. (The message was the one requesting more time to publish the original article, but the NSA didn't know that.) In fact, there was exactly one instance of Factor Man sending a message to which there had been no response.

The Feds could tell that it was a short message. We couldn't read it, but I learned much later that it said, "Albert Einstein, perhaps?"

The recipient was Robert Hasday of Duane Morris.

We had found Factor Man's lawyer, and we were all over it.

Factor Man
June 8, 2018

I sat in the parking lot, going through the mental list I had made of what I needed to do. Defeat GPS. Defeat following me by car. And defeat satellite.

One. I had to make sure that no one approached the car.

Two. I had to access the online documentation for this make and model of Toyota.

Three. I had to wait for the mall to close.

Following me using GPS would involve an actual device, attached either to the car or to me. I had been careful to ensure that no one had any significant physical contact with me from the time I left Sparta Safes until I bought the car, and there was no way the car could have been tagged before I started driving it. So the risk was that someone put a tracker on the car now, while I was sitting in it.

I was approached only once while I was parked, by a security guard for the mall. I just started the car and drove to another remote location in the parking lot.

There are GPS jammers, incidentally. But they work by putting out a random signal on the same frequency that GPS systems use, and I figured that anybody trying to track me could track that signal just as easily.

Accessing the online documentation for the Toyota was easy. I used the burner phone to create a hotspot, logged onto TOR, and was pretty much safe. Once I found the documentation, I located the fuse box to the left of the steering wheel, and found the fuses for the brake lights, interior lights, and directionals. In theory, I could simply not use my turn signals, but I was afraid that I might do so out of simple habit. Not a spy. I left the fuses in for now.

And then I waited. It would have been boring, if I hadn't been so nervous. I did take time to factor the day's five numbers and post the results, of course.

Liu
June 8, 2018

The subject drove to the mall, and parked. Parking for the mall was a multilevel structure; he parked on the top level, which was the least occupied, and simply remained in the car.

Surveillance was relatively straightforward. One other agent and I, in our vehicles, followed him to the top floor and parked some distance away, keeping him in sight. The remaining agents were on lower floors, near the exit. The fact that there was only a single exit would eventually make it easy to resume the tail.

Mall security also noticed the isolated vehicle, and approached it. The subject started his car at that point and parked closer in. The mall cop left, and the subject vehicle returned to a point (albeit a different one) on the edge of the lot. The subject remained in the vehicle. We had to maintain a reasonable distance, which made it difficult to determine what he was doing, although he seemed to be using a laptop computer. This provided some measure of confirmation that the subject was indeed Factor Man.

The subject appeared to manipulate something under the dashboard on the left side of the vehicle, but it was impossible to determine what he was doing.

Everyone waited.

The mall closed at nine. The subject vehicle left and proceeded to a rest area on the A1, just west of Vienna. He parked in a relatively remote location in the rest area and waited. The two closest agents drove by the rest area and pulled to the side of the A1; the third agent pulled into the rest area and parked in a fairly central location. The other three vehicles remained somewhat behind. From this point on the A1, there was virtually nothing until you arrived in Zurich, about seven hours' drive away.

He began driving again shortly after eleven.

* * *

We all traded off fairly regularly. Following a lone car at night on a nearly deserted highway is a challenge, but it is a challenge for which we had all been trained. We had practiced this.

A late night environment confers advantages to both the hunted and the hunter. It made it easier for the subject to spot any single car that was tailing him. But it also made it easier for the tails, since we could track the target vehicle from nearly a mile away without the use of special equipment. We could even follow from in front if need be, especially on sections of the road where exits were separated by significant distances.

It went just as it should. We followed the target. We leapfrogged it. We fell back, and sped up. As much as possible, we resembled a handful of other cars also traveling from Vienna toward Switzerland late at night.

About sixty miles before reaching Ötztal, the subject pulled to the side of the road, apparently to relieve himself. He switched his headlights off and I was driving the vehicle that passed him as he got out of the car. I pulled to a stop about a mile down the road, along with another agent that was also in front. The four remaining agents were behind. None of us were terribly close, but we didn't need to be. We remained in our cars and resumed waiting.

After about ten minutes, I had a vague sense of a vehicle passing, but saw nothing. Our windows were rolled up; had there been the sound of a car going by?

I instructed one of the agents who had stopped a mile or so back to proceed forward; when he got to the location where the subject vehicle had been parked, it was gone. All that was there was a discarded cell phone.

About twenty minutes behind now, we drove frantically toward Zurich. In spite of our speed, we passed no one. Perhaps he had pulled off the road to spend the night. We stopped just outside Zurich and waited for the blue Toyota.

Factor Man
June 8, 2018

There was too much traffic on the highway out of Vienna. And to make matters worse, there always seemed to be more cars behind me than in front of me, and more traffic leaving Vienna than arriving. It seemed to me that just before midnight, it should have been the other way around.

Sadly, it appeared that I was being followed.

Yes, I had a plan. Yes, I thought it was a pretty good plan. But I'm not a spy and, hopefully, never will be. These folks were trained, and I was an amateur. I had hoped (a lot) that my plan wouldn't be necessary; that I would somehow pull the whole thing off while remaining quietly and absolutely anonymous. Well, you know what they say about the best-laid plans.

I got back into the car on the shoulder of the A1 and found the three fuses I had identified earlier. I popped them out of the little plastic holders where they lived. No more brake lights, directionals, or interior lights. I wiped down the burner phone and tossed it. It wouldn't lead to me, but it could be tracked itself. Then I took the night vision goggles out of the backpack. They worked pretty much like I expected. Hopefully invisible, I returned to the A1 and proceeded toward Zurich. I got off at the next exit, but then took the onramp back toward the freeway, stopping far enough back that I could see the A1 traffic without being seen myself.

Sure enough, one car took the exit that I had used and proceeded into the town. The remainder stayed on the A1 toward Zurich, going much faster than they had before. I waited for them all to pass and then got back on the road myself.

There was nothing in front of me as I proceeded. I kept checking my rearview mirror as well; nothing there, either.

I drove as quickly as I dared, which was still significantly below the speed limit. I eventually reached the Ötztal exit shortly before five. It was still dark, and I hadn't seen another car in miles. So much for GPS, and for a physical tail. But anyone following me knew the car, and the car could potentially be found on satellite images.

Ötztal was dark and empty as I navigated my way back to the hotel. I parked in the covered parking and carefully wiped down all of the surfaces I had touched while driving. For good measure, I removed the license plates. I wished I could figure out a way to just drive the car into the Ötztal Ache river. They make that look easy in the movies, but I had no idea how to do it in actuality. Driving off a bridge just didn't seem practical, and the water here was so clear that it wasn't obvious to me that I could hide the car that way in any case.

But I couldn't see how it mattered. I put the wig and goggles in the now empty backpack, and tossed it into a small dumpster behind the hotel. The dumpster cover would ensure that the backpack didn't show up on any satellite imagery, and it would be gone in a day. Believing fairly solidly that I had returned to the DMZ unscathed, I went back to my room and crashed. I had been gone less than twenty-four hours.

The next morning was delightfully uneventful. I arose somewhat later than usual after not nearly enough sleep and shaved.

The hotel waiter smiled as he brought my breakfast. "No beard today?"

I smiled back. "Time to rejoin the outside world," I explained. The waiter laughed and we agreed that all good things must come to an end.

My face once again matching my passport, I caught the RailJet to Zurich. Safely back in the private circle, I returned home under my own name, just one more American tourist traveling during the summer. With any luck, the two circles would never touch again.

Liu
June 9, 2018

The Toyota never appeared. By the next morning, it was clear that we had lost him.

I had only poor choices. We could retrace our steps toward Vienna and hope to somehow stumble across the car, but that seemed unlikely.

I could do a satellite search. That also seemed unlikely. We had last seen the car about 350km from Zurich, and had no certainty that our subject would eventually arrive in Zurich in any event. Zurich was simply the first large international airport in the direction he was last known to be heading.

Finally, I could enlist some assistance. This was also unlikely to be successful, but had perhaps the best chance of my various possibilities. It was also, unfortunately, the most fraught with political peril. Chinese operatives are not expected to need help. And when they do, they are not encouraged to actually request it.

I played it out in my mind. I would leave the hotel and purchase an untraceable cell phone, trivial in any large metropolitan area. Zurich public transport, the VBZ, would take me to a random location, and I would call the Zurich police.

I would tell them, in Arabic, that I was a member of a fictional Islamic extremist group, and that I had left a dark blue Toyota at an undisclosed public location in Switzerland. The license plate was K-799 RY. The vehicle was filled with explosives and was set to detonate in five hours.

What would happen next was less certain. They would surely trace the cell call to the location from which it had been made, and search all of the nearby security footage. It was possible that they would discover that I had been the one making the call.

They would find the seller of the car in Vienna. He would report that the driver had indeed seemed to be in a hurry and had paid for the car with cash. He would report that the buyer appeared to be Semitic. But he would also report, unfortunately, that the buyer spoke flawless English with an American accent.

Even if neither of these things transpired, and the police decided to find the car, it struck me as unlikely that they would. The vehicle was surely hidden at this point, if not actually destroyed. It could be almost anywhere in either Austria or Switzerland. And the chances that it still carried its original license plates were surely nearly nonexistent.

On balance, the political risks would be substantial and the practical benefits seemed at best modest.

Factor Man had escaped us.

Factor Man
June 11, 2018

I got off the plane from Zurich to be greeted by an email. (Much as I loved TOR, checking the Factor Man email from a plane seemed to be pushing my luck.)

```
From: Robert Hasday (rjhasday@duanemorris.com)
To: Factor Man (factorman0@gmail.com)
Re: new client?

Courier has package, instructed deposit funds our Vienna
office.
```

Vienna was hopefully now well and truly behind me.

8

HUDSON
JUNE 11, 2018

So: Factor Man had a lawyer.

Big New York law firms have a reputation for being tough, and their business often depends on that reputation. I expected Hasday and the other Duane Morris attorneys to be even less cooperative than Google had been, at least initially. They did not disappoint.

No, they would not provide me with a list of Hasday's clients.

No, they did not care that national security was at risk. No, they didn't care that there was legal precedent to the effect that the simple name of a client was not protected by attorney-client privilege. If the FBI or anyone else wanted a client list, they would have to get a warrant.

I got a warrant.

Duane Morris appealed.

We argued that an imminent terrorist threat meant that Duane Morris should turn over the client list while the appeal was resolved.

Duane Morris argued that there was no evidence of any kind that Factor Man was a terrorist, and there was plenty of evidence that he didn't intend to do anything until he had factored 255-bit numbers on the blog. That was still months away, so it was hard to see any sense of imminence in any case.

The judge agreed with them.

We started following Hasday. Duane Morris threatened us with a harassment suit, and we stopped.

Hasday's office was at 1540 Broadway, a big New York office building. (Is there any other kind?) We eventually tried reaching out to the building's security firm and asking to see all of the security video since six months before the Factor Man blog began.

Duane Morris had no problem going toe to toe with the federal government. Midtown Office Security was a lot easier to deal with; no security firm wants to aggravate law enforcement. Gone are the days when the tapes were recycled every week or so; security video was stored forever. And Midtown Office Security was quite willing to share it. We sent the video to the NSA for analysis.

The NSA has better than state-of-the-art facial recognition software, and they have a picture of virtually everyone. Let's just say that if you have a driver's license, the NSA knows what you look like. They know what you look like if you've got a passport. And they know what you look like if you've visited the United States legally in the past fifteen years.

Seven agents checked the list of names of everyone who had been to the Duane Morris building, especially those who had gotten off the elevator on Hasday's floor.

We found Brian Finn, who was a Hasday client and who, unbeknownst to us, had recommended Hasday to Factor Man. We thought nothing of the fact that Finn had visited Duane Morris; he was reasonably well known on Wall Street and it was in no way surprising to see him on the list.

And we also found a woman named Janet Liu, which was odd for two reasons.

First, the NSA had a strong suspicion that Liu was in fact a Chinese operative. They had her under intermittent surveillance, but had never sought to tap any of her phones because she had never merited the attention. That now changed.

Second, Liu's visit had occurred during normal working hours. But a few nights later, another Chinese national had visited the office, apparently as part of a cleaning crew. The second Chinese national had entered the country only a week earlier, however. That this was a coincidence was quite a stretch.

* * *

Hasday was not thrilled when we showed up to meet with him yet again, but took the meeting. My guess is that he decided (rightly) that the meeting would take less time than a refusal.

I went in with Ron Livingstone, who had accompanied me to Burkett's apartment a few weeks previously. I did most of the talking.

"We have some disturbing news," I began, and continued to explain that there had likely been a break-in at Duane Morris and that we were concerned that some of Hasday's files had been compromised.

"Which files?" Hasday asked.

I didn't claim to know.

Hasday didn't know either, although he looked like he had a suspicion. It was a suspicion that he certainly wasn't going to share with us.

Normally, we deal with situations like this by simply waiting. The person being questioned often feels a need to fill the gap, providing information they otherwise would have been unwilling to relinquish.

Sadly, Hasday had seen as many depositions as I had seen investigations. He had learned to never provide information to an adversary, or to a potential adversary, unless you needed to. People who get paid $1000 an hour whether they're talking or not are better at waiting patiently than a couple of GS-14's.

Ron eventually broke the silence. "We've got pictures of the group that we believe may have been responsible for the break-in. Are you willing to take a look?"

Hasday was, and was shown a picture of Janet Liu. "Do you recognize this woman?"

Hasday revealed nothing. "Who is she?"

"That's what we were hoping you could tell us."

Hasday pushed the picture back across the table. "I'm sorry," was all he said.

Next came the picture of the Chinese cleaner. Hasday responded similarly, but I suspected he actually meant it this time.

Livingstone and I considered this and looked at each other. Maybe an appeal to Hasday's patriotism would work.

"These people are suspected Chinese agents," Livingstone said. "We believe that the Chinese may have taken an interest in one or more of your files."

"Unless you can tell me which file, it will be difficult for me to help you."

"The reason we're here, Mr. Hasday, is that we would like to know the identities of some of your clients."

Hasday stood. "I'm sorry," he said. "We appear to be at an impasse. Perhaps if you can be more specific about your concerns, I will be able to help."

I suspected that not a word of that was true.

Factor Man
July 25, 2018

From: Robert Hasday (rjhasday@duanemorris.com)
To: Factor Man (factorman0@gmail.com)
Re: new client?

FBI visited. Chinese may have broken into your file. Thoughts?

I smiled. Hasday appeared to believe that shorter messages were more secure than longer ones. Perhaps the terseness of my Albert Einstein message had convinced him.

Factor Man: No need to be so brief; either our messages are being watched, or they aren't. It's unlikely that the messages themselves are being read, although it is reasonably likely that people see them go by (but can't read them).

First, please find my original letter. You know those movies where someone writes something on a piece of paper and the hero then rubs a pencil over the piece of paper under it to see what they wrote? The letter I sent you should have "FM" written that way in the lower right corner. Is it?

Hasday: No. Just the original letter.

Factor Man: Just a *copy* of the original letter. Why does the FBI think it's the Chinese?

Hasday: They have pictures from the security camera at the entrance to the building.

Factor Man: Should be fine. Thanks for the heads up.

None of this could be good news, but I wasn't sure that it was such bad news, either. In fact, it might not be news at all.

It certainly appeared that *someone* had followed me when I dropped the money at Sparta Safes. If that happened, then someone had presumably found the original letter to Hasday and the break-in shouldn't even surprise me. All that had happened, really, was that I had learned that it was the Chinese.

Another nail in the coffin of my hoped-for quiet and anonymity, though.

I didn't think that the letter could hurt me. I had printed it off at a Kinko's, which was surely untraceable. The label on the envelope had been printed at the same shop. I had mailed the letter while changing planes on a business trip through Salt Lake City, and had been careful never to touch anything. I didn't even think my prints were on the mailbox in the Salt Lake airport, although they were surely rubbed off by now in any case.

Time passed. The Chinese must have realized that they had lost me in Zurich, but there were no apparent consequences of that.

February 15, 2019

In early 2019, that changed. Video of me leaving Sparta Safes appeared on the Internet. Someone speculated that it was I, and a prize of half a million dollars was offered to anyone who could identify the fellow in the picture.

Would it work? I certainly hoped not. In the video, I had long hair. I had a beard. I had sunglasses. And I had a limp, because a person's gait is almost as distinctive as his fingerprints. I had spent six weeks hobbling around with a cane in college after a knee injury playing volleyball, and figured I had given a pretty good impression. (I have no idea why computer scientists have such a frequent affinity for volleyball, but they do.)

But it ticked me off that people were looking. I don't deal well with that.

Anonymous is a group of activist/hackers, also known as "hacktivists." They claim to have a social conscience and, for example, shut down the Cleveland city web site after a twelve-year-old Cleveland boy named Tamir Rice was killed by a policeman.

In many ways, Anonymous is like me. They have a fairly high public profile, but are fundamentally incredibly secretive. They do appear in public on relatively rare occasions, generally wearing Guy Fawkes masks as in the film *V for Vendetta*. At least, people claim to be members of Anonymous and wear the masks; it's impossible to tell for sure.

Anonymous even has a web site, anonhq.com. They have a contact address, which is contact@anonhq.com.

```
From: Factor Man (factorman0@gmail.com)
To: contact@anonhq.com
Subject: assistance?

I could use some help. Interested?

FM
```

The reply took about an hour.

```
From: Contact (contact@anonhq.com)
To: Factor Man (factorman0@gmail.com)
Re: assistance?

ftp.anonhq.com
user factorman

The password is the smaller factor of
31901077902561505296729874728386769785784457264035505043
881415529088564608023.
```

I liked these guys already.

* * *

Back before there were Internet browsers like Explorer and Safari, people communicated by sending files to one another. They used something called the File Transfer Protocol, or FTP. Not many people used it any more, but it still worked.

The Anonymous guys had set up a user on one of their computers that I could access using FTP. They had given me the user name, and given me enough of a hint that if I had the abilities I claimed, I could generate the password.

The password was 97552088883039660558320728539627925591. Kind of them to use the smaller factor, saving me one digit of typing.

I logged into the account they had created, and looked around. There was one file there, called README.txt. I copied it back to my own machine and opened it.

What can we do for you?

I made another little file called answer.txt. (There is a general convention that README files have their titles capitalized but little else does, unless you're an AOL customer from the 90's.)

That depends. For a start, can you trace the origin of the video that claims to be me?

The response was in answer2.txt and was surprisingly quick.

We thought you might ask that. :) China.

They weren't surprised by the question, and I wasn't surprised by the answer.

Factor Man: If I get you IP addresses and root passwords for about fifteen boxes, can you bring them down?

Anonymous: We would obviously need to identify the boxes. But we like it and yes, we can do that.

A "box" is slang for a computer somewhere.

The Factor Man blog

42863529557607052827226122062970101789930721760879858203588 9331 = 300824589368253332418044377808069×14248678822307247709 240790275799

(requested by Sam Elliot)

430115888144930284802219293192354725350626714793856754010763 359 = 290637121930152348673773906699411×14799069206592897220 875257111299

(requested by Sylvester Stallone)

473190972979958543270703882276405044511057969972897659957191 553 = 258404931922036179806676291480067×183119946457804392473 89331806859

(requested by Jimmy Fallon)

486302771593855890657898732624588219991234832797752236098430 989 = 353765195115472649927775855645559×13746484343524003067 180162884771

(requested by Matt Damon)
5372498495025555999666691683357255892646249596667512018032738769 = 27858426320756570381508439025951×1928500351443991891643864 7080719
(requested by John Hennessy)

210-bit numbers will be factored in two days.

When I began this blog, I made it clear that I wished to remain anonymous. That is still my wish.

Certain individuals working on behalf of the Chinese government have posted video purporting to be of me on the Internet, and a reward has been offered to anyone identifying the figure in that video.

If you know the individual in question, I encourage you in the strongest possible terms to keep that information to yourself.

China's attitude toward privacy (and intellectual property) is unacceptable. I am a private non-Chinese citizen and am not willing to have my privacy challenged in this fashion. What I do outside of China is simply none of China's business.

I therefore have the following demands of the Chinese government:
1. You are to withdraw the prize for determining my identity.
2. You are to immediately cease all acts of cyber espionage.
3. You are to return the material that was stolen from my attorney's office in New York City.

You have three days to comply.

This web site has been visited 103,298,817,326 times.

* * *

If you pick up the phone and call London, the call is routed over one of a relative handful of cables running under the Atlantic Ocean. Those cables all need to begin and end somewhere, and each of the terminations is monitored by a computer.

The Internet is similar and at the international level, it is actually remarkably sparse. Any particular geographic region is generally connected to the rest of the world at a handful of points. This is especially true for China, which carefully monitors all of its Internet traffic with the outside world.

There are fourteen computers through which all Chinese Internet traffic has to pass. Each of those computers could obviously be accessed remotely, if you knew the password. Computers have super-users, who have the privileges to do whatever they want to the machines in question – reboot them, shut them down, delete all the files, you name it. These superusers are typically called "root" in the computing world, so if you know the root password to a box, you can crash it.

The day after the above blog post, a response appeared in every paper published by Xinhua News, which is China's official press agency. All told, it appeared in twenty newspapers in Chinese, English and six other languages.

The terrorist calling himself Factor Man yesterday made certain groundless claims against the People's Republic of China. He accused the People's government of espionage and of theft. He demanded that the government provide certain unnamed documents to an attorney in New York, and that they withdraw a prize for identifying the individual in a particular video.

The accusations are offensive and without merit. All available evidence indicates that China has abided by both international law and those treaties to which it is a party. China has also abided by the specific agreement regarding cyber activities that was made by Presidents Obama and Xi in September of 2015.

It is not appropriate for an individual to threaten a state, or to interfere in the affairs of a state. It is especially inappropriate for an individual to do so while hiding behind the mask of anonymity that the Internet can provide. We urge the parties who control this individual's access to the Internet to terminate such access. Freedom of speech should not be confused with freedom to meddle in international affairs.

We do not expect the Chinese government to comply with these demands. An independent state need not be concerned if someone has misplaced materials exchanged with an attorney. But an independent state *should* be concerned if an attempt is made to interfere with that state's desire to reward a third party that has assisted in anti-terrorism efforts.

Terrorism, in all of its forms, is an anathema to modern civilized society. We encourage all nations to join together in a determined effort to eliminate it.

9

BURKETT
MARCH 6, 2019

To paraphrase Shakespeare, some people are born to investigative reporting, and others have investigative reporting thrust upon them.

I was definitely in the second group.

It was safe to say that my life didn't improve when the video of Factor Man (or whomever) hit the Internet. All the people who had been bothering me continued to bother me, but with greater fervor. They were joined by some new ones. Everyone seemed to think that I should recognize the guy in the video, which I didn't.

So I decided I would figure it out. I didn't have a plan for figuring it out, and I especially didn't have a plan for what I would do if I *did* figure it out. But knowledge is power, and I could certainly use some of that. Plans would come later.

So I declared myself to be an investigative reporter. But before I could start investigating, all hell broke loose.

China Goes Dark – Briefly
William Burkett, The *New York Times*

> At 11:58 Eastern Standard Time last night, China disappeared from the Internet. That was three days to the minute after the individual known as Factor Man gave the Chinese government a three-day ultimatum that the Chinese government ignored.

China was off the Internet for seven seconds at 11:58AM Chinese time. (In spite of its size, there is only one time zone – the "People's time" – in China.)

Internet traffic internal to China was not disrupted. The Shanghai and Hang Seng markets continued trading as usual, although they both dropped approximately 5% after the outage was discovered.

The hacking group Anonymous has taken credit for the attack, which appears to have simply rebooted every computer connecting China's Internet to the outside world. It is generally assumed that Factor Man provided crucial information that allowed Anonymous access to the machines that make up the Chinese gateway. Anonymous has taken credit for a variety of Internet attacks in the past, including attacks on government computers in Canada and Tunisia.

Extremely tense discussions are rumored to have taken place between Beijing and the White House, with the Chinese demanding that the US government take steps to prevent future disruptions and the US government telling China that they will be happy to take any specific steps that China is able to suggest. Sources inside the White House report that the somberness of the official response may not reflect the government's actual attitude.

Liu
March 8, 2019

The previous two days had been anything but pleasant.

General Zhao had been extremely disquieted to learn, months previously, that the break-in at Duane Morris had not gone undetected. He had been more concerned still to learn firsthand of the apparent vulnerability of China's ability to communicate with the rest of the world.

My position in the Fourth Department, inevitably tenuous because of my gender, had been more precarious still since the Duane Morris incident. No one was able to ascertain the method by which the break-in had been detected, but there was a clear and justified consensus that the responsibility was mine. The Internet disruption exacerbated the situation further.

The Fourth Department had no intention of reducing the breadth of its important cyber-security related activities, but did reluctantly withdraw the prize for identifying the figure in the video. The responsibility for the remaining task of returning the original Factor Man letter to the Duane Morris offices fell to me, and honor required that I discharge that responsibility personally.

The New York skies were overcast as I emerged from the Times Square subway station, three blocks southwest of the Duane Morris building. I made my way to the Duane Morris building and to Hasday's floor, where I told his receptionist that I wished to see him. I then had the pleasure of waiting for nearly an hour before being shown into Hasday's office.

"Good afternoon, Ms. Liu," Hasday said. "I must confess to being somewhat surprised to see you again. I thought you had decided to take your business elsewhere."

"I simply brought the paperwork that you requested." It was Factor Man who had made the request, but I saw no reason to say so.

"Did you, indeed?" I handed over an envelope containing Factor Man's original letter to Duane Morris. Hasday looked inside and confirmed its presence. "How very kind."

I waited for him to indicate that our business was now concluded, but no such concession was forthcoming. "Thank you," I eventually said.

"Not at all." He continued to wait. Eventually, I simply excused myself and left.

Americans are mannerless.

* * *

My involvement in the Factor Man matter had not been completely without success, however. Although we had not managed to identify him in Vienna, we did have video. That the person in the video was Factor Man seemed to be confirmed by his reaction.

The video showed a man with a beard, long dark hair, and a limp. The sunglasses were unfortunate, as was the fact that his hair had covered his ears. The beard, hair and limp might all be artifacts of one sort or another. Nevertheless, there were certain things we knew.

Factor Man was indeed male. Whatever the mechanism of disguise, he could never be *taller* than the man in the video. In fact, the video showed that there were no lifts in his shoes, so we were looking for a Caucasian male, approximately 180cm in height.

His clothes were made in America. That, too, was something of a pity. There are slight stylistic differences between clothing in one country and in another; had his clothing been (for example) French, our search would have been significantly reduced. And while surveillance cameras are reasonably prevalent in the United States, they are far more prevalent in Europe, especially at the national level to which we can generally obtain access.

He weighed no more than 82kg which, in America's overindulgent society, was surprising for someone of his height.

Most important, however, was the video itself. China has the best facial recognition software in the world. It is an amalgam of techniques developed elsewhere, and methods developed in China and not distributed further. The software allows Chinese authorities to maintain the societal structure from which all Chinese citizens benefit.

An American in Vienna would have a passport. And like the American spy machine, we also had access to the photographs that American passports contained. Because of the likelihood that some of the features had been obscured, running them through the relevant software might take longer than usual. But it was certainly still possible.

Burkett
March 26, 2019

A seven-second Internet disruption caused all of us to hold our breaths for about two weeks.

The Chinese authorities continued to maintain that Factor Man was a terrorist. They announced that just as America seemed to delight in wiping out terrorists with the touch of a button, they would have no qualms about acting similarly if they could locate him. The United States responded just as strongly, tersely informing the Chinese that should Factor Man turn out to be an American citizen, he would be entitled to both due process and the full protection of the American government while he got it.

Everyone was being totally two-faced, of course. The Americans seemed to have little interest in due process for the people they targeted with drones, and the Chinese were threatening a state-sponsored assassination as retribution for a seven-second Internet outage that was, if the blog was to be believed, retribution for a theft from Factor Man's attorney in any case.

In the States, at least, public sympathy seemed to be mostly with Factor Man. The usual polls found that 83% of the American public hoped Factor Man was an American and supported what he was doing, and the usual pundits made the usual comments about Yankee ingenuity, mavericks, the Wild West, and the importance of diplomacy.

It might have been entertaining, had the stakes not been so high.

After a couple weeks, the world settled back to somewhat normal, and I prepared to begin my new career as a crack investigative reporter. I decided that I would start with a visit to complexity theorist Scott Aaronson, who you may recall jumped ship from MIT to work at UT Austin. My trip would be cleverly disguised as a visit to old friends from my graduate school days. The FBI was still following me, I figured, and for all I knew, the Chinese now were as well. I bid Emma farewell, promised to be careful, and off I went.

* * *

Austin was much as I remembered it, a liberal bastion in the right-wing insanity that is generally referred to as Texas. March is arguably the most pleasant time of year; while the rest of the country slowly thaws, the Austin highs are generally around 70 and the lows about twenty degrees cooler. The rains that will begin in May have not yet arrived.

I wandered onto campus and did indeed visit my thesis advisor and a couple of other folks I knew in economics before drifting over to the computer science department. This was my technique for losing a notional tail: I drifted aimlessly. My hope, I guess, was that they would simply lose interest. In actuality, of course, I had no real idea what I was doing, but I couldn't think of a reason that investigative journalism should be so different from everything else.

Aaronson taught complexity theory. No surprise there. The class met Tuesday and Thursday mornings at 10:30 and I cleverly arrived on a Tuesday afternoon because I hadn't formed even the minimal plan of checking course schedules via the Internet. I spent a day learning just how hard it is to return to graduate school. All of my friends had obviously moved on to other things, and the only people I knew were faculty who were in general pleased to see me but only for a limited amount of time. They all asked identical questions about Factor Man and then the conversations faded quickly.

Thursday morning eventually arrived, and I learned that Aaronson's class was being taught by a graduate student for whom English was clearly not a native language. I approached him after class and he explained that Professor Aaronson had been called away, and that he would be teaching the class until the professor returned. He had no idea where Aaronson was, or the reason for his absence.

I figured that maybe this investigative reporting stuff wasn't so hard after all. Then I tried to figure out what to do next, and concluded that maybe that was wrong.

* * *

What crack investigative reporters do in situations like this is find someone else to bother. I decided to bother Bruce Porter, the chairman of Austin's Computer Science Department.

People outside of academics probably believe that being the head of a department is a good thing. Status, upward career mobility, like that.

They're wrong.

Academics *hate* being department chairs. Schools of medicine are the only exception. First off, there isn't any status. Status in academics is pretty much a matter of the strength of your publication record, and department heads generally have so much political crap to deal with that they don't manage to do any research at all during their time as head.

Academics generally aren't interested in upward career mobility, either. They have what they view as the perfect job, doing research and perhaps teaching, with tenure offering them the promise of a job for life as long as they don't sleep with any of their students.

It sounds like a sweet deal, and it is a sweet deal. It's especially sweet for someone who wants nothing more out of life than to get up in the morning and try to solve hard intellectual problems, interrupted only by the occasional student or lecture.

Being chair disrupts all of that. As an example, Porter's web page included a list of papers he had written in artificial intelligence, and the publications pretty much stopped at the time he became chair.

Artificial intelligence. A field that has been described by one of its founders as, "An attempt to get machines to do badly what people do well." AI gets a ton of press these days, what with machine learning allowing Amazon to know our buying preferences better than we do, and machine vision allowing Teslas to drive us around, killing us slightly less frequently than we manage to kill ourselves.

Artificial intelligence and complexity theory are sister disciplines. Making algorithms run faster matters when you're looking at databases as big as the one Amazon (or Google) maintains on all of us. And if your goal is for a program to do something truly intelligent – write a symphony, say – then the classic P vs. NP question of whether creating a great work of art is as easy as recognizing one is obviously relevant indeed.

So it was fair to expect that Porter would have at least a passing acquaintance with complexity theory. In addition to knowing Aaronson, he would probably also have some view about how Scott might fit into the whole Factor Man story.

Porter was also busy, but his admin said that he could fit me into his schedule in a couple of hours. I decided to spend those hours at Texas Coffee Traders, an on-campus coffee shop where I had spent far too many hours during my years as a UT graduate student.

TCT was essentially unchanged from my student days, although I have to confess that the women appeared considerably more attractive than they had back then. One struck me as particularly stunning, drinking her drink by herself and reading a book. Ah, to be a few years younger and unattached.

I drank my coffee and wandered the web for an hour and a half, and then headed back over to computer science.

* * *

Porter turned out to be a genuinely nice guy, in the geeky way that is common to computer scientists. Mid- to late-fifties, welcoming smile, casually dressed with sneakers instead of shoes. A tennis racket was in the corner of his office but seemed mostly to be gathering dust. The office itself was a typical academic's, with cases full of books, and every surface covered in books or research papers. Diagrams with arrows covered the whiteboard, which had "DO NOT ERASE" written in the top right corner. Investigative reporters notice this stuff.

Porter shook my hand and invited me to sit. "William Burkett," he said. "Austin Ph.D. student who introduced Factor Man to the world. What can I do for you?"

"I think I liked it better when people thought of me only as an economics graduate student," I answered. "But Factor Man is certainly why I'm here. I'm looking for Scott Aaronson. I was hoping to get his take on it."

Porter got up and walked behind me, closing the door to his office. Clearly about to reveal great secrets, like Aaronson's location or perhaps the identity of Factor Man himself.

"Scott's away on a personal matter." He paused. "That's all I know."

This is how you can tell the great investigative reporters. If that really was all he knew, why did he pause before saying so? Why did he close his door?

Actually, that was probably how you could tell the mediocre investigative reporters. The great ones knew how to use that information to move the investigation forward.

"So why did you close your door?" Fundamentally, I had nothing.

Another pause. "Your question seemed to involve Scott personally. I always close my door when questions about a faculty member arise."

"Do you think this personal matter might have anything to do with Factor Man?" William Burkett, master of nuance.

"Scott is arguably the world's most visible complexity theorist. I would imagine that much of what he does these days is impacted by Factor Man in one way or another."

And that was basically the most I could get out of him. We danced around it for a few more minutes, but eventually I thanked Porter for his time and conceded that I had taken enough of it.

He opened the door to let me out. As I began to pass through it, he added one more thing. "William? You're not the first person to ask me about this. The NSA and FBI were both in here last week, with basically the same questions. And I gave them basically the same answers."

Terrific.

* * *

Next up was Aaronson's wife Rina, also a computer scientist at UT Austin. Not as mainstream a complexity theorist as her husband, but they worked in closely related areas. The two of them had jointly transitioned from MIT to Austin in the fall of 2016, a move that Aaronson had explained as being motivated by ten factors, ranging from the quality of the department to a comparison of the weather in Austin and in Boston. Mostly, though, Austin was a location where the Aaronsons could both get tenure in a respected computer science department.

Rina was a few years younger and a few inches shorter than her husband. And, when I found her in her office during office hours, a few notches more accessible. She was Israeli-born, dark hair and eyes, with excellent but gently accented English.

"Scott and I talked about you," she told me with something of a rueful smile. "You gave him a lift to his hotel years ago. It struck him as ironic you had been so helpful back then, and then the same man springs Factor Man on the world years later."

"Don't shoot the messenger," I told her. "Factor Man introduced himself to the world."

The bottom line was that Rina gave me no more than anyone else had. "Scott's out of town," she said. "A personal matter."

"Do you know where?"

"Of course I know where."

"Care to share?"

"Should I?"

I explained that I was trying to get to the bottom of things, nothing more. I wanted to talk with Factor Man, whoever he was. After what happened to China, I had no plans to reveal anything that he wanted to keep secret. I was a reporter; I just wanted to know what was going on.

She considered this. "Do you think Scott is Factor Man?"

"Do you?"

"Mr. Burkett, I know whether or not Scott is Factor Man. I'm his wife. I know. I'm asking what you think."

"You obviously realize I think it's a possibility."

The rueful smile again. "There are two possibilities here. One. Scott is Factor Man. If so, he's made it clear that he wants his identity to remain unknown. So I won't help you. Two. Scott is not Factor Man. In that case, let me assure you that you aren't the only one with these suspicions, and both Scott's and my lives would be considerably simpler if you could somehow, shall we say, clear his name."

"How could I do that?" I asked. "It's tough to prove a negative."

"You could find out who Factor Man actually is, Mr. Burkett. If you can't, it's not clear how you can help us."

Like I said, I had nothing. Rina politely showed me out, and I returned to my hotel.

* * *

I hung around and licked my wounds for a day, stopping in to see the few people I remembered personally and wondering what to do next. I knew at best incrementally more than when I had arrived in Austin three days earlier. Lots to consider, but little in terms of actual knowledge. I returned to the hotel after dinner, telling them that I planned on checking out the next morning.

Shortly after I got back into the room, there was a knock on the door. Rina Aaronson, to my surprise. She handed me a sheet of paper, told me to do the right thing, and left.

The sheet of paper said:

```
30.3657424 N, 98.1151105 W
receive further instructions
Thursday
come alone and unfollowed
```

It was Friday. William Burkett, crack investigative reporter, extended his hotel reservation.

10

Factor Man is the pseudonym of an anonymous individual who claims to have resolved the *P=NP* conjecture by developing and implementing a polynomial time algorithm for solving satisfiability problems. He claims to have been using that algorithm to factor numbers of increasing size, and has offered to sell a license to the technology, exclusive for one year, to the highest bidder in mid-2019.

If true, this technology would have a profound impact across modern society, allowing for the more efficient solution of a wide range of technical problems. Among these advances, however, would be the ability to break most or all modern public-key encryption schemes, potentially wreaking havoc with Internet commerce and Internet security generally.

1. History
2. People named on the Factor Man blog
3. Identity
4. Public and academic perception
5. Controversies
6. Value of the technology

...

3. Identity

Although the subject of intense worldwide speculation, little is known about Factor Man's identity. It is generally believed that he is an adult Caucasian American male. On February 15, 2019, the Chinese government circulated a picture they stated to be of Factor Man, offering a reward of $500,000 to anyone who could identify the individual in the photograph.

The reward offer was withdrawn on March 7 after a demand to that effect from Factor Man himself.

It is possible that virtually all of the features in the photograph are artificial, except for the height (about 180cm, 5'11") and weight (about 82 kg, 180 lbs) of the individual in question. The Caucasian skin color is presumably authentic as well. Individuals familiar with the location of the photograph have identified it as a set of shops in downtown Vienna. The date of the photograph is uncertain.

It is believed that Factor Man has a personal relationship with William Burkett, a reporter for the *New York Times*. This is because the first mention of Factor Man in the public domain is in an article that Burkett wrote on May 17, 2017 titled, "How to Find a Crackpot." The now infamous *Factor Man blog* appeared simultaneously with Burkett's article, and it is assumed that Factor Man himself told Burkett about it. Because all of the early readers of the blog claim to have gotten the location from the *Times* article, it is reasonable to think of Burkett as "Patient Zero" of the Factor Man phenomenon. Burkett has refused to comment on this element of Factor Man's history, and has achieved a considerable amount of celebrity as a result.

Recent speculation regarding Factor Man's identity has swirled around complexity theorist Scott Aaronson, a member of the computer science faculty at the University of Texas at Austin. This is in part because of Aaronson's reputation within the complexity community, although his stated position has generally been that P and NP are distinct. More importantly, however, Aaronson vanished without a trace in March of 2019. His wife, computer scientist Rina Aaronson, disappeared approximately a week later. Aaronson is known to have given a talk at UT Austin while Burkett was a graduate student there in 2012.

4. Perception

Initial response to Factor Man's claims was extremely negative, the general consensus being that there was little chance those claims were valid. As time has passed, however, it has become increasingly likely that Factor Man can indeed do what he says.

This change in perception has been accompanied by a corresponding modification of the public's perception of Factor Man's activities. A Gallup poll in March of 2019 indicated that 92% of respondents believed that Factor Man was trustworthy and could do what he claimed, and that 87% had a favorable view of the course of action Factor Man had taken generally. 56% of those polled felt that Factor Man had been justified in his response to the apparent Chinese break-in at his attorney's office (see *Controversies*, below). Similar polling in other countries (other than China) gives comparable results, although slightly less favorable.

The results in China are drastically different. A slight majority of Chinese (52%) believe that Factor Man can do what he claims, but he is only viewed favorably by 13% of the Chinese population.

The Chinese government has stated that they consider Factor Man to be a terrorist and a threat, and that they will treat him as such if they are able to learn his true identity. This position has been criticized sharply by the American administration, which has said that Factor Man is believed to be an American citizen. He is therefore entitled to the full protection of the United States government until his crimes – if any – are evaluated by the American justice system.

This dispute has led to a significant increase in tensions between the two nations, with China continuing to maintain that they will take whatever steps they feel to be in the interests of Chinese security.

5. Controversies

In response to a perceived Chinese threat, Factor Man is believed to have severed all of China's Internet connections for seven seconds at 11:58AM Chinese time on March 6, 2019. Opinion varies widely as to whether this action was justified and whether reprisals are appropriate. Factor Man's claimed technology would give him an almost unlimited ability to disrupt Internet service in any way that he chose.

A more far-reaching debate has surrounded the question of whether the Factor Man technology should be in the control of a single individual or private entity. This question is made somewhat more urgent by Factor Man's stated plan of providing an exclusive license to his technology to the highest bidder for a one-year period commencing on July 10, 2019. After the year is up, the United States government will supposedly also get a license for one year, after which (on July 10, 2021), the technology will be released into the public domain and Factor Man will reveal his or her identity to the world.

A variety of individuals have argued that this will concentrate too much power in the hands of a small number of individuals between now and the

2021 date. Virtually all foreign governments have objected to the release of the technology to the government of only the United States.

The United States government has also involved itself in this controversy directly. The Factor Man technology has been classified as top secret by the American military, meaning that it will be, at least according to some experts, a crime for Factor Man to sell or otherwise distribute it. Other experts claim that since the technology itself appears to be Factor Man's invention, his rights to distribute his own work are protected by the First Amendment (freedom of speech) of the U.S. Constitution. It is impossible to litigate this matter until Factor Man does indeed attempt to circulate the technology in question.

The American Congress has gotten involved as well, passing legislation making it illegal to sell the technology. It is not clear that this legislation will have any effect beyond the consequences of the top secret classification, but Congress was forced to respond to a general public demand for action of one sort or another.

6. Value of the technology

All of these questions are made considerably more pressing by the fact that the technology is of extraordinary value, and the amount of Factor Man's fee for a one-year license to the highest bidder is likely to be immense. Current estimates of the value range from $1B (one billion) to $1T (one trillion) US dollars. If the transaction proceeds as Factor Man apparently plans, he is likely to be one of the richest (if not the richest) person on the planet at a single stroke.

...

Liu
2019

When you disrespect the Chinese government, you disrespect the Chinese people. Chinese leadership had been right to declare Factor Man an enemy of the Chinese people and to allow us freedom of action in dealing with him.

First, we had to find him.

At any given moment, some 500,000 Americans are visiting Europe. Half of those are women, and about 70% of the remainder are shorter than 175cm or taller than 185cm, which safely bracketed the height of the individual we had seen in Vienna. That left 75,000 individuals.

The footage we had made it difficult to estimate Factor Man's age, but it was probably safe to say he was at least twenty and no more than sixty. That cut the number by about a factor of two, say 40,000 people.

We were also aided by the American obesity epidemic. The man in the picture was at most slightly overweight, something of an anomaly for Americans. While passport data does not include weight, it can be inferred from the photograph. This allowed us to eliminate half of the remaining individuals. 20,000 names remained, give or take. From passport data alone, we had 19,729 people to consider.

Race also helped. Factor Man appeared to be a non-Hispanic white man, and non-Hispanic whites make up 62% of the U.S. population. Eliminating those left us 12,377 potential targets.

12,377 is both a large number and a small one. It was small enough that we could apply our most sophisticated facial recognition technology to the problem, even though that technology ran sufficiently slowly that it would take almost a second to analyze each passport image and compare it to the Factor Man video.

But 12,377 was large enough that it was impractical to analyze the images by hand. We certainly had the necessary staff available, but it was simply too likely that errors would be made by a single individual responsible for examining perhaps 250 photographs. That was especially true given that in all probability, none of any particular set of 250 images would be the individual whom we were seeking.

Unfortunately, our vision software was unable to identify Factor Man among the candidate passports. In many senses, only Factor Man's nose was available for analysis; everything else was potentially artificial. A detailed comparison between a nose on a front-facing passport photograph and a profile image from our video was simply not yet possible. Noses also lacked the many distinguishing subfeatures that were present in mouths or in ears. The one area that generally provides reliable secondary information is the philtrum, the vertical groove between the nose and upper lip that varies in both width and depth. It was unfortunately obscured by Factor Man's mustache.

We therefore needed to resort to conventional techniques. Approximately 2% of males in the American workforce are computer scientists. While such individuals would likely be somewhat overrepresented in the fraction of Americans visiting Europe on the day we had seen Factor Man in Vienna, we expected that restricting our focus to computer professionals of one sort or another would reduce the number of Factor Man suspects to well under a thousand.

Surreptitiously determining the livelihood of some twelve thousand Americans would involve tens of thousands of phone calls. It would require thousands of individual visits. It would take time.

But, perhaps above all else, China is patient.

The blog
April 3, 2019

339524017662683972487361425337689949542654612673566437592600 14757337 = 8641545093141119215461766484057041×392897351113943 2480338511586866057

(requested by Nathan Fillion)

342694389787627618004323558349711790316065201522598846702991 78195651 = 8909126050460870726517292588441261×384655450878821 0200413402600946991

(requested by Summer Glau)

309014993800868226721201352948499495242499427814951481422774 27840473 = 1011741995029674942485804977895 6563×30542865208615 23090548671399161571

(requested by Alan Tudyk)

304947561564793935861839223606337045684967835467688586337331 40650589 = 1020061269055056480722706849120 0329×29895024035888 06269209226620429941

(requested by Adam Baldwin)

391978144085342841723366483579529581936786524698266135285722 48216297 = 1000582843509563318887045497828 4789×39174981524815 28265542434710910373

(requested by Jewel Staite)

Five of the original cast members of *Firefly*. My apologies to Mr. Maher, Ms. Torres and Ms. Baccarin. Mr. Glass is unfortunately no longer with us.

226-bit numbers will be factored in three days.

In 90 days, bidding will commence on a license to use the technology I have developed, exclusive but non-transferable for one year. I would like to provide some additional details on how that process will work.

The bidding method I will use is a modified Vickrey auction. Basically, it's like eBay. Assuming that there are at least two bids, the technology will be licensed to the highest bidder and the price will be the offer made by the second highest bidder. If the highest bid is made more than once, whoever made the bid first will be treated as having outbid the others.

In the event that the highest bidder for some reason does not complete the transaction, the license will be issued to the second highest bidder at the price that bidder offered.

Unlike eBay, bidding for the technology will be a two-step process.

1.   First, all bidders must be qualified by me personally. This means that I need to determine that if awarded the license, you will use it to further the interests of the citizens of the United States.

If you are a public entity (such as a publicly traded corporation or a famous person), I will make that decision based on the record of your past actions. If there is no such record, please provide me with whatever you choose, and I will make the best decision that I can. All of my qualification decisions are final.

In spite of the consequences of the technology I have developed, I am a great believer in privacy. So you need also to convince me that you will not use the technology to further erode the privacy of each of us – myself included.

In order to be qualified, you must place $1M (one million US dollars) in escrow through my attorney, Robert Hasday of Duane Morris in New York. Duane Morris has retained Wilmington Trust as the escrow agent to handle these funds, and the escrow agreement will be made available upon request. Money escrowed during the qualification process will be returned to you as soon as a qualification decision is made, whether it is positive or negative.

Consortia are not permitted. My goal here is to license the technology to a single entity, not some conglomerate of all of the stocks in the S&P 500. I will not qualify potential bidders that were not already in existence as of the time of this blog post.

Qualified bidders will be provided with the detailed terms of the license on which they are permitted to bid.

2.   After you are qualified (assuming that you are), you are free to place any bid that is higher than the current second place bid. (This amount will be known; see below.) Whatever your bid, 10% of that amount must be placed in escrow through Duane Morris. Interest on the escrowed funds will be donated to the National Alliance to End Homelessness. Bidders will also be required to waive any conflict of interest that might prevent Duane Morris from representing me as negotiations proceed.

Each day, I will announce via the blog the current second-highest bid. When bidding is complete, I will announce the identity of the winning bidder, and will inform the winning bidder of the identity of the second place bidder so that they can confirm that the price is as declared.

The license will be issued as soon as contractual negotiations are complete. The winning bidder will be required to transfer to me on July 10, 2021 that amount of stock in certain publicly held companies that could have been bought on July 10, 2019 with the funds corresponding to the second-place bid, together with a reinvestment of any dividends. The licensing agreement will include instructions regarding the exact number of shares, and companies in which they are to be purchased. If the winning bidder is a publicly held company, no less than 15% of the stock to be transferred will be shares of the company obtaining the license.

This web site has been visited 126,211,231,262 times.

11

BURKETT
APRIL 4, 2019

As forecast, Wednesday in Austin was rainy; an early-in-the-season storm of the sort that I remembered all too well. Thursday arrived with clear skies but still muggy. Factor Man's blog post of the previous day had given me all manner of things to check out, but they would just have to wait until I went wherever it was I was going.

Investigative reporters are planners. I had planned carefully for the trip, which meant that I had pulled up the location on Google and figured out that it would take me about an hour to drive there. It looked to be squarely in the middle of nowhere, desert surrounded by scrub. Dirt roads that would probably be more miserable than usual because of the previous day's rain. In a paroxysm of organization, I even picked up a pair of binoculars.

I also checked the Google directions to the location, which was a good thing because they left me about a mile short. Google didn't know about dirt roads, so it just dropped me at the closest point on a road with a name. Wasn't all that close. But a tedious hour spent with Google's satellite imagery had let me figure out a route that would work, and I set off as early on Thursday morning as I could stagger out of bed.

An hour and a half of potholes later, it was 10:30 and I was where I was supposed to be. I hadn't had a cell signal for around ten miles. The location was pretty much as I expected, with the primary attraction being a rock about a foot across. One good thing was that I was at the highest point for maybe five miles around. In this part of Texas, that meant I was maybe fifteen feet higher than the lowest point for five miles around. But it made it pretty easy to grab the binoculars and tell if I had been followed.

Which I had.

I had no idea what to do about that, so I got back in the car and ran the air conditioner while I thought about it and hoped that something good would happen.

Nothing good happened. I waited another hour and the only thing that changed was that the sun was more directly overhead.

So I waited another hour, which had pretty much the same effect as the previous hour.

The guys who had followed me were, somewhat predictably, parked on the road back to civilization. I decided to go talk to them, and ask if maybe they'd be willing to drive back to civilization without me.

I pulled up alongside them, and could tell that their air conditioning was on as well as I rolled my window down. They did the same, and I found myself staring at a couple of suits with sunglasses. They stared back.

"Help you?" one of them finally asked.

"Are you following me?" William Burkett, master of indirection.

"Yup."

"You willing to stop?"

"Nope."

I thought the conversation was going well.

"Why are you following me?"

"Told to."

I decided to play my cards carefully. No point telling them everything about what I was doing out there.

"I'm trying to meet someone."

"Figured that."

"They're not going to show up if you're following me."

"Probably not."

It was a classic Mexican standoff. I couldn't give in because it was Thursday. They couldn't give in, I suspected, because they had nothing better to do.

I could go back to where I was supposed to be. I'd have to turn the a/c off, though, or I'd risk running out of gas.

So that's what I did. I didn't move and, a mile away, they didn't move. At sunset, they turned their lights on, but they still didn't move.

I conceded without a word, and drove back to my hotel in Austin.

I started Friday by looking for Rina at the Austin computer science department, only to be told that she, too, was on a mysterious personal leave. With nothing better to do, I drove back into the desert. Actually, pretty much anything was better but none of it seemed likely to be useful.

Same result. Same two guys, same two suits, same sunglasses. Same rock. It wasn't Thursday, and I had no idea if it mattered.

Saturday was different. I started it by sneaking out of the hotel and taking a cab to a car rental agency. I rented a car and drove to the spot with the rock.

Then Saturday turned out pretty much like Thursday and Friday. The only difference was that it rained again.

* * *

Sunday actually was different, because I slept in until noon. I figured the FBI might just as well watch me sleep as watch me drive into the middle of the Texas desert.

Shortly after noon, the phone rang. A woman's voice I didn't recognize asked for me and then said that she had a message.

"What?" I asked.

"Persist." And she hung up.

* * *

So I drove back toward the desert. The suit guys followed after me, and I turned around to talk things over.

Same suits, same sunglasses. Their days had as much variety as mine did.

"Hey." Investigative reporters are chatty like that.

The suits were far less loquacious.

"Listen," I said.

Nothing, they said.

"Everyone knows what's going on here.

"I'm trying to meet someone, and you're making it impossible. We can do this thing in the desert every day, and all we'll get is older.

"My guess is that your bosses, whoever they are, want this meeting to take place. Their first choice is that you get to watch, but that's clearly not going to happen. I bet their second choice is that the meeting takes place without you. They prefer that to no meeting at all.

"So. Before we leave cell coverage, how about if you check in with them?"

They stared at me as if I was a space alien, so I walked back to my car and sat down.

Ten minutes later, they drove off.

* * *

Same dirt road intersection. Same rock. Same bunch o' nothing.

I sat there, air conditioning running, and waited for something good to happen.

Nothing happened.

I got out of the car and looked with the binoculars. I was by myself. I looked in the sky for that stealth helicopter that the CIA is always sending out after people like me and couldn't see it. Unless it was the washed-out blue of the desert sky, it wasn't there.

I got back in the car.

Eventually, I got out of the car and turned over the rock. William Burkett. No stone unturned. Pretty easy when there's only one stone.

There was a piece of paper with hand-written directions. I didn't know whether to be elated or embarrassed.

* * *

The directions brought me to a small-town diner with no cell coverage and one waitress. She looked like she had been a waitress for a long time. Seen it all, but still greeting incoming patrons with a warm smile and appearing to be genuinely pleased to see me. Her nametag identified her as Luisa. "Table for one?" she asked.

I recognized the voice. Same one that had encouraged persistence.

I also recognized Rina Aaronson, sitting at a corner table. Back to the wall, eyes to the door. She had gotten up and walked over as I entered.

"That's fine, Luisa. This is the friend I had you call. He won't be staying."

"Of course, Mrs. Aaronson. I'll look forward to seeing you when you come back."

As we headed out, Rina told me she had assumed I wanted to see Scott as quickly as possible. I told her that she was right; it had taken me four long days to get this far.

She smiled. "Big mistake. They've got the best food in three counties."

We remained standing as Rina continued. "Sorry about all the cloak-and-dagger stuff. As I expect you know, I am Israeli-born. Every Israeli citizen is expected to serve in the Israeli Defense Forces; women serve for two years and men for slightly longer. But given my history of Israeli military service and Scott's history as a complexity theorist, I am sure you can imagine that the United States government has treated us … intrusively of late."

Rina asked that we take her car. After an hour and probably a grand total of ten miles over roads that felt like they hadn't been maintained in a decade, we got to a small cabin next to something bigger than a creek but smaller than a stream. The little brook supported a variety of greenery, and solar panels appeared to provide power to the cabin itself. As I might have predicted, there was no cell signal. There wasn't a satellite dish or any other obvious way of contacting the outside world.

The cabin itself was small but lovely; a bedroom with a desk that allowed it to double as an office and a kitchen/dining room combination. Scott Aaronson was typing away at a computer as we entered (is there even any point using a computer with no Internet connection?), and rose to greet us.

A hug and kiss with Rina preceded a handshake with me.

"Factor Man, I presume?" I asked.

"'Fraid not," he answered.

* * *

Who is Factor Man?

William Burkett, The *New York Times*

> I have just spent two days with someone who is not Factor Man.
>
> Not so impressive, I hear you say. And normally, I'd agree with you.
>
> But this particular someone was Scott Aaronson. A complexity theorist at the University of Texas at Austin, he's pretty high on everyone's list of Factor Man candidates. Or at least, he used to be.
>
> Let me begin by telling you something I know from personal experience: Being a known member of Factor Man's social circle – let alone Factor Man himself – comes with virtually no

benefits. Expect a serious hit to your privacy, and a big increase in attention received from various three-letter government agencies. Expect significant strains on any personal relationships you hold dear, as your boyfriend, girlfriend, spouse or whatever realizes that the simplest way to avoid your fate is simply to get out of Dodge. (If he or she *doesn't* cut and run, be sure to tell him or her often how much you appreciate their steadfast nature.)

In Aaronson's case, his wife's history as a member of the Israeli military made things worse still. Not only was the American government concerned that Scott was Factor Man, but they were also concerned that the Israelis would get their hands on the technology before the Americans did.

So Aaronson decided to prove that he *wasn't* Factor Man. He retreated to a three-room cabin he and his wife Rina own a couple of hours outside of Austin, and set up a video camera in every room. Far away from the nearest cell tower, he stayed there for a week, videotaping his every move to prove that he did none of the things Factor Man did. Factor Man even obliged by being a bit less predictable than usual, gathering the cast of *Firefly* to provide the numbers to be factored one day.

Of course, with Aaronson and his wife disappearing into the Texas desert, the three-letter guys were more convinced than ever that they had identified the mysterious-and-assumed-to-be-a-terrorist Factor Man. An intensive search was set up, and yours truly was even caught up in it briefly. The Aaronsons were hiding, and they didn't want to be found.

They eventually brought me out to the cabin, and I spent a couple of days with them. Here's what I learned.

First, Scott Aaronson is not Factor Man. I watched much of the video of him for the week ending April 7. It was very boring. Aaronson didn't leave the cabin. He didn't log onto the Internet. He didn't get any email, and he didn't make any phone calls. He met with his wife, but it was all too clear that no documents or other information was exchanged. They just talked and did what married couples do.

Second, I spoke with Aaronson at some length about Factor Man himself. I asked Scott if he now thought that P and NP were identical. He smiled and told me that his views were unchanged.

Since Factor Man's appearance, P and NP have become household words. We all understand that P means "easy", like checking that a particular route of travel visits every state capital in the continental United States and is 6,813 miles long. We all understand that NP means "hard", like finding the shortest road trip that does indeed visit the capitals of all 48 lower states. We even understand that some problems in NP are so hard that if you can solve them, you can solve all of the other problems in NP as well. We know that Factor Man claims he has solved one of these "superhard" problems.

Number factoring, however – which is all that Factor Man has *proven* he can do – is not known to be one of the superhard problems. It might be superhard. It also might be in P, one of the easy problems.

Aaronson believes that number factoring is in P, and that Factor Man has proven that. That would be interesting, and it would indeed be awkward for Internet commerce. But it would be nothing like as far-reaching as proving that $P=NP$.

So Scott Aaronson is not Factor Man. Neither is his wife. Neither am I.

Three down, 6,999,999,997 to go.

The day after this article appeared, Steven Rudich (complexity theorist at Carnegie Mellon University, and also a leading Factor Man candidate) contacted Aaronson and asked to borrow the cabin. He arrived, government entourage in tow, three days later.

Rudich spent a pleasant two weeks in the cabin, and the entourage spent a rather less pleasant two weeks outside.

Four down, 6,999,999,996 to go.

The Factor Man blog
April 15, 2019

62144836556726854621030588612709602025247074409769390644792124107913189 = 22221186809358295696397846842374492 1×27966479500889598576160684690781 80909

(requested by Dwayne Johnson)

75929427388846458810398369009721310673173193117020421713526293713365479 = 3178260139293152884230274058410692 07×23890249400960996444578974044917 3297

(requested by Olivia Wilde)

63157289044995885240907683903321372886380674541584490405063160836344827 = 2652130238133637621961059811471105 33×238137962219536618940131122052705 919

(requested by Emma Watson)

78189999769399726248484919802848410205197013119327423511629559173819621 = 2679055197945879823585219253855690 29×291856621055626564325906629016266 849

(requested by Angelina Jolie)

80854241359520937877717789206399870681672011704813766921239294602538597 = 2575503765096772828004845151858645 39×3139356364190090552748267976207578 23

(requested by Lin-Manuel Miranda)

237-bit numbers will be factored in two days.

In a recent interview, Scott Aaronson suggested that I have not in fact proven that *P=NP*, but have instead only shown that number factoring is in *P*. This is such an eminently reasonably view that it is exactly what I would expect Scott to believe.

It is also difficult for me to disprove. I considered offering, through this blog, to solve arbitrary problems in SAT, but such problems would inevitably be special cases, relatively meaningless, or of such obvious commercial value that solving them would overreach my goals in this phase of the project.

Here is what I am willing to show: The code for which I will issue a license is a general-purpose Boolean satisfiability engine. It is the technique I have used to power my demonstration thus far, and that can be validated by the licensor of my technology. Given that the licensing fee is due a full two years after the license is granted, the licensor need pay nothing if these statements prove to be untrue.

It is reasonable to ask why I don't just use the software to prove that $P=NP$. There are two reasons.

First, it's not efficient enough. The code itself was written by hand (and by me), and is about 5,000 lines of C++.

More important, it is completely possible that $P=NP$ but there is no proof from the standard axioms of arithmetic. (Indeed, there were thoughts that Fermat's Last Theorem was in this class, until Andrew Wiles came along.)

All I know for sure is that I have code that works. Presumably the fact that it's moderately inefficient will actually make it *more* valuable. First time I've ever gotten paid for being lazy.

This web site has been visited 171,299,382,217 times.

12

How much is the Factor Man technology worth?

William Burkett, The *New York Times*

The auction for Factor Man technology starts in two weeks. Where is it likely to end up?

The fundamental value of the technology itself is now relatively unquestioned. Factor Man continues to factor numbers of gradually increasing size, and every e-commerce site has switched to 256-bit encryption at least. (In fact, some 80% of the largest e-commerce sites have switched to 1024-bit encryption or more, although it's not clear that it matters.)

The question of whether the technology can solve more than just number factoring problems remains open, but the clear consensus of the scientific community is that it probably can. "Converted to SAT," Carnegie Mellon complexity theorist Steven Rudich told me, "why should number factoring be special?

"Look at it this way. You buy a car, take it to a test track, and it goes 287 miles an hour. Would you expect it to behave substantially differently when you brought it home?"

Rudich also explained Factor Man's somewhat cryptic comment that the code should be more valuable because it's inefficient.

"You need to understand," he told me. "This technology, if it's as described, isn't just about factoring numbers. It's about solving pretty much *anything*.

"Any quality that you can recognize if it's in front of you, this code can produce.

"One of the things that we can recognize is efficient code. So if you want a more efficient version of the Factor Man code, you can use the code itself to create it."

I asked him why that made it more valuable, as opposed to less.

"Because whoever gets the code first will have at least a one-year head start on making that happen. The code they make – the code that the tech itself makes, actually – will be that much better than the code the government gets in a year. And it will be better still than the code the rest of us get in two years."

I asked Rudich how much he thought the code was worth. "It's worth whatever you pay for it," he replied. "Break open your piggy bank."

The British betting markets appear to agree with him. Their latest rage is a market where you pay in a certain amount of money, and you get back one billionth of the winning Factor Man bid. As of this writing, you have to pay $94.37. They also have the usual sorts of bets where you can wager, for example, that the final price will be between $75 and $100 billion; the numbers there suggest an expected price of $87.3 billion for the technology, so that the $94.37 betters are paying a bit more than they actually might need to.

The American stock market appears to have chimed in as well. Most of the free cash held by American companies is held by a handful of them:

Company	Cash on hand ($B)
Apple	236.4
Microsoft	102.6
Google	75.2
Cisco	58.6
Oracle	52.7
Pfizer	39.3
Johnson & Johnson	38.4
Amgen	36.9
Intel	31.3
Qualcomm	28.4

All of these companies would presumably be interested in the Factor Man technology. The software companies are obvious. The drug companies could use it to design better drugs. Drug design is in large measure a matter of figuring out how to make a molecule of a specific shape, but once you have the molecule, recognizing that it has the necessary shape is easy.

If Rudich is right about breaking the bank, each of the companies will make a bid at least equivalent to their cash on hand. So Apple will wind up handing Factor Man $102.6 billion (the value of Microsoft's presumed second place bid), getting a one-year exclusive license in return and a two-year head start on everyone except the U.S. government.

Four notable companies are not on the above list, but have market capitalizations large enough that they could raise large amounts of cash by issuing additional stock. Those four companies are Facebook, Amazon, AT&T and the Alibaba Group, the NYSE incarnation of the Chinese e-commerce giant. No one expects Factor Man to accept a bid from Alibaba, which has served only to deepen the national tensions between the Americans and the Chinese.

Apple is currently valued at about \$680B by Wall Street. The day of the Factor Man announcement, Apple stock jumped 18% – a bit over \$100 billion. The obvious interpretation is that the Street expects Apple to license the technology for \$100 billion, and for it to be worth about \$100 billion more than that. So Wall Street's estimate of the value of the technology is \$200 billion.

The blog
June 9, 2019

```
From: Factor Man (factorman0@gmail.com)
To: Tim Cook (tcook@apple.com),
  Larry Page (larry@google.com),
  Satya Nadella (satyan@microsoft.com),
  Chuck Robbins (crobbins@cisco.com),
  Larry Ellison (ellison@oracle.com)
Re: Factor Man offering

Gentlemen:

I obviously have no idea whether you will bid on the
license to my technology that I will make available in
about a month. In the interests of supporting such a bid
if you decide to make it, however, I can guarantee that
if you submit a suitable number for factorization on the
last day of my demonstration, I will provide an answer.

FM
```

33001715969582375095009592670209582447566969513345469294940876521726351307607 = 19533128571720988121614070119271531131×168952535424153623073162953212148732839
  (requested by Tim Cook)
4733488175204595409258151547484636419065579144360044952365503276933296775216 = 278221272171897955783822415145064157233×170133941889246618326065262415128842417
  (requested by Larry Page)

33442895455114903399535297282049796899850405125285403541986362228562592505493 = 2620845725296916333499005541047850848270×127603449269514513562763167420263734159

(requested by Satya Nadella)

33961816262878148599942318331855077594431919467338180353771080136945015164101 = 2215528995023103515030019360550915244930×15328987496516151487749578549603767605/

(requested by Chuck Robbins)

39007763895250933515155780430381494356557030123873808465555797061175942093359 = 23886826210246497404552668589404451019100×16330241427602531756517322390130063404/

(requested by Larry Ellison)

Bidding for a license to this technology is now open.

There are 26 qualified bidders. The second-place bid is currently $0.

Bidding will close in 30 days.

This web site has been visited 212,314,295,387 times.

13

What price power?
William Burkett, The *New York Times*

The Factor Man technology auction is five days old, and bidding currently stands at $3.17 billion. What will the final price be?

Surprisingly little is known about the life cycles of online auctions. eBay, for example, does not publish information about the relative prices of items while the auction is ongoing and when it ends. In fact, the only online information available appears to be from a single individual, Troy Davis, who charted the value of a digital camera he sold in 2009.

What Davis found was that when the auction was one-sixth over (one day in, for Davis' seven-day auction), the price was 20% of the final price. Based on that, Factor Man's technology will eventually sell for about $16 billion. No one believes that for a second.

Online auctions often end with a brief period of what is called "sniping". This means that a variety of bidders make their bids via computer programs, telling the program to place the bid at the last possible moment. By doing this, they hope to avoid situations where emotions take over and two parties wind up in a bidding war, bidding against each other and eventually paying much more than a particular item is worth.

That seems unlikely to happen here. Computerized bidding is impossible, given the requirement of depositing 10% of the bid in escrow through Duane Morris. In addition, while it is well known that the Factor Man auction will end on July 10, no one is sure exactly *when* on that day the auction will conclude. This makes sniping impossible, and email to Factor Man asking for more specifics about the end of the auction has gone unanswered.

General wisdom remains that the final price is likely to be a little bit north of $100 billion. The economics of that number are staggering. Assuming that he has no major partners, Factor Man will, at a stroke, become the richest man on the planet, and it won't be close. Factor Man will, by himself, have a larger GDP than Costa Rica or Luxembourg. Also larger than a whole bunch of countries that you wouldn't want to visit.

The number will also have a major impact on Wilmington Trust and the National Alliance to End Homelessness. Assuming that 10% is deposited with them, Wilmington Trust will be holding $30 billion – a presumed $10 billion from Microsoft and double that from Apple – for at least a day or so. If they manage to invest it at a mere 0.5%, they, and therefore the National Alliance to End Homelessness, will make five million in interest. Personally, I wouldn't know where to park a cool $30 billion at any rate. It's not as if you can walk down to your local branch and hand over a bunch of 20's. It would be a bit over 1500 *tons* of 20's, and would also be about 15% of the $20 bills in circulation, doubtless causing a national crisis of one form or another.

Wilmington Trust will presumably find a way to cope. And the rest of us really seem to have no choice but to keep watching the blog.

Liu
July 3, 2019

The terrorist whom we had failed to capture in Vienna intended a three-step journey by which his code would be released upon the world.

The initial release would be to the highest bidder, doubtless an American multinational corporation. That organization would presumably safeguard the code as carefully as possible, and we suspected that it would be successful in doing so.

The second release would be to the United States government. They would presumably also attempt to safeguard the code, but their ability to do so in practice was far more questionable.

The third release would be to the public at large.

The view of my government was that each successive step was more perilous than the previous one, both in terms of the potential disadvantage to China and in terms of potential interference with our government's need to moderate the information flowing to the Chinese people. We had attempted to participate in the absurd bidding game via the Alibaba group, a Chinese company with a presence on the New York Stock Exchange. Alibaba was denied even the opportunity to make a bid.

It was not clear what steps we could take to interfere with Factor Man's overall plan, however. He might have arranged for his plan to proceed even in the event of his death. He might have arranged for some or all of the releases to be performed by surrogates.

But he also might be planning to take each of the steps himself. He was sufficiently arrogant that the view of my government was that it was at least reasonably likely that eliminating Factor Man would eliminate the threat. Given the damage that his stated plan would cause China at large, the decision was made to remove Factor Man if possible.

Eliminating Factor Man after the first release might give one American multinational a competitive advantage over the others, but that was of little concern to us because most such corporations had interests fairly well aligned with those of China. Of course, putting a halt to Factor Man's activities before the code was released at all was more attractive still.

My instructions from the Fourth Department therefore changed. Instead of attempting to acquire the technology, General Zhao ordered me to use whatever methods were necessary to destroy it. I was to achieve this before the Factor Man auction concluded if at all possible, which meant that I had one week left.

The 12,377 potential matches for the Vienna video had each been evaluated independently three times. One individual was considered a viable possibility under all three evaluations, and two others were considered viable under two of them.

One of the three was a computer scientist named John Kind. He had been educated at Stanford but currently worked for a startup in Seattle. Kind had been eliminated by one of the investigators because a small mole on the bridge of his nose did not appear in the Vienna video. Moles can be hidden with makeup, and I decided to place him on the active list.

The second was a Carnegie Mellon graduate student named Anthony Muraco. Muraco was a student of complexity theorist Steven Rudich. He had been traveling with his wife in Europe at the time the video was taken.

One of the investigators had noted that while Muraco might well have been the character in the Vienna video, there was a restaurant charge to his wife's credit card on the same day in Paris. An examination of the restaurant's records indicated that Mrs. Muraco had been dining with a single companion, and an examination of security video from outside the restaurant confirmed that the companion had been her husband. Muraco was removed from the list.

The final possibility was something of an outlier, a fifty-year-old high-tech entrepreneur named Dale Miller who lived outside of Miami. He had gotten a Ph.D. under UCLA computer scientist Rich Korf, who worked in an area of artificial intelligence related to complexity theory and algorithm development.

I felt that Kind, as a lower level employee, would likely be the easier target. My timing would therefore be more predictable if I started with Miller, and I planned a trip to Florida.

* * *

My investigation of Miller showed him to be a paradigmatic example of everything ugly about America. Recently divorced and mired in what appeared to be a permanent midlife crisis, he drove a bright red Ferrari, and drove it poorly. He lived in an absurdly large house surrounded by other absurdly large houses, each no more than six meters from its nearest neighbor.

I parked my nondescript rental car around the corner from his house and waited for him to return from work. When he did, I drove back around the corner and told him I was lost, trying to find an address a couple of blocks away. He seemed only too glad to help.

I appeared to notice his car for the first time. "Nice ride," I told him.

He grinned back. "The nicest."

I looked at the Ferrari, clearly wanting to check it out but seeming not to know what to say.

"I'll tell you what," he finally said. "I'll be happy to run you over to your friend's house. You can leave your car here and shoot me a text when you're ready for me to pick you up."

I accepted, and it was only the Ferrari's handling that kept us on the road as we took as many corners as possible en route to the address I had provided.

"I'll tell *you* what," I said, placing one of my hands on one of his. "How would you feel about going back to your place now? My friend will surely still be there in an hour or so."

We returned to the cookie-cutter mansion. I wanted badly to drive, a request that would undoubtedly have been granted. But I could not bring myself to mishandle the car, and the end result would only have been to embarrass the overenthusiastic Mr. Miller.

In the end, I spent significantly less than the suggested hour. Miller grinned clownishly throughout, right up to the point that I wrapped my hands around his neck.

My basic mission complete, I removed any potential fingerprints from the surfaces I had touched, including those in the Ferrari, and found Miller's computer in a back room. It was not password protected, so I simply copied the contents to a flash disk and erased the hard drive.

* * *

Kind was indeed easier, but also far more difficult.

I drove from Miami to Tampa and then flew to Portland, Oregon using one of a variety of pseudonyms for which I had suitable identification. I then drove to Seattle, where I found that Kind lived in a modest home outside of Bellevue with his wife and two young children. I arrived on a Friday, and on

Saturday his wife thankfully took the children out, all of them laughing as they headed to a park or some other enjoyment.

I knocked on the door; the bell somehow seemed inappropriate. Kind answered, unsuspicious. He was in his mid-thirties and approximately the same height as Miller had been, of course. Athletic looking. The small entry-way included a table with a handful of family photographs.

I looked him in one eye and shot him in the other. His family would find him, but there was little I could do to avoid that. I took the backup drive connected to Kind's computer and erased his hard disk as well.

Needing to report to my superiors, I returned to Portland and, as Janet Liu, returned home.

On the long flight over the Pacific, I had to wonder. Had I killed Factor Man? Perhaps. Was his code on a hard drive in my carryon? Perhaps. If so, were the other copies now gone? Also perhaps.

But two men had died. The chances that China now had the only copy of the Factor Man code were surely not zero, but they were at best modest.

China's needs are paramount; if it were possible to return to the day before I got on the flight to Miami, my actions would be unchanged. But sometimes, it feels that China is not so patient after all.

14

THE FACTOR MAN BLOG
JULY 8, 2019

Bidding for a license to this technology is now open.

There are 40 qualified bidders. The second-place bid is currently $137 billion.

Bidding will close in two days.

Qualification has been denied to fourteen potential bidders. Most of them have accepted this decision with reasonable grace, but two have not.

The Alibaba Group is a Chinese corporation and, as such, is presumably a shill for the Chinese government. The nature of my relationship with the Chinese government is well known, and it is clearly not in my interests, let alone those of the American people, for the Chinese government to have access to my technology before the people of China do as well.

Facebook has also been quite vocal about its displeasure at being disqualified. I simply point out that whatever value Facebook has provided to the world, it would hardly be appropriate to describe them as championing the cause of individual privacy. I made clear in a relatively early post that a history of defending the interests of privacy was a prerequisite to qualification.

This web site has been visited 236,298,155,214 times.

Burkett
July 10,2019

The price of power
William Burkett, The *New York Times*

The Factor Man auction is now over. In the end, there were forty-one qualified bidders, and the final price was $147 billion. Apple was the winning bidder, and it is generally assumed that Microsoft or Google was second.

Apple's price dropped slightly after the winning bid was revealed, but then the Street realized that at least 15% of the $147 billion – some $22 billion – would essentially be reinvested in Apple stock. Since Apple could issue this stock without actually paying for it, the net price was more like $125 billion in actual cash. Apple stock rebounded to near its highs for the year.

Factor Man required that the terms of the license be made public, and Hasday's skills as a draftsman have been apparent. The document is written in something remarkably close to plain English, but has been confirmed by a wide range of attorneys as being bullet proof.

The license is for a two-year period beginning on the day that Apple won the auction. It is exclusive for the first year, although Factor Man himself retains the right to use or modify the software. The initial one-year period is followed by a second year of co-exclusivity with the United States government. After this, the code will presumably be in the public domain and no license will be needed. Apple is not permitted to share the code with any third party under any circumstances. It is also required to provide Factor Man with a description of all of the uses to which the code is being put; in the event that Factor Man feels that the code is not serving the interests of either privacy or the citizens of the United States, an arbitration procedure exists to decide who is right. No application can be fielded or even developed unless either Factor Man or the arbitrators approve.

It is generally assumed that Apple will purchase the $125 billion of non-Apple stock immediately, so as to avoid being exposed to the risk of that stock being more expensive two years from now, when the stock must be transferred to Factor Man. The license agreement specifies that the stock to be transferred consist of shares of all 500 stocks in the S&P 500 index, in amounts proportional to the current capitalization of each of those companies. Dividends (which will amount to over $2 billion annually) are to be reinvested on a similar basis.

On the day of the Factor Man Coming Out Party, which is now universally known as FCOP, Apple is to transfer ownership of all of the stock to the individual identified as Factor Man. Any dispute over Factor Man's identity is to be resolved by documents already in the possession of Duane Morris.

Finally, Apple is required to retain at least $50 billion in cash for the duration of the license, and not to take any actions that could reasonably be expected to risk bankruptcy.

The general legal consensus is that the document itself guarantees that Factor Man will eventually be paid, that the license will not jeopardize the secrecy of his identity prior to FCOP and, perhaps most importantly, that Factor Man himself will not owe income taxes on the stock in question until he has the resources to pay them. At that point, he will presumably be the richest man in the world by a considerable margin.

Speculation is rampant over the question of whether Factor Man has any partners. No one has a clue. But if he does, they are likely to join him on the list of the world's richest people.

Factor Man had made it clear that the terms of the license were not negotiable, and Apple did not try to negotiate. Buying pressure on the stocks in the S&P 500 pushed the index up by almost 5% within 48 hours of the license terms being agreed. A day later, Apple announced that the code had been received as an encrypted attachment to an email from the factorman0 Gmail account, with the decryption key being the password of the Apple CEO. Apple decrypted the message and reported that it appeared to be as Factor Man had described it.

Apple also described the extraordinary measures that they will be taking to ensure that the code does not get "out". For a start, any Apple machine with access to the Factor Man code will be a machine that has never been connected to the Internet.

When Apple wants to give a problem to the Factor Man code, the problem will be put on a new thumb drive and loaded onto the Factor Man machines by hand. The thumb drive will then be destroyed. The answer provided by the Factor Man code will be loaded onto a fresh thumb drive and returned to a "normal" computer for analysis and evaluation. The Factor Man machines are presumably somewhere in Apple's massive Sunnyvale facility, but the actual location is known only to a small handful of individuals. The thumb drives will be transferred to and from the machines using a special room known as the Airlock, where a handful of trusted employees will gather or deposit the thumb drives in question and move them to or from the location of the Factor Man computers. Even the identities of the employees handling the transfers are a closely guarded secret.

15

FACTOR MAN
JULY 11, 2019

From: Factor Man (factor.man@yandex.com)
To: Brian Finn (finnbrian@gmail.com)
Subject: transaction

Dear Brian:

I make your cut to be $7.35B. Not a bad rate of return.
Thank you for transfering the money into the Swiss account
according to the schedule that we had agreed. Please let
the bank know that I will be withdrawing it shortly.

Thanks. This has been a pleasure, and I'll look forward
to seeing you in a couple of years.

FM

The hard part was over, I figured. Denise and I flew to the Cayman Islands
for a week.

Officially, we went for the diving, which is as good in the Caymans as
anywhere else in the western hemisphere. The Caymans are known for it.
We dove with manta rays in the mornings and drank cool drinks by the pool
in the afternoons. (Diving is better in the mornings worldwide, before the
day's currents stir up the water and reduce visibility.)

We flew first class because we bought first class tickets, not because the
airlines decided to upgrade us. We stayed in a one-room "romantic cottage"

at Le Soleil d'Or, a five-star hotel right on the beach. The pool with the cool drinks was ours alone. Two more well-to-do American tourists in paradise.

The Caymans are also known for the privacy of their banking system and the excellence of their lawyers. On one of the afternoons, I did without the cool drinks and asked Timothy, the hotel chauffeur, to take me to James Trask of Dixon Cayman, the lawyer the hotel concierge (and the Internet) had recommended.

Mr. Trask, a British export to the Caymans, met me in a luxuriously appointed office and I explained that I needed to move funds from a Swiss bank account to me personally. The funds were clean and while I didn't need complete anonymity, some measure of discretion was essential. I had no objection to paying income tax in the United States as the money arrived; I simply wanted it to be difficult to impossible to trace the money back to the original Swiss account. My expectation was that I would move the $24M in question to the Caymans now, but then withdraw the money only gradually; my tastes were fairly modest.

Trask set up two shell companies. In both cases, he was the main point of contact. Cayman Island Luxury Real Estate and Development (CILRED) was the first, and I had a silent but controlling interest in it. It would be the initial point of deposit for the funds that were currently in Switzerland. Trask called CILRED the "hidden" company.

International Export and Import Consulting Services (IEICS) was the second (and, according to Trask, "visible") company. IEICS contracted to provide CILRED with consulting services. IEICS contracted with me to provide those services, and it was owned entirely by Trask.

Any time I wanted, the visible company IEICS would send the hidden company CILRED a bill. CILRED would pay the bill, Trask would keep 3%, and the balance would be paid to me for the services I had notionally provided to IEICS.

It was clean, it was legal, and it was safe.

It was clean because the funds in the Swiss account, which would shortly be transferred to the hidden CILRED, were themselves clean. They weren't some shady cash deposit made by a South American drug kingpin; they were a clean deposit made by Brian Finn.

It was legal because the visible IEICS could charge CILRED whatever it wanted for consulting services, and I could charge IEICS whatever I wanted.

CILRED and IEICS both had no legal responsibilities to anyone other than their shareholders, and neither Trask nor I was about to complain.

And it was safe. I was protected from the public because while my tax returns and other documents would show income from the visible IEICS, there was no way to trace the money back through Trask to the hidden CILRED. Trask owned IEICS, and any inquiries would simply end there. It was true that Trask would have control of the money as it passed from CILRED to IEICS to me, but if he failed to complete the transfer, the deal would fall apart and he would (obviously) lose his 3% commission on any remaining funds. So I was safe from Trask as well. And even if everything did fall apart, both of the companies could lead no further than to the original Swiss bank account and to Brian Finn. People might wonder why Finn had decided to make me a gift of $24 million, but we could cross that bridge if we ever came to it.

The whole arrangement also had to last only two years. After that, my identity would be well known and Trask would be, well ... surprised.

Setting everything up took maybe an hour. Trask asked me how much I wanted to transfer to CILRED to get things started, and I told him $5 million. He had me sign a form authorizing the transfer and stepped away for a few minutes. When he returned, he told me everything was complete.

* * *

Now, there are some things I should probably explain here.

I'm not rich.

I'm not famous.

I'm not powerful.

I'm a computer scientist, and I'm good at it. I figured out how to do something hard. I figured out – I hope! – how to capitalize on that. But that's sort of it.

I looked at Trask and, in all honesty, I didn't know how to ask the next question. "Can I ... try it?" was the best I eventually produced.

"Of course," was the answer. "How much?"

I told him half a million.

"Very good. Please wait here."

Trask was gone for a few more minutes, and came back with two bills and a wire instruction sheet. One bill was from IEICS to CILRED and was for $515,000, the half million plus Trask's 3%. The other bill was from me to IEICS for $500,000. The wire instructions were so that IEICS knew where to send the funds. I filled them in with account information for my bank back home, and handed all the paperwork back to Trask.

"Excellent," he said. "You should see the funds in your account in about an hour." He stood. It took me a moment to realize it, but we were done.

I left, somewhat speechless. In just under an hour, my phone buzzed as my bank sent me an email, indicating that a wire for $500,000 had been received from International Export and Import Consulting Services in the Cayman Islands.

Denise and I had $24 million to spend over two years. I figured we could probably get by.

Hudson
July 11, 2019

The day the Factor Man auction ended, I was told I probably had two weeks to find him. The expectation was that he would basically go completely dark after the transaction with Apple was complete, not to reappear for at least a year. With no new data, the case would be cold. But cold or not, our interest in finding him would be unabated: Factor Man knew too much that was too important for the Bureau to be comfortable not knowing who and where he was.

I didn't have much. I had William Burkett, who was not cooperative and appeared to know virtually nothing in any case. I had Robert Hasday, who was even less cooperative and probably didn't know much more than Burkett. And, if the Chinese were to be believed, I had a picture of Factor Man's nose.

I figured that the nose was probably my best lead.

We tried just looking for the nose straight up. We looked for it in passports, and on airplanes. We tried driver's licenses and security camera footage.

And we found it. The problem is that we found it a *lot*. It turned out that about one person in 5,000 had a nose pretty much indistinguishable from Factor Man's.

So I decided to scale back. Instead of looking at everything, I just looked at police reports, with the kind FBI technical folks automatically scanning them for noses that might match.

Most of the matches were mug shots, and I decided fairly quickly that those weren't so interesting. Factor Man didn't seem likely to get arrested; he was too careful for that. But maybe he'd bump into the legal system in some other way.

I generally got a hit or two a day. But the day after the auction ended, I got three.

The first one was a missing person report in Arkansas. I was sitting at my desk, trying to decide if I cared, when the other two came in.

I think I was probably going to wind up deciding I didn't care. The timing was certainly interesting, but I couldn't imagine that Factor Man would up and disappear just as things seemed to be working out for him.

Check that. I couldn't imagine that he'd up and disappear in a way that would generate a missing person report. Again, he was just too careful.

The other two reports put the first one out of my mind in any case. Two murders, both in private residences and both without any apparent robbery motive. Florida and Washington, a continent away from each other but separated by only a day. Both occurred just before the Factor Man auction concluded.

I asked agents local to Miami and Seattle to get the files from the local police departments and send them over. They did, and I read through them.

Both victims had been at home when they had been killed. Dale Miller had been strangled on his couch. John Kind had been shot in the face, standing in his doorway. Kind's family, justifiably distraught, reported that nothing appeared to be missing. Miller had no family but there was no obvious robbery motive there, either. His wallet contained over $200 and a high-end home entertainment system was untouched. Keys to a Ferrari were on his nightstand.

The murders were both fresh, and the files only just getting started. There were photos of the bodies; Miller's was in pretty good shape. Kind appeared to have been shot on the side of his face, and the nose, which had triggered my receiving the file at all, was still visible. Some of the photos focused on the cause of death; others showed the bodies in their entirety as they had been found. There was something more, but I couldn't place it.

More or not, there was no reason to believe they were connected, either to Factor Man or to each other. I set the folders aside.

Factor Man had been my only case for what had been an exceptionally frustrating twelve months. The government wanted him found, but it was easy to sympathize with the guy. He certainly had my vote on what had happened with China. But my bosses said find him, so I would find him.

Maybe tomorrow. I went back to my apartment, heated up some leftovers in the microwave, and drank a couple of beers while watching the Red Sox pound the Yankees. Good for them. The game ended and I hit the sack.

* * *

It's amazing the work your subconscious can do while you're sleeping. I woke up fresh the next morning and realized what had been bothering me about the two murders. Pulling the files out, I could see from the bodies' surroundings that the two victims were about the same height and weight. I made them maybe six feet tall and 190.

I knew that Dale Miller was some sort of Internet fat cat, and the murder file said that John Kind was a programmer for an Internet startup that did credit analysis.

Two computer scientists had been murdered. They were the same height and weight, give or take. They had the same nose. They were both killed in cold blood with no apparent motive.

Someone had just tried to take out Factor Man.

* * *

Depending on who's talking, the FBI is a bunch of hard-working, reasonably inventive citizens working for love of country, or a bunch of power-hungry cardboard government employees. The truth, not surprisingly, is that we've got both types in reasonable abundance.

I work out of New York City, and had originally drawn the Factor Man assignment because William Burkett works out of New York, too. I just happened to be the agent available when Burkett's name came up and someone high up in the food chain decided he was worth a look. Then Hasday's name came up as well, and Factor Man rapidly became my only responsibility.

My partner in this work has generally been a Special Agent named Ron Livingstone. Livingstone and I get along fine, and we've worked a bunch of cases together in the past, generally successfully. But he's definitely from the cardboard side of the street. I like to believe I'm not like that.

Right now, Livingstone was working something else, a white collar accounting scam that appeared to be right up his alley. My boss, ASAC (Assistant Special Agent in Charge) Jennifer Willis, had given me a considerable amount of leeway in whatever I thought might help figure out who Factor Man really was. Surprisingly, that leeway included travel. Instead of always asking for help from an agent in another jurisdiction, I could actually head out there. Provided, of course, that I told the local SAC what I was up to. Bureaucracies are bureaucracies, and turf is turf.

I decided to use some of my leeway on trips to Miami and Seattle. I prefer seafood to Cuban – by a lot – so, after checking in with the Seattle SAC, I decided to start there.

Leeway or not, the paperwork authorizing my travel would likely take a couple of weeks.

Factor Man
July 22, 2019

```
From: Factor Man (factorman0@gmail.com)
To: Robert Hasday (rjhasday@duanemorris.com)
Subject: Factor Man Coming Out Party

Bob:

I need help organizing this. Can you find someone
appropriate?

Figure an event organizer on steroids. My guess is that
it rates to be the proverbial Big Deal.

FM

Hasday: You think?
Factor Man: I think. Choose well for me.
```

16

BURKETT
JULY 31, 2019

I'm good with numbers. If you need to know the impact that a new piece of technology has on credit card use, I'm your man. Analyze a bunch of tweets? Count me in.

But as an investigative reporter, I figured that I pretty much sucked.

There really was no better word.

I confessed my failings to Emma one night as we were wandering around The Strand after dinner.

Not the hotel. The bookstore.

The Strand is a New York landmark, an enormous bookstore carrying two and a half million titles. For Emma and for me, it's the perfect date. Emma had been promoted from manuscript screener to assistant literary agent, and we were out celebrating. And I confessed that investigative journalism appeared to be beyond me.

Emma looked at me with that cool gaze that makes me feel like I'm in high school again and smiled. "The key to being an investigative reporter..." she began.

Promotion notwithstanding, Emma continued to read an inordinate number of the manuscripts that made their way to her agency's e-doorstep. Mostly, she seemed to delight in reading fiction from heretofore-undiscovered authors, typically garbage from self-proclaimed experts in an obscure field who believe that they've written the next version of *The Martian*.

Their domains of expertise range from professional wrestling to opera. The plots are generally moronic. But Emma, bless her heart, is committed to ensuring that no diamond in this vast rough goes undiscovered. She reads each submission with a care that never ceases to amaze me.

One unfortunate upshot of this, however, is that she comes to believe that she, too, knows all there is to know about the back story of professional wrestling, or what it really takes to make it in the world of New York opera.

Or, in this case, investigative reporting.

"The key to being an investigative reporter," she told me, "is to never stop asking questions. Be indefatigable. Ask, and ask, and ask. Be a pest. Make it easier for someone to talk with you than to ignore you."

"So let's say I'm investigating a banking scandal," I replied.

"Exactly! The head of the bank knows. But he won't talk. So you find someone around him. If he won't talk, find someone around *him*. Eventually, someone talks. Then you wind it all back in and you have your story."

I want to be clear here. I love this woman with all my heart. Sometimes her enthusiasm just gets the better of her.

"Sounds easy," I said. Emma grinned.

"So let's say I want to figure out who Factor Man is."

"Exactly," she encouraged.

"Now, he isn't talking."

"That's fine. You find someone around him who knows. You ask," and she stopped, definitely mid-sentence and practically mid-word.

"Oh," she finally concluded. Back came the cool gaze, which was still entirely bewitching. She smiled at me and turned back to browsing the eighteen miles of bookshelves that the Strand offers.

* * *

I got up the next morning to find the following.

From: jess@jmac.com (Jess MacMurray)
To: wburkett@nytimes.com (William Burkett)
Subject: Fwd: help with a party?

Mr. Burkett:

Any idea what I should make of this? In all honesty, I haven't a clue who to ask.

Jess

From: Factor Man (factorman0@gmail.com)
To: Jess MacMurray (jess@jmac.com)
Subject: help with a party?

Dear Ms. MacMurray:

I got your contact information from my attorney, Bob Hasday. I need someone to arrange the Factor Man Coming Out Party, and have no idea how to do it.

Are you interested? There will be a variety of restrictions and certain unusual expenses, but the short version is that whatever you can arrange in terms of income from ticket sales and broadcast rights, after expenses, will be yours to keep as a fee.

FM

"You see?" I asked Emma. "That's how it's done."

She crossed her wrists behind my head and gave me the cool gaze again from as far away as her arms could manage. "Just like the rest of your life, bucko. Better to be lucky than good."

Love is a wonderful thing.

William Burkett, crack investigative reporter, was back.

Hudson
August 1, 2019

I've always liked Seattle. Maybe it was going up in the Space Needle as a kid on a family vacation. Maybe it's the rain. Some people just have an overcast personality.

I wouldn't want to live here, to trade the hustle and bustle of New York for the laid back of the Pacific Northwest. But I could deal with laid back in small quantities. I liked the weather, and I liked the clam chowder.

I especially like the clam chowder at Ivar's. It's a chain now, even with a branch in SeaTac. But it was just a family restaurant when I first went there thirty years ago, and I've been going ever since. A visit to family members in the Seattle area just wouldn't be complete without a stop at Ivar's. With any luck, I'll be going for thirty years more.

I checked in with the Seattle SAC and then headed out to Bellevue, where John Kind had lived. I met with the chief of police there.

These meetings are always a challenge. By and large, cops just want to be good cops. The sad thing is that the cops who want to be good cops tend not to become chiefs. Police chiefs all too often view the position as a stepping stone instead of a responsibility.

On those rare occasions when I travel to get involved in a local case, or the more common ones when I'm doing a New York favor for an agent elsewhere, I always start with the chief. Especially if it's a moderately small place like Bellevue. Then one of two things happens. Either I get handed off to the detective or other investigator handling the case that interests me, or I don't.

Getting handed off is good. It means that everyone involved is on the same page and that the goal is to solve the crime or, at a minimum, to understand it. Not getting handed off is always the first step in jockeying for turf. The people who care primarily about turf just don't understand that most people, including me, really couldn't give a rip about it.

The Bellevue chief of police didn't even ask me to sit down. Instead, he brought me to the desk of Detective Debbie Haller, who was handling the case. There I did sit, and Haller gave me the murder book. Told me I could take my time with it, copy anything I wanted, examine it right there or in an interrogation room. Just don't take it away with me.

The book was thin, which Haller found frustrating. Bellevue has an average of two murders a year, and she wasn't winning on this one. She had interviewed family and coworkers, and there was no motive. Kind's finances were clean. He and his wife owned their modest house and had a mortgage about the size you'd expect. They both worked, which is how they made the payments.

On the morning in question, Kind had been alone in the house when he was killed. As far as anyone could tell, he had answered the door and been shot right there. The murder book had a ballistics report indicating that he was shot with a Glock and a bunch of interviews with neighbors who had seen nothing. It wasn't surprising; the little community in which Kind had lived saw a reasonable amount of vehicular traffic at any time, including Saturday mornings. The killer was unlikely to have stood out in any useful way.

I took a predictable trip to the crime scene, which was no longer cordoned off with the usual yellow tape. I found a small middle-class house on a tree-lined street full of other small, middle-class houses. There was a for-sale sign in front of one of the houses; I couldn't tell if it was a response to the murder or just the usual turnover that accompanies suburban living.

The coroner's report indicated that Kind had been killed by a single bullet, which had passed through his right eye socket, entered the occipital lobe and expanded on its way toward the back of Kind's skull. It had then rattled around the inside of his head, and he had been killed instantly. The house had been unoccupied since the murder, and most of the evidence remained intact. The blood spatter inside the front door was consistent with the description of the shooting. Maybe the killer was left-handed; if you're shooting someone while standing face-to-face, you tend to shoot them on the same side as your gun hand. Maybe the killer was a few inches shorter than Kind's 5'11", based on the point at which the bullet first impacted the back of Kind's skull. Or maybe I didn't know a damn thing.

I made my way into the house and found three bedrooms, a master and two kids'. Everything appeared absolutely normal, almost boring. Some of the clothing had been removed, along with toiletries, but it was all done neatly and carefully. Haller had told me that she herself had gathered what the family needed so that they would not have to return to the house; they were staying with Kind's mother-in-law, who lived in Seattle proper. The pictures reflected a happy family, with a decent mix of groupings of the various family members and only a couple of individual shots.

I went into the office at the back of the house, where Haller had told me the computer had been located. She had also told me that the hard drive had been wiped. The Bellevue police had pulled it for analysis and determined that not only had all the files been deleted, but they had been overwritten with garbage in a way that made it impossible to recover the information that had once been there. Other than the fact that the computer was now missing, the office was as unremarkable as everything else.

All of this was consistent with my view that someone had concluded that Kind either was, or might be, Factor Man. Given that the murders had both occurred before the Factor Man auction concluded, and that Factor Man himself had presumably distributed the code to the winning bidder, it appeared that the killer had been wrong about Kind's identity.

Not that it helped much. There was essentially no physical evidence, and I decided that little would be gained by repeating Haller's interviews with the family and interfering with a healing process that would take something between years and forever.

I booked myself on a flight to Miami the next morning. On the way back to my hotel, I stopped at Ivar's, but the chowder wasn't as good as usual.

* * *

Miami was everything Seattle wasn't.

It was hot. It was sunny.

And the pace was like New York's, or maybe even worse. The retirees – and there were many – acted like they were in a tremendous rush, lest they keel over of a heart attack before they finished whatever it was they were doing. People who had not yet retired were in similar rushes, lest their customers keel over.

Bob Strickland was the chief of police. He didn't shake my hand, but he did ask me to sit down. "First things first," he told me. "We have an active investigation going on here. You think you can add to it, that's great. I'd love the help. But if you've got nothing to contribute, do everyone a favor and let us do what we've been trained to do."

Miami averages 81 murders a year. It took Strickland another hour to tell me how good they were at solving them, especially on his watch. The detective handling the Dale Miller murder was handling two others at the same time. Strickland called him up and asked if he wanted to make time to see me. Told him it was "totally optional." He paused for a few moments and I only heard his side of it. "Not a problem," he said. "I've got your back. Absolutely."

He turned back to me. "Sorry," he said. "The detective working that case has two other active murders on his plate as well. He can make time for you, of course, but it'll be a few days."

I thanked him for his time, and left. Cardboard.

Strickland had been pretty clear with his detective that his preference was to blow me off; it was hardly surprising that the detective had decided the safest way to avoid making waves was to do just that. But a detective was the same as a beat cop. The goal was to solve the crime and avoid the politics.

Miller had been a reasonably well-known Internet guy, and the case had gotten a predictable amount of play in the Miami press. It took about two minutes on Google for me to find out that the detective who pulled the case was Josh Wilson, who worked out of the Miami Beach precinct.

I drove down there and spoke to the sergeant who was manning reception. Showed him my credentials and said I was hoping to talk with Detective Wilson.

"I'm sure you are," he responded. "It's not so clear that the detective is hoping to talk with you."

"Every detective I've ever known hopes pretty much what the chief hopes," I told him. "I'm not looking to make waves here. It's just that I've got a case in Seattle that looks like it might be related to this one. Last I checked, we were all supposed to be on the same side."

The sergeant eventually decided that we probably were indeed on the same side, and told me that Wilson could often be found at the Lionesse Wetlab after his shift. It was a dive bar on the Rickenbacker Causeway.

* * *

Parking is always a challenge at a dive bar. I eventually figured out that I needed to park on the neighboring University of Miami Marine School campus, which turned out to be easy after business hours when the bar opened up anyway.

I recognized Wilson from a newspaper clipping when he walked in a little after six. Mid-forties, face that looked like someone you could trust but also someone who wouldn't take any crap from anyone. Overweight, because his street days were long behind him. But not much overweight, because he remembered what they were like and still saw a beat cop when he looked in the mirror.

I stepped up. "Detective Wilson? John Hudson."

He looked less than excited to see me. "Yeah, Sarge told me you might show up here. Not sure how I feel about that."

His response was simple and direct. I decided to try the same back and hope for some luck. "So tell me, Detective, was Dale Miller's killer left-handed?"

Wilson considered this. "Okay, Special Agent John Hudson. I'll buy you a drink, and you can tell me why you asked that particular question." He bought me a beer and we found a table in the back.

"Okay," he asked me. "Why that question?"

"I assume that the answer is, 'Yes.' "

"The answer is, 'Probably.' The strangulation marks suggest it, but it's not certain. Your turn."

"Same deal, actually," I told him. "There's a murder outside Seattle that I think might be related. Similar vague evidence of a left-handed killer."

We both waited. "Guy killed in his doorway, gunshot to the right side of the face."

"I see. And you think the killings are related ... why?"

It was a good question, and not one I was really willing to answer. I told Wilson that they had similar noses.

"Noses? You gotta be kidding me."

"God's own truth. Cut me a little slack here, okay? There was basically zero physical evidence in the Seattle killing. Nothing. Killer used a Glock. That's it."

Wilson just stared at me. I could tell that he had more in the Miami killing, but I had no idea what it was. My turn to wait while he decided what to share and what not to.

"We've got more than that." He paused. "But if we're gonna trade, we gotta trade. No FBI-telling-you-only-what-we-think-you-need-to-know crap."

"That's fair. But I'm out on a limb of my own here, Detective. My ASAC knows that I'm traveling, but I haven't even told *her* why I think the murders are connected. It's too thin. But if it firms up, you'll be the second to know. Good enough?"

"Good enough. And it's Josh." He finally offered a hand across the table, and I shook it.

"I'll trust you that there's nothing of interest in the Seattle case, but I'd still like a look at the book. You swing that?"

I told him I could. "And I'll even start," I said. "The hard drive in the Seattle case was erased."

"Same with us," Josh said. He stopped and grinned. "A *nose*?"

I smiled back. "A nose."

"Okay." He paused for a moment, and I waited for whatever it was he was considering telling me. "We've got a hair."

A hair was huge. Among other things, a hair meant a conviction if we could find the killer. "In the system?" I asked.

"Still waiting on sequencing. At this point, all we know is that it's long, it's straight, and it's black. Thick. Maybe Asian."

Sequencing meant DNA sequencing. My guess was that the Miami PD had more DNA than they could deal with, and it was handled strictly first-in, first-out. It might be a couple of weeks before they had results.

I told Wilson I could make it go faster. But I also told him I expected him to decline. He had to work with a roomful of guys waiting on their own DNA results, and he wouldn't make any friends by having the Feds help him jump the queue.

"I'm good," he told me. "And thanks for understanding."

We talked a little more as we worked on our beers. Josh told me that just like in Seattle, the murder had taken place in a quiet neighborhood and that other than the hair, there was basically nothing in the way of additional physical evidence. The neighbors hadn't seen a thing. We swapped vague feelings about the cases, which are often more important than the details in the murder books. We agreed to exchange books and keep each other informed.

I had a cubano on the way back to my hotel. It was better than I remembered.

17

BURKETT
AUGUST 2, 2019

From: jess@jmac.com (Jess MacMurray)

To: wburkett@nytimes.com (William Burkett)

Subject: Fwd: help with a party?

Mr. Burkett:

Any idea what I should make of this? In all honesty, I haven't a clue who to ask.

Jess

<message from Factor Man to Jess MacMurray>

From: William Burkett (wburkett@nytimes.com)

To: Jess MacMurray (jess@jmac.com)

Subject: Re: Fwd: help with a party?

Just confirming that this was actually intended for me.

William

MacMurray: Yes. You seem to know more about Factor Man than anyone else, I think.

Burkett: Thanks. I don't know much.

MacMurray: In the land of the blind …

Burkett: Flattering.

MacMurray: Charm is my middle name.

Burkett: Curious coincidence that we have the same middle name.

We went on like that for a while. I was surprised that Jess wanted my involvement; the story itself had to be worth a fortune. She explained that she never did anything like that; her standard procedure in designing a big event was always to ensure that she had absolutely no conflicts of interest in its execution. Between the ticket sales (50,000 tickets at $1000 each?) and the broadcast rights to something that rated to rival the Super Bowl, she was going to make a mint in any event.

We eventually agreed that she would cc me on her exchanges with Factor Man. In exchange, anything I wrote I'd have to run by her first. She had no editorial authority but could ask me to delay publication by up to a week. And I would be available to help her deal with whatever arose, to the extent that I could.

It would be almost two years before I realized how valuable those emails really were.

Liu
August 7, 2019

My mission to stop Factor Man had apparently not succeeded, and the responsibility for the failure lay with me. While there had initially been at least some chance that either John Kind or Dale Miller was the subject in question, it appeared unlikely that Apple had gotten the Factor Man code without his direct involvement. There was also nothing of interest on either of the hard drives I had brought back with me to China.

General Zhao's displeasure was apparent. It was recognized that I could claim success in identifying Factor Man and obtaining the video footage in Vienna, but my mission since had been an almost complete failure.

We still had no way of knowing if eliminating Factor Man would result in his code spreading no further than Apple. But as long as it was a possibility, our need to identify him would grow only more pressing as time passed. If Factor Man were alive to effect the exchange, it was a certainty that the United States government would gain access to the technology in less than a year.

Unfortunately for China – but fortunately for me – I remained the individual in China most qualified to find him.

We had investigated 12,762 individuals in our search. The 12,760 that were still alive would all need to be examined anew and with greater care. If we considered forty a day, our analysis would be complete well before the next deadline.

Factor Man
August 8, 2019

```
From: Jess MacMurray (jess@jmac.com)
To: Factor Man (factorman0@gmail.com)
Subject: Re: help with a party?
```

OK, you're on. Two conditions. First, William Burkett will be helping me. Mostly as a sanity check on what's going on, but you should expect him to have access to any email that you send me.

Second, you will be paying me an absurd amount of money to do this for you. I'm incredibly good at it. Your primary job is to give me the freedom to do my job.

```
Jess
```

Factor Man: Agreed on both counts. Tell William to behave responsibly. Shall we start with venue?

MacMurray: Yes.

Factor Man: You know the date. Venue actually up to you, provided it is in the continental United States. I'd like 750 reasonably good seats for myself, randomly grouped in blocks of two, three and four.

MacMurray: I would suggest either the LA Coliseum (93,607 seats) or the Rose Bowl (92,542). There are larger spaces, but they don't have the cachet of those two.

Factor Man: Are they available?

MacMurray: Nothing suitable will be available with this little notice.

Factor Man: ?

MacMurray: Everything will be booked, but money talks. My guess is that buying out either venue's current commitment will be $5-10M. Shouldn't be more; I'll call and tell them they'd better take it before I come to my senses and offer less to someone else. We certainly have that much to work with. My guess is that the seats will go for an average of maybe $1500. So I've got $150M in ticket sales to play with before we even talk about broadcast rights, which should be triple that. I'll make them an offer they can't refuse.

Factor Man: So we can go either way on the location?

MacMurray: I'd expect so. Is there likely to be anything special that I don't know about?

Factor Man: Security. Lots and lots of security.

MacMurray: I would go with the Rose Bowl in that case. They are a bit higher profile and probably in a position to do a better job there.

Factor Man: Sounds reasonable. Make it so.

MacMurray: As you wish. Two can play this game :)

Hudson
August 10, 2019

That an Asian had tried to eliminate Factor Man somehow felt right. That a Chinese had tried to eliminate him felt even more right. And one in particular seemed especially right.

Janet Liu had been mixed up with this from the beginning. She had been involved in the break-in at Hasday's office. An inquiry to my counterparts in the EU showed that she had been in Europe some time before the video, supposedly of Factor Man, had surfaced. And US Customs and Border Protection told me that she had flown from Portland, Oregon, to Beijing the day after John Kind had been shot.

Portland was an odd but perhaps sensible choice. Better than Seattle simply as a matter of tradecraft, but close enough to be convenient.

What was odd was that Liu wasn't on any of the flights arriving *into* Portland.

So I started looking at the security cam video. Finding her working her way to the Beijing flight was easy; I knew the time of day and the gate. There Liu was, plain as day in the CCTV recording of the security checkpoint. Portland has only one.

For her arrival, I had much less to go on. I did have the day, I expected, since the two murders had exactly one full day between them.

I didn't know the airline, but Portland's single checkpoint might mean that I didn't need to know it. I didn't think she'd take a redeye, and flights from the East Coast into PDX generally arrive between 11AM and 7PM.

The CCTV coverage of the passengers arriving on the ground to take a flight out of the airport is unfortunately much better than the coverage of the people arriving by air and then leaving by ground. The people going *out* past security were generally visible only from behind and, while there were other cameras scattered around the facility, I had no guarantee that Liu had walked by any of them.

I started looking for any woman about 5'9" with long, straight, black hair. There were too many of them.

There was one other thing I could try. Assuming that Liu even had used Portland as her point of arrival in the Pacific Northwest, I suspected that she had worn different clothes coming and going. But while she might have changed everything else, there was a pretty good chance she had worn the same shoes.

When she flew to Beijing, she was wearing black boots, dusky enough to be suede, just above ankle height.

Looking through the video of the people arriving into PDX and leaving the airport, there were four possibilities. They were at 12:45, 1:13, 3:44 and 6:32. Now I just had to look at the video for all the airport cameras for maybe the preceding ten minutes.

Bingo. She had come in on a United flight arriving at about quarter past six. Most likely, she had changed planes in Chicago.

Now it got easy. Of all of the passengers on the United arrival from Chicago into Portland, exactly one had come from Florida. Elizabeth Chu, leaving Tampa at 12:01.

And there she was on the Tampa cameras, plain as day.

Elizabeth Chu had rented a car on her arrival in Portland, returning it two days later. She had put 375 miles on it, just about right. She had put 425 miles on a car in Tampa, also just about right.

Easy, peasy.

* * *

I had two people to tell. Willis, my ASAC, would be easy. Josh Wilson was going to be hard.

I told Jennifer I needed to see her as soon as possible, which turned out to mean in a couple of hours. I summarized it for her: A Chinese operative named Janet Liu had apparently killed two American citizens, one in Miami and one in Bellevue. I didn't have it yet, but I fully expected to have DNA evidence placing her at the scene of the Miami crime. I could place Liu in or near both cities where the murders were committed. The Americans she had killed appeared to have committed no crime other than having a nose that looked like Factor Man's and being in the computer business.

I could see the wheels turning in Willis' head. This was about to be above her pay grade. Probably *way* above her pay grade. A Chinese agent had murdered two American citizens, on American soil, for basically no reason. And then she had returned to China.

I was glad that I would be out of it.

I explained to Jennifer that I needed to tell Josh Wilson that I had closed his case. She had known me for long enough to know that there wasn't any point in trying to talk me out of it.

"I hate the political ones, John," Willis told me. "The shitstorm coming on this is going to be unbelievable."

"Go ahead," she told me. "Fly to Miami on the government's dime. My guess is that the whole thing will be classified before you even touch down. I have no idea what you're going to say, but it'll be better if you say it in person."

No cardboard there. But I didn't have a clue what I was going to say to Wilson, either. We had solved his case, and he never would. And I wasn't going to be able to share a damn thing with him.

* * *

We met back at the Lionesse Wetlab, a little later into the evening than the last time. The college crowd was out in force, and I wished that I was twenty years younger. Hell, I'd settle for a decade.

Josh wasted no time. "Only one reason for you to come back here," he told me. "You've made progress, and I'm gonna get screwed."

"You mind if I order a couple of beers first?" I asked him.

"Go ahead. But tell me I'm wrong."

I told him I couldn't tell him that, and was rewarded with a stream of expletives and a rather unsanitary suggestion as to what I could do with the beer.

"Listen, Wilson," I told him. "I'm here, okay? I could have stayed in New York and stiffed you."

"I'm surprised you didn't do just that."

"Cut it out. I told you I wouldn't, and I didn't."

"Screwing me in person isn't any better than screwing me by phone, Hudson. You're not my type."

I told him he wasn't my type, either.

After all this, we were still standing at the crowded bar. Josh picked up his beer and stalked back to a table. I followed him and we both sat down.

"You're a prick," he told me. "You know that?"

"Yup."

"You gonna tell me anything at all, or just let me keep chasing my tail down here?"

I told him he could stop chasing his tail because his case was solved. Not surprisingly, this got me another stream of carefully chosen language. When he calmed down – a little – he asked if the same person had killed both his vic and the guy in Seattle.

"Yup."

"And you're not going to tell me who it is?"

"Nope. I'll tell you that they're no longer in Miami, and probably will never be in Miami again. But that's all I can tell you."

"Fuck you, Hudson. And the horse you rode in on."

And he went back to his beer, staring at me across the table.

There is a reason Willis is the ASAC and I'm not. I'm a good agent. I dig through things, and if something can be unraveled, I'm at least as likely to unravel it as the next guy.

But I have a fatal flaw. I believe that good people should be treated with respect.

In itself, that's not completely fatal. It's bad, but it's not fatal.

But I believe that treating them with respect is more important than following the rules.

And that's fatal.

I wasn't going to break the rules here, but I was about to bend them.

"Listen," I told Josh. "I figured this out yesterday. Yesterday. You understand?"

"What I understand is that you got on the next plane down to tell me the good news."

"What I'm trying to tell is that before I even got off the plane, the whole thing had been classified."

"Classified? Classified what?"

"Classified," I told him. "Like top-secret classified."

You're not supposed to do that. The very fact that information was classified was in general also classified.

Josh still didn't get it. "Top secret?"

"Yes," I told him. "But that isn't the point. The point is that this got classified *instantly*. Nothing ever gets classified that fast. And it got classified at a level where even if someone decided you should know, it would take about eight months to run the background checks on you to confirm that it was okay to tell you."

"Fuck me," was the considered response.

"Well, that's all of us," I told him. "You, me, *and* the horse I rode in on."

He looked at me with a bit more kindness. "You allowed to tell me any of this?"

"Tell you any of what?" I asked back. "Drink your beer."

We drank.

* * *

When you surprise the vast bureaucracy known as the federal government, two things are pretty much guaranteed to happen.

First, they will do whatever is necessary to make sure that no one else knows they've been surprised. This generally involves classifying the surprise, so that if someone else learns about it, people can be put in jail.

And second …

There is no second. The second thing that will happen is absolutely nothing.

Now, it's probably not *really* nothing. Meetings are taking place. Options are being weighed. Decisions are being decided.

But to the outside world, it looks like nothing.

I have never really understood this. I'm fundamentally a cop. Clues come with expiry dates. You're way more likely to solve a murder in two days than in two months, and the same goes for most other crimes. If you sit on something while twelve people have eleven meetings about it, it'll be worthless by the time you're ready to act.

My first partner explained this to me a long time ago. She told me that the world divided into two types of people: entrepreneurs and custodians.

The entrepreneurs always want to do things as quickly as possible. They solve crimes and form businesses. For an entrepreneur, four failures and one success is fantastic.

Then there are the custodians, who want to do things as *slowly* as possible. It's not because they're lazy or cowards (although some certainly are); it's because they're *careful*. For a custodian, four failures and one success is a disaster. In fact, four successes and one failure is a disaster.

What my partner told me was that the world needs *both* of these groups. Only custodians, and nothing ever gets done. Only entrepreneurs, and nothing ever works.

The higher up in government you get, the more likely you are to be a custodian.

Which is why after I told Willis what had happened in Seattle and Miami, I heard absolutely nothing about it for two months.

At which point, I was handed an airplane ticket to DC and told to report to the office of FBI director Richard Starkey.

Starkey had completed a double major in chemistry and religion before going to law school. From there, he had followed a fairly direct political trajectory, serving as a US Attorney and then as Deputy Attorney General before being appointed to head the FBI.

Mostly, though, he should have been a basketball player. The man is well over six and a half feet tall. Intimidating in person on many levels.

The shuttles from New York to Washington generally arrive at Reagan, and I took an Uber from there to the FBI headquarters at 935 Pennsylvania Avenue. Then I made my way upstairs and into what was probably the biggest office I had ever been in. Starkey's reporting path was there on the wall: he reports to Attorney General Kenneth Singer, and Singer reports to the president. Starting with Starkey, it's two steps to POTUS.

The office was spacious as well as big. There was no clutter, just space and a lot of really big furniture. Starkey's admin showed me in and the director stepped around from the desk to shake my hand. He sat at a conference table on the right side of the office and invited me to join him.

No one else was there. Willis wasn't there. Neither were any of the dozen or so people who were probably between Willis and Starkey in the governmental pecking order.

Normally, the whole chain of command would have shown up. If someone below you is having a conversation with someone above you in the hierarchy, you need to be there to know what's being said. But in this case, most of the reporting path was back in New York City, which meant that Starkey could leave them out and they had no effective mechanism for pushing their way back in. Just Starkey and me, two good ol' boys having a nice afternoon chat.

"So," he began. "You think an agent of the Chinese government killed two American citizens in cold blood because of how tall they were and what their noses looked like. Might just as well have been random, for no real reason at all. Right?"

"Yes, sir."

"Tell me about it."

I took out the pad I generally used to keep track of ongoing investigations. "Okay if I refer to my notes?"

"Absolutely. But I also want what's not in the notes."

"Everything's in the notes, sir."

Starkey smiled. "Special Agent Hudson, you may not believe me, but we're on the same side here. If an agent of a foreign government came onto American soil and killed two of our citizens, believe me. It transcends politics. We just need to make sure we have it right."

So I told him the whole thing, starting with the break-in at Hasday's office and ending with my connecting the dots at the Tampa and Portland airports.

He asked a few clarifying questions as I went along but pretty much just listened.

"I believe you. So tell me, Agent Hudson. What should we do about it?"

"Sir?"

"You heard me. Let's say you were sitting in my chair. What would be your recommendation to the AG?"

"I have no idea. Sir."

Starkey smiled. "Yeah, well that makes two of us. Includes everyone else who's seen this as well.

"Give it some thought, Agent Hudson. See what you can come up with. You're the only person who understood everyone's motivations well enough to piece the puzzle together. I can't promise you I'll follow whatever recommendation you make, but I *can* promise you I'd like to at least hear it."

"Yes, sir."

"Come back in a couple of weeks. Gladys will find you a time that works."

He stood.

I stood.

I left the office.

He stayed.

18

Factor Man
October 17, 2019

From: Jess MacMurray (jess@jmac.com)
To: Factor Man (factorman0@gmail.com)
Subject: FCOP

Rose Bowl secured. I need to contact both Pasadena and Los Angeles and let them know what's up. Please let me know if you have a problem with that.

Broadcast should probably be next. You have a preference?

Jess

Factor Man: On Pasadena and LA, that's fine.

On broadcast, do whatever you want. One network or many, doesn't matter to me. International coverage is fine. Please do ensure that the event is covered live by at least one major network on television, radio, and the Internet. One condition: I am viewing this basically as a two-hour press conference. No commercial interruptions until it's over. What time should we start?

MacMurray: It's a Saturday, but I think we're ok starting at 6PM Pacific time anyway. You good with that?

Factor Man: Sure.

MacMurray: On Pasadena and LA, I'd like to just handle things like this without involving you. My job. OK?

Factor Man: OK. I get plenty of email anyway. Trust me.

MacMurray: Anything else?

Factor Man: Yes. Before you announce the venue, please reserve 300 rooms for me for the nights before and after the event at a fairly wide range of upscale but convenient locations. I'll also need private jet transportation for a variety of guests; call it a hundred trips. Can you handle that?

MacMurray: Absolutely. Origins for the air travel?

Factor Man: Don't know yet.

MacMurray: Not a problem. Let me know when you can.

Factor Man: You bet.

Burkett
October 22, 2019

Rose Bowl to Host Party of the Century
William Burkett, exclusive to The *New York Times*

The Factor Man Coming Out Party, or FCOP, as it is now universally known, will take place at 6PM Pacific Time at the Rose Bowl on July 10, 2021.

This is the first we've heard from the mysterious character since Factor Man agreed to license his equally mysterious technology to Apple for $147 billion just under three months ago. Apple, long known for its internal secrecy, has also said nothing.

Rumors abound.

One of those rumors is that the technology is worthless, all a scam of some kind. But that seems at odds both with Factor Man's previous demonstrations and with his resolute progress toward FCOP.

FCOP itself is being organized by JMac, Inc., a boutique DC event-organizing firm led up by Jess MacMurray. She, too, has been quite tight-lipped about the whole affair. "For two hours in 2021," she told me, "everyone on the planet will be watching a single stage."

Another rumor is that Ms. MacMurray is in personal contact with Factor Man to arrange the details. Ms. MacMurray, when asked, has said that Factor Man is an email contact, nothing more, and that he uses factorman0@gmail.com to contact her, just like everyone else.

Ms. MacMurray may well be right that everyone will be watching. She is reportedly in discussions with multiple networks regarding the broadcast rights to FCOP.

The article appeared on a Tuesday morning. By that afternoon, every hotel in the L.A. basin was booked. Every airline flight within a week of FCOP was booked as well.

Wall Street seemed unimpressed by all the hoopla. Apple stock drifted quietly but steadily lower as investors wondered what Apple had actually gotten for its billions.

Factor Man
November 4, 2019

From: Factor Man (factorman0@gmail.com)
To: Jess MacMurray (jess@jmac.com)
Subject: FCOP

Glad to hear that the tickets, hotels and air travel worked out.

About the tickets in general: They are to be nontransferable, just like airline tickets. I would like security at the event to be incredibly strict. At least as strict as what TSA provides at airports, but hopefully much stricter. All tickets must be issued at least thirty days before the event, or they are void. Other than that, you are welcome to sell them in any way you want.

With regard to my 750 tickets, I would like them distributed as follows. First, every country in the world gets two, except China. Taiwan gets two. There are 195 countries including Taiwan but not China, so that is 390 tickets, and the recipients must be identified no less than six months before the event.

Kate Jackson and Robert Downey, Jr. each get two tickets. That's four.

I would like you to make a list of all of the computer scientists in the United States. Please interpret "computer scientists" broadly: anyone who has a CS degree, is CS faculty or a CS student, works as a computer scientist, or has been any of those things. Then I want you to select ten names from that list at random, and give each of them thirty tickets, including air travel (private jet) and hotel for them and their guests. That is 300 tickets, so I've got fifty-six left. The ten computer scientists and their guests are to keep their invitations secret; any of those ticketholders identified by the press in advance of the event is to be denied entry. All they need to do is to tell us where they and their guests live; we'll arrange air travel from there. That way, hopefully the press can't figure it out.

The names of those 300 ticketholders, along with any other corresponding security information, is to be provided to me. I will provide it, along with similar information for me and my guests, to the TSA (or whomever is handling security) the day prior to FCOP.

Food should be included with entry. It should be as good as the Rose Bowl is capable of providing to a group that large.

There should be microphones scattered around the stadium. This is, as I've said, basically a press conference. There should be a stage in view of the entire audience, with another mic and thirteen chairs on it.

There should be one special credential that gets the holder onto the stage. That's for me and, once you figure out what it should look like, please just email it to me and I'll print it out. When it's time for me to go on stage, I'll assume I can present my special ticket and get that done.

Please let me know if any of this is unclear.

MacMurray: All clear. I will look forward to meeting you on July 10, 2021. Am I allowed to share what you have told me with the public?

Factor Man: Sure.

19

HUDSON
NOVEMBER 6, 2019

I returned to DC on a rainy morning in November, having spent the requisite two weeks trying to figure out what the United States should do about what was, as far as I could tell, a hostile act by a foreign power.

The way I figured it, there were three options. We could call China out in public. We could call them out privately. Or we could do nothing.

There were no good options, because we didn't have Janet Liu's DNA.

Everyone who had seen the evidence was convinced that she was directly responsible for the deaths of John Kind and Dale Miller, but the Chinese government would obviously deny it. They would be incredibly offended, and Janet Liu would quietly disappear. Nothing would happen except the American government would be embarrassed, doubtless with Congress piling on in some way that I didn't even want to consider.

Approaching China privately would undoubtedly have the same effect, since they would have the option of making the whole thing public, professing complete ignorance, demanding an apology and so on. Congress would pile on, just the same.

So that left doing nothing, the final lousy choice.

Josh Wilson was presumably still upset that I knew who his killer was and he didn't. So he was a potential ticking time bomb in Miami.

Janet Liu might well never return to the United States.

And, most important, I had no idea if it was even legal for the president to ignore it.

Director Starkey met me as I entered his suite after getting out of the elevator. "We're going for a walk," he said.

I looked at him questioningly. "950," he said. "Right next door."

Fantastic. 950 Pennsylvania Avenue was Justice, where Attorney General Singer worked. The Washington pecking order was incredibly strict: No one ever met a subordinate in the subordinate's office. If we were walking over to Justice, Singer was going to be part of the meeting.

I could think of absolutely no way in which this was likely to make my life better.

The Department of Justice building looked like every other building in DC. It was built of beige stone and huge. There were flags all over the place, and various labels, like "Justice," "United States of America," and "Office of the Attorney General." The labels were all in capital letters. There were police out front, and anti-truck anti-terrorist blockades on the side streets.

No one was smiling. The guards manning the metal detectors when we went in certainly weren't smiling. Starkey wasn't smiling, just walking at the speed a six-foot-eight guy walks when he's in a hurry.

I wasn't smiling.

We were brought into a conference room containing one other person, whom I recognized as Peter Flier, White House counsel. Flier is thin, bald and in his mid-sixties. He's smart as a whip, according to anyone who's ever met him. Starkey introduced us formally, and we were about to sit down when Singer came in, accompanied by a woman I didn't recognize. She was introduced as Admiral Bobbie Spellman, director of the NSA.

My day just kept getting better.

We sat, and Singer started. "Thank you for coming down, Agent Hudson.

"As you can see, we've decided to keep this meeting as small as possible. Right now, we believe the information you provided to Director Starkey is only known to a handful of folks, and we'd like to keep it that way."

I looked at the people at the table. An absolutely minimum number of people, including the guy who told the president what he could and couldn't do. If I had to bet, I would bet that they had decided to go with option three. Do nothing.

I didn't want to be a yes man, but I thought they were right.

"So," Starkey continued. "I asked you to think about what we should do about this. Have you?"

"Yes, sir." I swallowed, knowing what a deer feels like in the headlights. "I think we do nothing, sir. We know what we know, but we can't prove what we know. If Janet Liu ever returns to the homeland, that all changes."

Singer looked at Flier. "Peter?"

"As far as I can tell," he said, "that's an option. But just because it's legal doesn't mean it's actually viable. If word of this gets out, the president will be impeached, and he'll be convicted. They'll call it treason, or a dereliction of his duty to defend the country, or some other damn thing. It won't matter what they call it."

"Does he have a preference?" Singer again.

"Believe it or not, he wants to do what's in the country's best interests. He agrees with you. Without proof, all we do is risk tipping our hand with nothing to show for it."

"What about it?" Singer asked me. "Any chance of getting some proof here?"

"I don't think so," I told him. "We've got pictures of Liu renting cars in Tampa and Portland. The mileage on the cars is consistent with her driving directly to the murder locations in both cases, dispatching the victims, and returning. She kept each car for a while, but the only video we can find of her anywhere is in Tampa and Portland. The roads she would have used to get to Seattle and Miami are freeways instead of tollways, so there's no video of her driving to the vics' locations.

"We grabbed the cars as soon as we put it all together, but almost a week had passed and there was no forensic evidence to be had. No fingerprints. No DNA. Nothing we could tie to either Janet Liu or the two murders." The six days it had taken me to figure things out was fast, and these guys all knew it. But in the life of a rental car, it was forever.

"The victims' locations themselves?"

"Same answer: Nothing. We've checked. They're both residential areas. We've spoken to all the neighbors, hoping that one had a lucky piece of video on a smartphone or something. All we need is one. We don't have to place her at both murder sites, just one. But we can't do it.

"We have a hair from the murder site in Miami, but forensics turned up nothing in Seattle. If we had Janet Liu, we could use the hair to link her to that crime with certainty. But without Janet Liu or her DNA, it's all circumstantial."

Flier got up and started pacing. "Here's the problem," he said. "The president is concerned that this happens again. Kind and Miller are already dead. He's not willing to risk the lives of any additional Americans. If there's a chance of that, he'll go toe to toe with the Chinese now."

They all looked at me, like I had a direct channel into the mind of either Janet Liu or the Chinese government.

"I'm not sure," I answered. "They have to know they missed. They may think they got away with it this time, but the risk is crazy. My guess is that they don't try again until they're sure. No more killing people based on guesswork."

Singer looked at Starkey. "Dick?"

"I think that's probably right," he answered. "It's certainly how I'd do it."

"What's the Agency say?" Starkey asked. The Agency was the CIA.

"The Agency doesn't say anything," Singer answered, "because they don't know anything. Telling them is the same as telling the world." He looked around.

"Okay," he continued. "Let's say we decide to play it that way. Who knows?"

Starkey answered first. "Agent Hudson, of course. His ASAC, Jennifer Willis. The New York SAC, my assistant director, and me. That's five. You and Peter make seven."

"And the president," Flier added. "Eight."

"That's six too many." Singer. "Anyone else?"

"Not on our side." Starkey.

I thought about Josh Wilson and the Lionesse Wetlab. "The Miami cop," I said.

Starkey was dumbfounded. "You're kidding me."

"He doesn't know much. He knows that the two murders are connected, because I told him about Seattle at the beginning of the investigation. He knows I solved it, and he knows everything got classified in a hurry."

"And he knows because you decided it was a good idea to tell him these things?" Starkey again.

"I had to," I answered. "I had to tell him about Seattle because he wasn't going to tell me anything unless I filled him in, at least a little. And I told him everything was classified because I was trying to get him to *stop* investigating, not start."

"All right," Singer said. "Call it eight and a half. Still way too many."

"Everyone in this room is good," Starkey answered. "I don't always trust my chain of command, but from Hudson up is solid. I don't think we have a problem there."

And then they all looked at me.

"The Miami cop is named Josh Wilson," I told them. "I don't think he's an issue. I can go down and talk with him, but I think he's best simply left alone."

"Okay." Singer again. "What else?"

Starkey answered. "Factor Man himself. All of this works until the Chinese figure out who he is. If they find him before we do, we have to assume they'll act against him."

"I agree with that. So how do we find him?" Singer asked.

Starkey looked at me. "I have no idea," I conceded.

"Are the Chinese ahead of us?"

"I don't think so," I answered. "I think they're trying harder than we are. But I don't think they have anything that wasn't in the video they put up a while back. The people who took that video saw Factor Man in person. But I expect if there was some other way of identifying him, they'd have said so."

"Where was the video shot?" Starkey.

"Vienna."

"So the Chinese know where Factor Man was. We don't."

"I agree," I countered. "But Factor Man knows he was spotted there and video was taken. I can't imagine he'll go back."

"Okay," Singer said. "Are we ahead of the Chinese?"

"Absolutely." Starkey. "He's an American citizen, as far as we know. We assume that he lives and works here. Eventually, he'll show up in a video or some other media that we monitor."

"And will the Chinese have access to the same video?"

Spellman finally spoke up. "They probably will. We don't know for sure how successfully they've infiltrated our various surveillance systems, but we think they've probably done pretty well. But in seven months, that all stops."

"Explain." Singer.

Spellman did. "Looking for vulnerabilities in a computer system is like factoring big numbers. It's hard to do, but easy to recognize an answer when you've got one. We're going to use the Factor Man code to ensure that all of the American cyber systems are completely secure."

Starkey asked if it would take a while to figure out how to do that.

"It would. But the input language to the Factor Man code is supposedly SAT, which is universally understood. We've spent the last year translating the hacking problem into Factor Man input. As soon as we get the code on July 10 next year, we'll be ready to go."

"And the other way around?" Singer asked. "Will the Chinese be able to protect themselves against us?"

"Not without access to the Factor Man technology," Spellman answered. "In fact, we'll be able to use that technology to exploit their systems more effectively than we ever have."

No one said anything, as the consequences of that sank in.

"Of course," Spellman continued, "we wouldn't ever do anything like that. It would be up to the Agency."

"Good to know, Bobbie," Singer commented.

Starkey again. "But for the next seven months, we have to assume that the Chinese know what we know."

"We do," Singer answered. "And more than anything else, we have to keep Factor Man alive."

"Understood," Starkey answered.

Spellman. "And that means we have to find him."

All of a sudden, I had the uncomfortable feeling that everyone in the room was looking at me.

Burkett
February 21, 2020

Apple Releases "Final" Patch for iPhone and Mac
William Burkett, The *New York Times*

> Apple today released what it claimed was the final security patch that would ever be needed for the iPhone and for Apple personal computers. They were able to do this because it turns out that vulnerabilities in computer code are like the factors of big numbers: easy to recognize but hard (until now) to find. Apple had used the Factor Man code to find all of the ways

someone could hack into an Apple device. Every such potential hack was repaired.

"This is the first payoff from our investment in the Factor Man code," Apple CEO Tim Cook announced. "First, we used it to find vulnerabilities in our code, and then we had our engineers fix them.

"As of two days ago, I'm pleased to announce that the Factor Man code has confirmed that it is now impossible to hack into any Apple product."

Google's Android smartphone operating system, which is open source and available to all, was not so fortunate. Apple also announced two "critical" vulnerabilities that would allow a third party to obtain full access to both Android phones and all of the personal data that they might contain.

Security experts have confirmed that Apple's claims appear to be valid, at least as far as Android goes.

Not surprisingly, Apple got everyone's attention.

Wall Street noticed. With the Factor Man technology finally paying dividends, Apple stock jumped on the news.

Google noticed. One week after Apple announced the flaws, Google provided a patch.

And Apple noticed that. An hour after the patch was released, Apple announced two additional flaws in Android.

The flaws announced by Apple were remarkable, because security experts who investigated them reported that they were extremely difficult to either fix or to exploit. So Apple wasn't really doing anything that jeopardized Android users. Apple was just harassing Google, forcing them to spend substantial engineering resources fixing things before other folks could exploit them.

The dance went on for months. Google would fix things, and Apple would break them. Apple's share of the smartphone market started to increase, as customers proved themselves unwilling to tolerate what appeared to be a virtually endless series of critical updates.

Google sued Apple for business interference. Apple's defense was that it was performing a public service by identifying problems with Android and that it certainly wasn't Apple's responsibility to help Google fix things. (As of this writing, with FCOP days away, the suit has not been settled, and Apple currently has about 80% of the smartphone market, up from 15% when all of this began.)

About a month before Factor Man was due to release his technology to the US government, Apple made another announcement.

Chess is a Draw but Go is Not, Apple Announces
William Burkett, The *New York Times*

> Apple has announced that with perfect play on both sides, chess is a draw. This surprised no one. Apple also announced that with perfect play in Go, the first player wins. This surprised everyone.
>
> Well, everyone who had an opinion. My personal expertise ends with tic-tac-toe.
>
> These conclusions are Apple's latest results obtained using the Factor Man code that Apple has licensed, as Apple continues to harass Google by identifying vulnerabilities in the Android operating system.
>
> Factor Man himself has essentially disappeared from the public eye, although he is scheduled to release his code to the United States government in a few weeks' time.
>
> Meanwhile, details about FCOP have begun to emerge. The tickets are apparently all in the hands of one Jess MacMurray, who is handling all of the details involved in the event. Continuing the minor Iron Man tradition introduced by Factor Man in his original blog post, a variety of folks have begun to refer to Ms. MacMurray as Pepper Potts.
>
> Ms. Potts-MacMurray has announced that the tickets will be sold at auction beginning shortly after the Factor Man code is released to the US government. The Rose Bowl accommodations will be broken into groups of comparable seats, with sets in each group sold in an eBay style. Multiple seats bought by single bidders will be guaranteed to be together.
>
> Initial estimates are that the price of seats will range from $1,000 to at least $50,000, with an average of perhaps $2,500. With almost 100,000 seats available in Pasadena, some $250

million is up for grabs as the Factor Man story takes its latest turn.

In general, broadcast rights for "sporting" events go for approximately triple the aggregate value of the seats themselves, and rumor has it that in exchange for organizing the event, Ms. Potts is to receive the proceeds. If so, the world is likely to welcome another billionaire.

Liu
July 8, 2020

I had been searching for Factor Man, and doing little else, for a bit over two years. The size of my team had grown, and been reduced, depending upon my perceived progress and the proximity of one of the Factor Man deadlines.

The next such deadline was two days away.

The last year of my life had been spent in virtual house arrest in Beijing, a situation that I did not expect to change over the next few days. If I found Factor Man, my responsibilities would shift to the task of ensuring that he was unable to transfer his technology to the American government. If I failed to find him, I would be expected to have spent at least eighteen hours daily attempting to do so.

We had been through my original list three times. It was distressingly clear that neither Kind nor Miller had been Factor Man, but no one else on the list could be a match. Their noses were wrong. They weighed too much, or were too tall or short. Of the 12,762 original individuals, two had been eliminated by force, and 12,760 were negatives.

We had reviewed our assumptions multiple times, and they all appeared to be conservative. But given that Factor Man was clearly no longer in our sample, we needed to relax them.

Two weeks before Factor Man was due to provide his code to the American government, we expanded all of our ranges by 5%, so that instead of limiting Factor Man's weight to 86kg (already more than the apparent weight of 82kg in our images), we allowed it to be 90kg. Instead of 180cm, we allowed his maximum height to be 189cm. And we watched unhappily as our collection of possible individuals jumped to almost 100,000 members.

Two were known to be dead. 12,760 were known not to be Factor Man. There were 86,525 remaining.

One at a time, we began to examine them. We would obviously not finish in our two-day time frame; in fact, it was unlikely that we would finish before Factor Man released his technology to the world at large.

We did not meet the two-day deadline. And it turned out not to matter, because in keeping with a previously undisclosed condition of Apple's license to the Factor Man code, it was Apple, and not Factor Man, that provided the Factor Man code to the American authorities.

And three days after that, there was a drop in the number of US government machines we could access surreptitiously.

To zero.

* * *

The auction of tickets to FCOP occurred in the two months following the American government's acquisition of the technology. China, having been absurdly excluded from the list of countries receiving tickets directly, was forced to purchase two.

We obtained two front-row, midfield tickets on opposite sides of the stadium at a price of $125,000 each. The ticket holders were listed as Li Qiang Wu and Ma Yong Feng.

Burkett
October 9, 2020

Congress Passes Factor Man Act
William Burkett, The *New York Times*

> Three months after the United States government obtained access to the Factor Man code, Congress has passed the so-called "Factor Man Act," which requires that all government operations be optimized using the Factor Man technology to the extent "reasonably practical."

The vote in the House was 318 to 117; in the Senate, it was 72 to 28. In both cases, a relatively large number of Republicans joined Democrats in supporting the bill.

The argument in favor of the bill was that according to the Office of Management and Budget, it will cut government spending by some 7% without any impact on the quality of services. The stated argument against was that the bill was simply another example of government overreach through additional regulation. In practice, the real argument against the bill appears to be that many government suppliers provide services on a "cost plus" basis, so that they get reimbursed for their costs, plus some profit margin.

The larger the costs, the larger the profit.

Numerous amendments excluding certain industries from the requirements were proposed, but all such amendments failed. The arguments were the most heated for the notoriously inefficient American shipbuilding industry; the Jones Act requires that US Navy vessels be built in American shipyards, even though the cost per ton of such vessels is double what the cost would be in virtually any competing foreign yard. Congressional Budget Office (CBO) estimates are that the Factor Man technology will reduce the Navy's $16.5 billion annual shipbuilding costs by a bit over $1 billion annually.

The bill includes a timetable for the optimization of various industries, with both shipbuilding and flight planning slated for optimization next year. In addition to shipbuilding savings, flight plans optimized to minimize fuel consumption are expected to reduce the Air Force's $8 billion annual fuel bill by some 3%. All told, the savings from the use of the technology are expected to be just north of $200 billion annually by the time the technology is fully deployed in 2022. This will cover about 25% of the currently projected United States federal deficit, although the CBO is also estimating that the broader economic impact of the technology can be expected to reduce the deficit to levels not seen since the 1990's.

The absurd amount of news notwithstanding, the world continued to spin on its axis. Young men fell in love and got married. Investigative reporters investigated.

I was arguably a member of both of these groups.

* * *

I had no idea I was going to propose to Emma.

It was a surprisingly balmy Saturday afternoon, and we were at an antique market on Long Island. Emma was there because she loved antiques. I was there because I loved Emma.

We came to one booth that was entirely – and I know you will find this difficult to believe – Cracker Jacks prizes.

Now the first thing you may not know here (if you are under, say, 25) is that Cracker Jacks used to come with little prizes in the boxes or bags or (if you are over 25) that these treasured prizes from our collective childhood have now been replaced with QVC codes encouraging you to download an app from Frito-Lay.

I'm in the over-25 group. I remembered the prizes fondly from being a kid, and had no idea that they had been replaced by these crappy little pieces of paper. (I clearly need to go to more major league baseball games, where Cracker Jacks are such a staple that they have been immortalized in song.)

I did vaguely remember that the prizes had gotten worse from the first time I got one until the last such event. They used to be little plastic things that were clever but worthless, and they slowly got replaced by tiny paper joke books or such that were just as worthless but not nearly as clever. I had no idea that they were now gone completely, with no kid ever to dig cheerfully through his Cracker Jacks wondering excitedly what he will find. Beauty and innocence, they say, have no enemy but time.

I also had no idea that back when all of this started, the prizes were actually very cool.

Cracker Jacks itself has been around since 1896. There is an urban myth that it, or a similar product, was introduced at the Chicago World's Fair in 1893. "According to legend…" is the description on the crackerjack.com web site, and the legend is sufficiently pervasive that the Chicago Cubs celebrated the 100th anniversary of Cracker Jacks during their June 16, 1993 game against the then-expansion Florida Marlins. The immortalization in "Take Me Out to the Ball Game" occurred in 1908.

The prizes were introduced in 1912, and have included baseball cards, the little plastic toys I remember, and a variety of other things. There is a definite collector's market, and the old prizes include watches, engagement rings, decoder rings, and all sorts of other cool stuff.

Engagement rings.

I was standing there, checking out these rings that must have been nearly a hundred years old, and looking at Emma across the way at another shop. The sun broke through the clouds and came off her hair just right. She had that bearing that I had come to know all too well – somehow a little bit haughty and a little bit shy at the same time. She stepped up to the counter of the booth she was visiting and said something to the guy behind it. He smiled.

Emma was like that. You didn't notice it at first. But everywhere she went, it was like this cloud of happiness surrounded her. Not that she was so deliriously happy all the time, just that the people around her, however happy or sad they were, always seemed to be just a little bit happier after she had touched them in some way.

Sort of like Pigpen, but with happiness instead of dirt.

So she was just there, being Emma, and in that moment – and the moments since, I must confess – I loved her more than I could bear. So I bought one of the silly Cracker Jacks engagement rings, walked across the aisle (no pun intended), got down on one knee, and asked her to marry me.

She looked at the booth from which I had emerged, and looked at the ring, and I could see in her eyes that she had figured it all out and was trying incredibly hard not to laugh. She knelt down on one knee facing me.

"William Burkett," she told me, "I will marry you. But I want more than just that ring."

I didn't know what to say.

"I want the Cracker Jacks that go with it."

"A hundred-year-old Cracker Jacks? Gross."

She looked at me. "Wilbur," she told me, "Of the last eleven words out of your mouth, five have been, 'Will you marry me?' and 'Gross'. But yes, I will marry you. I will listen to you mangle the English language forever."

Mangle? Who mangles? But all I cared about was the answer.

I returned to the Cracker Jacks booth and bought a decoder ring, on the grounds that my personal cause had been helped immeasurably by the engagement ring and perhaps related caramel magic would support my professional needs as well.

It didn't work.

I could report on Factor Man all I wanted. And, thanks to Jess MacMurray, I often had something novel to say. But in terms of unmasking his identity, I was absolutely nowhere. My strategy in such moments, as I have explained, is to find someone else to bother. In this particular case, though, I seemed to be out of someone elses.

When we got home that evening, I realized that wasn't quite right. There was someone else. It was a call I hated making, but Emma had agreed to marry me and I was personally unstoppable.

I dug through some old paperwork and found the warrant that, two and a half years earlier, had cost me my computer and phone. John Hudson's card was still attached.

20

HUDSON
OCTOBER 11, 2020

There were many folks who might call me on a Sunday afternoon, but William Burkett wasn't one of them. Mutual suspicions notwithstanding, we agreed to meet the next morning at the Starbucks at 3rd and First Avenue.

I knew, obviously, that Burkett had been involved with the Factor Man story from its beginning, just as he knew that I had. I suspected he wanted to share information, and spent the evening trying to figure out just how much I was willing to tell him, and what I wanted in return.

* * *

I was a few minutes early for our 9AM meeting, but Burkett was earlier still. I passed on his offer to buy me a cup of whatever I was drinking, and we found a table near the back. We sat down, and I waited for him to begin.

"For a start," he asked, "What do I call you?"

"You can call me John. Or Agent Hudson. Whichever you'd prefer."

"John. Thanks. I'm William. And thanks for leaving that other guy at home."

I told him that the invitation didn't seem to include Agent Livingstone. And I waited.

"So," he finally continued. "John. Am I supposed to ask you about the wife and kids?"

"What's on your mind, William?"

Another pause. "I'm looking for Factor Man. I assume you still are as well."

"We still are," I told him.

"Getting anywhere?" That one didn't even need a response.

"Fine," Burkett eventually continued. "I figure standard protocol has to be for you to bring another agent with you. If you didn't do that, you're presumably stuck. I'm also stuck. Maybe we could get unstuck if we worked together. Shared information. You know."

"Share away," I told him.

"Two-way street?"

"That depends on what you've got for us," I answered.

There was yet another pause before Burkett answered. "I've got nothing."

"Hardly," I responded. "How about a list of all of your email contacts?"

"You know I won't do that."

"How about the text of the emails themselves, with the names stripped out?"

"Same answer."

"So tell me, William," I asked him, "How do you propose that this be a two-way street when there's not a single thing you're willing to share with us?"

Nothing.

"William," I continued, "information exchange means information *exchange*. It doesn't mean that we tell you what we know now, and maybe you tell us something you figure out later. But I'll tell you what. There is one thing I'll share with you.

"I've got a picture of someone we think is somehow involved. How about if I show you the picture and you tell me if you know the person. You willing to do that?"

Burkett said he was.

So I showed him a photo of Janet Liu. He went white as a sheet, and claimed to have no idea who she was.

Burkett
October 12, 2020

Hudson suggested we meet at a Starbucks in the East Village. I guess he thought that meant trendy. We both arrived a bit early; I was earlier. The only bit of good news was that he didn't bring his goon with him.

We traded supposed pleasantries and agreed to work on a first-name basis. Then he belittled the fact that I didn't know squat. Basically a "what's in it for me?" attitude. Gotta love the FBI.

And then he showed me a picture of the stunningly attractive woman from the coffee shop in Austin.

I attempted, surely unsuccessfully, to take it in stride. But it was hard to imagine an innocent reason for her to have been there.

Hudson didn't say anything while I tried to figure it out. His attitude toward the woman in the picture somehow suggested that she wasn't a good guy, or even a neutral. Not as if she was somehow involved with Factor Man in a positive way. Almost as if she was a threat.

So what could she have been doing in Texas Coffee Traders? She clearly wasn't with the FBI, so that almost certainly meant that she was either following the FBI or that she had been following me. I doubted that people followed the FBI all that often.

That left one possibility, and I can't say I liked it much. I just don't get followed around by gorgeous women all that frequently. This has always struck me as a somewhat surprising and somewhat sad aspect of my existence generally.

So I had been looking for Factor Man, who had picked a fight with the Chinese, and this gorgeous Asian woman who had attracted the interest of the FBI had been following me.

None of this was good.

I handed the photo back to Hudson and tried to buy some time by telling him – truthfully, I hasten to add – that I had no idea who she was.

"Come on, William," he told me. "Don't kid a kidder. It took you that long to figure that out?"

I told him I was being careful.

"Careful enough to look like you just saw a ghost?"

That one was a bit harder to answer.

"Who is she?" I asked.

"So you do know her."

"I didn't say that. I asked who she was."

"And I asked if you knew her."

I thought about it. "John, I don't know much, but it's more than nothing. You obviously know more than nothing, because you showed me the picture.

But my guess is that you don't know much, either. So I'll tell you what I know, and you tell me what you know. Fair?"

Hudson agreed, and I told him I had seen her in Texas Coffee Traders. He told me she was a Chinese national who appeared to be looking for Factor Man.

"That's it?" I asked.

"That's it."

"That can't be it, John. Where is the picture from?"

"It's a file photo."

"If it's a file photo, you have a name."

He told me her name was Janet Liu.

"So if you have a name," I answered, "she has to have shown up somewhere else."

He looked uncomfortable, at least. "I can't answer that."

"You can't what? I thought we were telling each other what we knew here."

"Yeah. I told you she's looking for Factor Man, and you confirmed it. You want more, give me something I can actually use."

"That's all there is, *John*. At least I told you everything I had."

"When did you see her in Austin?"

"You know damn well when I was in Austin."

"Was she alone?"

I thought back. She had been. Gorgeous girl, sitting at a table, drinking a cup of coffee and reading a book. But Hudson appeared not to know that, appeared not to know if she was a solo operator.

"I don't know that I want to tell you that," I told him, "unless you tell me how you know she's involved."

"Do you know who Robert Hasday is?" he asked me. I told him that everyone knew who Bob Hasday was.

"Ms. Liu is a person of interest in a break-in at Mr. Hasday's offices. We believe she may have been looking for Hasday's Factor Man file."

"When did this happen?"

"Two-plus years ago."

"And where is she now?"

"To the best of our knowledge, she's out of the country. So tell me, William, was she alone or not?"

"She was alone."

"You're sure?"

"I'm sure."

"No companion in the bathroom?"

"I was in the coffee shop for over an hour. Would've been quite the excursion."

Hudson waited, but I had nothing to add. Eventually, he asked if we were done. I told him that I thought we were.

We stood, and he offered me a hand, which I shook. He told me I was a pain in the ass. I told him that my fiancée felt the same way, and we went our separate ways.

February 10, 2021

If You're Going to FCOP, You Know It
William Burkett, The *New York Times*

> With five months to go, all of the (non-transferable) tickets for FCOP have now been sold. Total ticket sales were $267,369,219, which makes this event the 16th highest grossing concert tour in history, after adjusting for inflation.
>
> The thing is, every tour that made more money involved at least sixty-nine individual concerts. That was One Direction's "Where We Are" Tour in 2014. Except for that, every higher grossing tour involved at least eighty-four events. FCOP is *one event*.
>
> Other comparisons aren't even really meaningful. The tour with the highest average gross per event was U2's 360° tour, which ran for three years, 110 shows, and grossed an average of $6.7 million per show. That's about 2.5% of what FCOP is bringing in.
>
> Broadcast revenue for the event has been disappointing, at least in comparison to the industry standard of approximately tripling ticket sales. Factor Man's prohibition on advertising has resulted in total media revenue of only $132,300,000. The $399,669,219 total makes the event the 122nd highest grossing *film* of all time, between *Crocodile Dundee* ($175M in 1986 dollars) and 1921's silent classic *The Four Horsemen of*

the Apocalypse ($9.2M dollars at the time, but $397M after adjusting for inflation).

A variety of Chinese nationals were among the ticket purchasers, so every nation on earth will be in attendance. The United States government purchased an additional dozen tickets, and the new First Couple will be among the attendees.

Through all of this, Factor Man himself has remained completely silent. The blog has not been updated.

But the impact of his technology continues to spread. Apple's Siri has become legitimately intelligent, and the iPhone is now almost unchallenged in the smartphone market. A computer-composed symphony opened to rave reviews last month at the San Jose Center for the Performing Arts. Rumors are that Apple has renewed its interest in autonomous driving and that a legitimately autonomous vehicle operating system is slated for release shortly after FCOP.

The American government has also been busy. In addition to the efficiency gains mandated by the Factor Man Act, the most surprising impact has been on the improvement in tax collection.

In 2016, some 19% of federal taxes went uncollected. Last year, that number was 9.3%, and it is expected to fall further still next year. The impact has been an additional approximately $300 billion flowing into the federal coffers, and there is some chance that the government will show a surplus in the near future. This would have been virtually unthinkable a few years ago.

The impact on terrorism has also been profound. Prior to the appearance of the Factor Man technology, 2015 showed a 13% drop in the number of terrorist incidents when compared to 2014. With vastly enhanced abilities to track individual terrorists, however, this year is on track to show a full 52% reduction.

But perhaps not all of this is progress. While there is no new information being collected by government agencies, those agencies' ability to use what they know is unprecedented. If the IRS can find tax cheats, government agencies can find other people in whom they have taken an interest, and this surely corresponds to a general degradation in privacy. Similar arguments can be made for terrorists.

Apple's apparent domination of both the smartphone and automotive markets may have similarly chilling effects. Smartphones provide both handset manufacturers and telephone companies with vast amounts of data about their users, and it cannot be appropriate for one organization to either collect the bulk of this data or to have hitherto unheard of abilities to exploit it. There are suggestions that Apple may already be using its dominant position in the handset market to impact both the nature of its relationships with the telcos and to dictate terms regarding the data that Apple is permitted to collect.

A stifling of competition in the autonomous car market would be similarly profound. This technology is currently estimated to be worth some $560 billion annually, as it has the potential to completely rework the ways in which all of us travel and interact. As with other examples, the overall technological effects are positive, but having the technology in an isolated set of hands is troubling at best. Apple's stock has skyrocketed in the period since it acquired the Factor Man technology, and Apple is on the verge of becoming the first company with a capitalization in excess of one trillion dollars.

In five months, of course, that will all change – again. Assuming that Factor Man is true to his word, the technology will be made available to everyone. Let us hope that this transition goes without difficulty, since it is not clear that either Apple or the United States government would take a similarly generous approach if Factor Man were not around to require it.

Factor Man
March 15, 2021

FCOP was about four months away. As far as I could tell, I remained undiscovered.

There had been some surprises. The first was that having access to Brian Finn's $25 million (or the $24 million that was left) wasn't nearly as much fun as I had hoped it would be.

I couldn't spend it. The quality of my vacations had certainly improved, but not enough to include transportation by private jet or similar extravagances. That had to wait until FCOP, both because I'd be attending FCOP itself by private jet and because after the party was over, I could be as flamboyant as I wanted.

Well, as flamboyant as my wife Denise could stomach. She would want to give all the money to charity.

But that was all for later. For now, the $24 million just sat in the bank in the Caymans, and James Trask waited for me to spend it so that he could get his 3% cut.

I didn't have to worry about money. But I had plenty of other stuff to worry about. Mostly, I had to worry about FCOP, and about remaining undiscovered until it happened.

The biggest thing I could do to help in that regard was to just release the code early. I hated the fact that I had promised both Apple and the US government a full year to work with it before the next release took place. But science moves much more slowly in real life than it does in the movies, and less time probably wouldn't have been enough for them to actually do anything interesting. So two years total it was.

The second thing I could do was to set up some kind of a dead man's switch, something so that if I were killed or otherwise removed from the picture, the code would get released anyway (or perhaps immediately). That seemed like an incredibly good idea, since it would remove the incentive for the Chinese (for example) to figure out who I was and take me out.

But I just couldn't figure out how to do it. And I had spent an inordinate amount of time trying.

The fundamental problem was that I couldn't just put the code on the Internet somewhere, because the risk was too great that it would be found. If it were unencrypted, then any random idiot could discover it. If it were encrypted, finding a way to release the encryption key was basically the same as finding a way to release the code itself.

If I couldn't put the code on the Internet, I would have to basically stick it in an envelope and either give it to someone or hide it somewhere.

Giving it to someone I trusted, like Bob Hasday or a family member, wouldn't work, either. If the Chinese found me, they would have found my family members as well. Eliminating me would simply encourage them to eliminate my family also. And everyone knew about my relationship with Hasday. Giving the code to a person would simply expose that person to the risk that I should have borne myself.

All that was left was hiding the code under a rock or something. I could set up an automatic email just after FCOP: "The Factor Man code is an envelope buried next to the biggest oak tree in Glenwood, Maine (population 3)." It would be like a treasure hunt.

The problem is that it would be *exactly* like a treasure hunt. I would be eliminated, the email would go out, the world would descend on Glenwood, and someone would get the code.

Someone.

One person.

That wouldn't work at all.

Maybe I was missing something, but I'd been worrying about this since before that first email to William Burkett, and I just hadn't been able to solve it. But there was one thing I could do to convince people I was serious about the lack of a dead man's switch.

The Factor Man blog

The Factor Man Coming Out Party is about four months away. The tickets have pretty much all been distributed, but I would still like to clarify what's happening with the technology.

As is well known, I will be placing my technology in the public domain on July 10, 2021. And I mean what I say here: *I* will be placing the technology in the public domain.

It's not already on the web somewhere waiting, because I'm concerned that someone else will find it and use it prematurely.

And it's certainly not in the hands of any of my acquaintances or family, because I don't want to burden them with either the responsibilities or the risk associated with holding the technology for me.

But it is out there. Go to www.thiscodeisours.com, and you'll find it. It's encrypted, and the decryption key is Tim Cook's current password.

He's the CEO of Apple and Tim, you probably want to change that password before I reveal it at FCOP. Until then, I'll keep it a secret.

So everyone just has to wait. For better or worse, I'm waiting, too. Whatever my life is going to be like after FCOP, I'm looking forward to getting started.

This web site has been visited 226,388,257,314 times.

It would be a pretty obvious mistake for me to distribute the Apple CEO's password to third parties, so hopefully this would convince people that I really was the keeper of the key.

Liu
April 9, 2021, three months to FCOP

Factor Man's stated intention was to release his code to the world in three months. And in the past three years, I had been singularly ineffective at identifying him.

My superiors had replaced me twice. On each occasion, my replacement had unfortunately made less progress than I had. And on each occasion, I had been returned to lead a group with increased staffing and resources. On one occasion, I had actually received a promotion.

I now participated in meetings at all levels involving the steps required to resolve the Factor Man issue. The Chinese authorities had decided that the terrorist act of releasing the Factor Man code was one that needed to be avoided at all costs. If Factor Man were identified prior to the release of his code, he was to be eliminated. Given Factor Man's blog post of a month previously, explaining his decision to conduct the final release personally, my superiors and I believed it to be reasonably likely that eliminating him would suffice.

This was a matter not of national pride, but of national expediency. Without Factor Man himself to release the code, we expected that both Apple and the United States government would decline to do so. While it was anathema to us that both the largest American multinational and the American government have access to the technology, such an outcome was still vastly preferable to one where the release was widespread. Although the cost to China of eliminating Factor Man was likely to be immense, especially if the elimination occurred on American soil, that cost was less than the estimated cost of having the technology escape into the wild.

We had three plans for resolving the issue, depending on when Factor Man himself could be identified. The simplest involved the use of any of the Chinese agents who were currently waiting at geographically distributed locations in the United States. Given the increased effectiveness of the American counterespionage efforts since the US government had obtained the Factor Man code, there were only five such agents available. This was far fewer than previously.

We expected that our ability to identify Factor Man would likely increase, for one reason or another, as the FCOP event approached. If it were impossible to intercept Factor Man prior to that time, our government's two attendees at FCOP itself would be available. The tickets were in the names of Li Qiang Wu and Ma Yong Feng, common names for Chinese men and for whom specific individuals had yet to be selected. It would be easy to produce backdated passports and other documents once China's needs were identified more precisely.

The difficulty with this second option was that it might be too late. By the time of FCOP itself, the code might conceivably have been released. So an additional option had been developed.

Factor Man presumably traveled by air at times. If need be, we would destroy the aircraft in question.

Doing so would require the use of Chengdu J-20's, the sole stealth fighter in the Chinese Air Force. The J-20 was the approximate equivalent of the American F-22, and the J-20 design had been compared carefully to that of the American Lockheed F-35 after the F-35 specifications had been obtained from compromised Lockheed computers.

Unfortunately, the J-20 was not carrier capable.

China's only blue water aircraft carrier was the Liaoning, built beginning in 1985 by the then-Soviet Union. Construction was halted when the Soviet Union broke apart and, after a relatively lengthy journey, the vessel came to us. It is used primarily for training purposes, but deployment is within its potential scope of use.

The Liaoning can carry up to 24 Shenyang J-15's. Unfortunately, the older J-15's are not stealthy aircraft and are unsuitable for any mission in United States airspace.

We did, however, have one J-20 that had been modified to use the new WS-20 jet engine, further equipped with curved nozzle technology. This would give the J-20 nearly vertical takeoff and landing capabilities. Although there would be some damage to the ship, it would be able to take off from the Liaoning, execute a mission over the United States, and return to the Liaoning, where the pilot would eject and the aircraft would be abandoned. The actions themselves would be attributed to the behavior of a renegade Chinese airman. The loss of the J-20 would still likely pale in comparison to the diplomatic cost of the mission, but would be far preferable to taking no action at all.

And if all of the plans failed, and Factor Man succeeded in releasing his technology to the world? There was no fourth plan. There was no need for one; once the code was out, it would be too late.

21

BURKETT
APRIL 22, 2021, TWELVE WEEKS TO FCOP

P=NP, and the Riemann Hypothesis is True
William Burkett, The *New York Times*

Apple today announced that it had proven both the Riemann Hypothesis and that *P=NP* using technology the tech giant licensed from Factor Man just under two years ago. In both cases, the proofs were generated automatically by software derived from the original Factor Man code.

The Riemann Hypothesis is like Fermat's Last Theorem, although a bit more obscure, which is saying something. Fermat's Last Theorem says that if *n* is an integer greater than two, there are no positive integers *a*, *b*, and *c* such that $a^n + b^n = c^n$. The Theorem remained unproved from the time it was suggested by French jurist and mathematician Pierre Fermat in 1637 until the British mathematician Andrew Wiles proved it in 1994. The Riemann Hypothesis has been unproven since the German mathematician Bernhard Riemann conjectured it in 1859.

The proof discovered by Apple is approximately 3,000 pages long and is currently being examined by a variety of respected mathematicians. Apple has also indicated that the same software discovered a proof of Fermat's Last Theorem, confirming Wiles' result. The Fermat proof is considerably shorter, some 1,000 pages. It, too, is the current subject of considerable scrutiny by the mathematical community.

Both Fermat's Last Theorem and the Riemann Hypothesis are of little practical value, although the Riemann Hypothesis bears on the distribution of prime numbers and could therefore be expected to have had some impact on encryption technology. However, Factor Man's ability to factor numbers of arbitrary size renders that technology moot.

Apple's claimed proof that *P=NP* would be quite different, finally validating the Factor Man work in an irrefutable way and having immense practical value as a result. Apple, however, has declined to release the proof in this case, stating that the proof is "constructive" in that it reveals a mechanism for building software equivalent to Factor Man's. Apple claims that because of this, their license agreement with Factor Man precludes their releasing the proof to either the international mathematical community or to the public at large. They have promised to release the proof on July 11, the day after FCOP.

Factor Man
May 1, 2021, ten weeks to FCOP

From: Factor Man (factorman0@gmail.com)
To: Erin Keenan (erinok@gmail.com)
Subject: FCOP

Dear Mr. Keenan:

It is my pleasure to invite you, together with twenty-nine friends or colleagues of your choice, to FCOP. I will provide you with rooms near Pasadena for the nights before and after the event, and transportation to and from FCOP by private jet. Please arrange for your guests to meet in one or two cities on the day prior to the event so that they can be brought to Los Angeles.

I do ask that you provide me with the names of your guests no later than one calendar month before FCOP, along with the location of the second city from which transportation is to be arranged if needed. I will assume that the first city will be the city in which you yourself reside.

I also ask that you keep your attendance confidential. If the press learns of your attendance, all of your tickets will be canceled. If the press learns of the attendance of any of your guests, that guest's ticket will be canceled. If three or more of your guests are identified by the press, all of your tickets will be canceled.

All I need is for you to provide me with the names of your guests and the location of the second airport. If you are not interested in attending, you need not even reply to this message.

FM

In the end, all ten of the computer folks Jess picked accepted my invitation. I had never heard of any of them, and the press discovered nothing. On the day of FCOP, I would be able to hide in plain sight.

Liu
May 8, 2021, nine weeks to FCOP

We had painstakingly eliminated 13% of our expanded list of Factor Man candidates. Unfortunately, we had used the bulk of the time available before FCOP. Our lack of access to the American computer network had proved to be a surprisingly large impediment.

There were 75,236 names remaining and, based on our current rate of progress, we had enough time to examine about two thousand of them with the care reasonably required. Our chances of identifying Factor Man in time were slim.

I knew that this was an unacceptable result. What I did not know was what I might do about it.

There was little that greater China could do as well. Announcing that we were opposed to the release of the code would be pointless. Tentative inquiries had been made of the United States government, indicating that China would cease investing in American debt if the code were made public. The new American president made a widely televised speech in response.

> ... As many of you know, the code that has allowed us to do these things, the computer program, is scheduled to be made publicly available in a little over two months.
>
> America welcomes this. While it is true that having exclusive access to the Factor Man code has allowed us to make unprecedented strides both in national security and in the stability of our economy, it is time for these abilities to serve all of us, not just those fortunate enough to live in a particular country.
>
> Nor should the benefits be restricted to a particular industry. Yes, Apple has done amazing things over the past couple years. But Google, and Facebook, and Microsoft, and the automakers, and the pharmaceutical companies, and every element of American industry can operate more efficiently given this technology. They can provide better products, and provide them for less money. In America and abroad, citizens – all citizens – will benefit from these advances. Science does not distinguish on the basis of race, or creed, or age, or religion, or disability, or sexual orientation. This technology should belong to every one of us, every man, woman and child on the face of the earth.
>
> And it will.
>
> Of course, not everyone feels this way. Some nations exist by oppressing their citizens. By limiting their knowledge and, through those limitations, by limiting their freedoms.
>
> To those nations, I say, "Enough." I say, "No longer." I say that knowledge belongs to all people, and that it is not the place of government to deny it.
>
> Right now, this technology belongs to one man. I am pleased that he has chosen to share it with the American government, and more pleased still that he has chosen to share it with the

world. This government applauds those actions and will do everything it can to support them.

Privately, the president had let us know that with the US government about to be running at a surplus, if the Chinese no longer wanted to purchase US government-backed securities, that was just fine with him.

We had serious doubts about the American government's commitment to releasing the code if Factor Man were not around to ensure that such an event transpired, and all of our viable options thus depended on identifying Factor Man himself prior to FCOP.

I was brooding over this when Xu Yan knocked on my office door.

Xu had been added to the team in the most recent reorganization. He was pale and bookish, what Americans would call a nerd. Average height, hair slightly longer than average and slightly less well-kept. I had seen nothing to distinguish him from his colleagues, and looked up wearily as I invited him in and to sit down.

"I've been thinking about Factor Man's passport," he began.

"And?"

"We know he was in Vienna on June 8, 2018. That is one of the biggest clues we have, an American in Europe then."

"Yes." I had no time for this.

"And we know that because he visited the box at Sparta ... Sparta whatever it was called."

I waited for him to tell me something I *didn't* know.

"And you saw him there. The one time someone has actually seen him."

"Your point, Yan?"

"How did he rent the box?"

An absurdly simple question, which no one previously had thought to ask.

"Here's what I think," Xu continued. "I think he rented the box in person. How else would he get the keys? Surely he wouldn't have given the Sparta people an address and asked them to send them to him. So he's been to Europe before."

Of the Americans visiting Europe, only a small fraction has been there before. For most, it's a once-in-a-lifetime trip. I turned to my computer, to find out what fraction of Americans in Europe were return visitors.

"But wait," he said. "There's more. *When* did he rent the box?"

Another obvious question that we had neglected to ask.

"I think he rented it just before the first William Burkett column. Consider. By the time Factor Man contacted Burkett, he certainly had his entire plan worked out, or nearly so. We've seen that at every turn. The whole plan was established in advance. What's more, I think he contacted Burkett that first time *as soon as he was ready*. We've seen him operate. He enjoys this. He enjoys the attention, and he enjoys belittling China. My guess is that as soon as he knew his technology worked, he put everything in motion. He went to Vienna, got the safe deposit box, and contacted Burkett."

It made sense. "So that means that we can restrict our attention to Americans who were in Europe not just on June 8, 2018, but around May 14, 2017 as well," I responded. I had long since committed the date of the first Burkett article to memory.

"Exactly."

I turned back to my computer, wondering how much of a difference that additional piece of knowledge might make.

"I already know," Xu said. "I ran it, looking for Americans who fit our existing profile but also were in Europe within two weeks of May 14, 2017."

"And?"

"And we no longer have 75,000 names remaining. We have 2,461."

Burkett
June 5, 2021, five weeks to FCOP

Graduate school is different in this age of technology.

As an example, Google "buy a term paper" and see what you get. There is a whole host of organizations out there that will write one for you for a fee.

EssayViking.com, for example. For $13 a page, they'll write an essay, an article, a college entrance essay, you name it. Everything is confidential. Their writers are professionals. Actually, they say, "We hire only graduated with MA and PhD diplomas."

So maybe they aren't the best choice after all.

But there are a ton of such services out there, all happy to do your homework for you. For a fee. In today's overly competitive world, people simply don't take honor codes as seriously as they used to. Just a side note here: Oxford University in the United Kingdom didn't even give you a diploma until recently. The feeling was that no one would ever lie about having an Oxford degree. Ah, for gentler days ...

When I was a graduate student, this was becoming a problem. And then one of the professors decided to strike back.

He used stylometry.

What?

Stylometry, according to Wikipedia, is "the application of the study of linguistic style ... to attribute authorship to anonymous or disputed documents. It has legal as well as academic and literary applications, ranging from the question of the authorship of Shakespeare's works to forensic linguistics." Vassar professor Donald Foster used this technique to conclude (correctly) that the book *Primary Colors* was written by Joe Klein.

Primary Colors, while purporting to be a work of fiction, was clearly an exposé of sorts about Bill Clinton's first presidential campaign. The author was "Anonymous", a prudent choice given the book's description of, for example, sexual infidelities on the part of a presidential candidate clearly modeled after Mr. Clinton.

In spite of Foster's stylometric analysis, Klein initially denied being the author. But an early version of the *Primary Colors* manuscript contained handwritten notes that confirmed Foster's conclusion, and Klein was outed.

One of my UT Austin professors decided to do something similar with term papers. A guy named Neil Yager – living in Oxford, curiously enough – put together an online tool where you could analyze various writing samples and see which appeared to have a common author. By using this tool with some essays from his introductory sociology course, the professor found that most of the students had, not surprisingly, a fairly distinctive style. The software identified each of them as the most likely author of each of their essays.

But there was one group of students for whom this wasn't true. An essay submitted by student 1, for example, might resemble an essay submitted by student 2 more closely than it resembled any of student 1's other assignments. What's more, the students in question were all friends. The professor concluded – correctly, as it eventually turned out – that they were all using one of these essay generation services, and getting one of a relative handful of authors to write all of their papers. The students were all forced to leave the university, and are doubtless now busy exercising their lack of morals elsewhere.

It occurred to me that I could try something similar with the Factor Man blog. I had a reasonably large sample of the guy's writing, and I had kept all of my email from time immemorial. I could run it through Yager's tool (or any of a variety of more sophisticated stylometric tools that I would eventually find) and, assuming that Factor Man was a correspondent of mine, I could figure out who he was.

Well, it was at least worth a shot.

The whole thing took about a week. At the end, I was no wiser than I was at the beginning. Factor Man's blog posts didn't read like any of my e-correspondence.

I received this delightful news at about two on a Thursday morning. I had this vague feeling that there was something else I could try, but nothing came to mind. I was too tired, and crawled into bed next to Emma. She mumbled incoherently and I joined her in sleep.

Hudson
June 11, 2021, four weeks to FCOP

With just under a month to go before FCOP, I was summoned back to Starkey's office. There I found Director Starkey, CIA director John Harbison, and a Navy officer I didn't recognize.

Harbison had been appointed CIA director after a somewhat contentious Senate hearing that had included a filibuster by Kentucky Senator Rand Paul. Paul's complaint was more with the American drone program (which Harbison had overseen starting in 2012) than with Harbison himself. The drone program offended Paul's isolationist tendencies. After a modest concession from the Obama White House, Harbison was confirmed.

I was introduced to the Navy officer, Admiral Mark Blackaby. The bald Admiral Blackaby was COMPACFLT, the commander of the US Pacific fleet.

And I was a Special Agent.

Harbison spoke first. The Chinese, he said, had decided to eliminate Factor Man, even if that meant doing so on American soil. Their goal was to prevent the release of the Factor Man technology by any means necessary.

I asked if such a plan would work. Wouldn't the US government simply honor Factor Man's wishes in such a case by releasing the code on his behalf?

No one answered.

"Result notwithstanding," Starkey continued, "Factor Man is presumably an American citizen within our national boundaries. Protecting him falls to us. And to protect him, we have to find him."

I could tell where this was going, and I didn't like it much. But what was COMPACFLT doing here?

Admiral Blackaby answered by sliding a large picture across the table and asking me if I knew what it was. I told him that it looked like an old aircraft carrier.

"It is," he told me. "Satellite picture. Commissioned by the Russian Navy in 1985, decommissioned in 1992. Bought by the Chinese and relaunched in 2012. It's their only deep water carrier, and right now, it's five hundred miles off the California coast."

He pointed to a plane on the carrier's deck. "And you see this? It's a Chengdu J-20, China's one and only stealth fighter. It's not even carrier capable. We figure it's good for one takeoff and then it'll wind up ditching in the water.

"That J-20 is going to fly exactly one mission. And it's not too hard to figure out what that mission is meant to be."

Blackaby went on to explain that the *Liaoning* was currently being shadowed by CSG-2, Carrier Strike Group 2 centered around the USS George HW Bush. A satellite had been diverted to provide surveillance as well. But with all the precautions possible, the odds were still no better than even that a launch of the J-20 would be detected, and smaller still that it would be possible to track the plane as it embarked on its presumed mission into American airspace.

If we couldn't track the mission from its beginning, we would have to track it from its target. Again, protecting Factor Man meant finding Factor Man.

"So, John," Starkey began.

When the director of the FBI calls you by your first name, you know you're screwed.

"We need, more than ever, to find Factor Man," he continued. "To figure out who he actually is. You've been looking at this for years. Tell us. Who is he?"

I confessed to not knowing. "We have the same video the Chinese do. We have access to more data, and to more Americans, than they do. That's especially true since we improved our system security. But he keeps an incredibly low profile, lower than ever for the past year or so. Nothing works. He's a ghost."

"If nothing you've tried works," Starkey told me, "Try something else. As many agents as you need. As many resources of any kind. Coordinate it through your SAC."

I wished only that Starkey had told me what the something else was that I was expected to try.

22

I told Emma I was no longer speaking to her.

"Why not?" she asked. "Oh, that's right. You're not talking to me, so you can't explain it."

"You make fun of how I talk."

"I do. It's adorable. You write all these columns, all these technical things with beautifully turned phrases. But face to face, it's different." She kissed me. "I think your mouth gets ahead of your brain."

She had a point. I opened my mouth to respond, but thought better of it.

"That's good," she said. "Practice that."

I write one way, but speak another. Everyone does that. We all have unique mannerisms, be they spoken or written.

That was it.

A blog isn't the same as email. Maybe the reason none of my correspondence matched the Factor Man blog was because Factor Man himself was different when he was blogging and when he was just writing a note.

And I could do something about it.

Factor Man had never really corresponded with me; just that short note from an eternity ago. But he had corresponded with Jess MacMurray. He had corresponded with her a lot. And I had all of it.

So I repeated all of my effort of the previous weeks. But instead of trying to match the blog, I matched my email contacts with the emails Factor Man had sent to Jess.

And two days later, I knew.

* * *

Knowing was one thing. Knowing what to do with that knowledge was something else entirely.

I told Emma, thereby pushing the problem slightly into the future. She didn't know what I should do, either.

Who else could I tell?

I could tell the world. My career as a journalist would be set. But I suspected that Factor Man had good reasons for wanting to protect his privacy for a bit longer. He had thought all of this out far more carefully than I had, and it seemed likely that I should trust his judgment here.

I could tell John Hudson.

No way.

The only person who really needed to know was Emma, and I had already told her.

So in the end, I decided to tell no one.

Well, not quite no one. I told Factor Man.

I just sent him an email. Not to factorman0@gmail.com, but to his personal email address. It said simply, "Please remember to invite me to your party."

The reply was predictably brisk. I was already on the list, he said.

* * *

The message I got a few days later was considerably more detailed.

```
From:
To: William Burkett (wburkett@nytimes.com)
Subject: FCOP

Hey William:

Well, guess what.

A bunch of computer scientists — including me! — got
selected at random to go to FCOP. Not only that, we each
get to invite 29 friends. It's truly an all-expenses paid
vacation, including a hotel stay before and after the
```

event, and transportation to and from. Transportation including a ride by PRIVATE JET from an airport of your choice.

Do you want to go? Sorry for the short notice, but I only heard fairly recently myself. You even get to bring a guest. (I heard through the grapevine that you're engaged; bring her!)

One caveat: This has to be a secret. If the press finds out you're going, your invitation gets canceled. If they find out the identities of three or more of my guests, we all get canceled. Please don't do that to me!

So: what say? It would be great to see you again, and it is, after all, the party of the century.

Or so I'm told. :)

Hudson
June 19, 2021, three weeks to FCOP

We had all these bits of forensic evidence. Based on the date that Janet Liu had left Europe, we knew Factor Man had been in Europe on approximately June 8, 2018. We knew how tall he was, and how much he weighed. We knew what his nose looked like.

And we had the best computers on the planet.

Unfortunately, none of it was worth squat.

You win some, you lose some. But when you're being watched by the directors of the FBI and the CIA, along with the commander of the US Pacific Fleet, that really wasn't when you wanted to be in "lose some" category.

Yeah, we had a ton of physical evidence.

Screw the physical evidence. I decided to do what we did before everyone carried a supercomputer around in their pocket.

I would follow the money.

On about June 8, 2018, Factor Man had appeared in a video taken at a market square in Vienna. One of the shops in that square was Sparta Safes, a private safe depository. It wasn't too much of a stretch to conclude that Sparta had been Factor Man's destination when he visited.

If that was true, Factor Man was presumably using the contents of a safety deposit box to buy services of some kind. He had no need to simply stash anything; Apple was effectively doing that with (at latest count) about $200 billion on his behalf. So he was putting something in the box that an employee could take out and use. Cash was way better than anything else for such purposes.

It was thin, but it was all I had. Shortly before June 8, 2018, Factor Man had withdrawn some amount of cash, presumably from another bank somewhere on the Continent. If I had to guess, I'd guess Switzerland.

There are three Swiss banks with significant overseas presence and with substantial assets under management. They are UBS AG, Credit Suisse, and the Julius Baer Group. UBS holds about 400 billion Swiss francs, Credit Suisse about 900 billion, and Baer about 250 billion. A Swiss franc is worth about a buck.

I had no time for subtlety. The next day, each of the three banks got a personal telephone call from Pete Muller, the chairman of the US Federal Reserve. Muller asked if there had been any large cash withdrawals in the three weeks before June 8, 2018.

All three banks balked. Muller told each of them to stop screwing around, and they provided him with the dates of any relevant transactions and the names of the account holders. So much for the famed anonymity of Swiss banking.

I got a list with thirty-seven names on it. The withdrawals ranged from one to seven million dollars.

I cross-referenced the list against the computer records of the ongoing investigation, and one name came up. A Credit Suisse account opened by Brian Finn a year or so earlier had seen a million in cash withdrawn about a week before Factor Man made the Vienna drop off.

And five months ago, Brian Finn and William Burkett had met for coffee.

I had been relocated to Los Angeles until FCOP was over, but Finn and Burkett were both in New York. By the time I could book a flight, I found myself on a redeye out of LAX bound for JFK.

I called Burkett and he agreed to meet for coffee the next morning. Same Starbucks, and Livingstone would as usual stay home. Finn I figured I'd just drop in on.

Burkett
June 23, 2021, seventeen days to FCOP

About a week after I told myself I would never tell the FBI who Factor Man was, John Hudson asked to meet with me. He suggested the same tacky Starbucks as previously. I agreed, as previously.

Our last meeting had ended pretty well. I had been fine telling him pretty much everything I knew about Factor Man, and he had seemed to do the same about Janet Liu, whoever she turned out to be.

This meeting would be harder.

It wasn't too hard to figure out why Hudson wanted to get together. I had no idea how, but he must have learned that I knew who Factor Man was. It was a safe bet that he didn't know himself, or he wouldn't have bothered arranging to talk with me. So he didn't know *what* I knew, but he apparently knew *that* I knew, which was pretty much just as bad.

I had no intention of telling him. None.

Zero.

Hudson and I arrived about the same time. We shook hands, and he acted a lot friendlier than he had at our previous meeting. Even bought me an Americano. Double shot, half-caf, with room. We found a table and sat.

He got right to it. "Listen," he began. "I've got a question for you. You aren't going to like it, but I have to ask."

Outstanding. I waited, and Hudson eventually passed a picture of Brian Finn across the table.

"Do you know this man?"

Okay, Burkett. Reset. Total reset. Definitely not the question I was expecting.

"I don't think so," I answered. William Burkett, master of deception.

He smiled. "Come on, William. Don't kid a kidder. We know that you and he met for coffee in January. You don't seem like the type to share a drink with a stranger."

"Oh, yeah. That's right. That's Brian Finn."

"That's better. What did you meet about?"

"We talked about Finn's role in the leveraged buyout of RJR Nabisco."

"And he gave you a large manila envelope."

"Financial disclosures from the buyout." William Burkett, master of deception.

"I see. Why didn't he just email them to you?"

"The Nabisco takeover was from when, like the 80's? It was all paper."

"1987, William. And the records were all electronic. Care to try again?"

"Not really." William Burkett, master of deception?

"Listen. When I showed you Janet Liu's picture, you cooperated. When I show you Finn, you clam up. What gives?"

"Honest answer?"

"Honest answer."

"I don't know Liu from Adam. Or Eve. Whatever. Finn I know, which means that he might be – *might be* – a source. So I can't tell you a thing."

"Can't, or won't?"

"Can't. Journalistic rules, John."

He stood up and walked away.

Maybe it was just me, but it seemed like Starbucks was losing its touch. The coffee wasn't nearly as warm as it had been on our previous visit.

Hudson
June 25, 2021, fifteen days to FCOP

My interview with Burkett was a bust. I made up a date for the Nabisco buyout (only off by a year, as I learned when I eventually checked), and bluffed him into confirming that the documents he had received from Finn had nothing to do with the buyout itself. It had to be Factor Man, I figured. Anything else would be too much of a coincidence.

So a visit to Finn was next. Teamed up with Livingstone once again, we arrived at his estate on Long Island on a Saturday around dinnertime. Two weeks to the day before FCOP.

The long driveway was lined with mature trees and eventually deposited us at a palatial stone mansion. There was no doorbell, just a huge knocker on the front door in the shape of a dragon's head.

We knocked.

The housekeeper answered the door and regretfully told us that the Finns were away. She was not terribly inclined to tell us where, but the authority implicit in our FBI credentials eventually swayed her. The Finns were at their summer house in Aspen.

* * *

I flew coach from JFK to Denver, and suspected that my seat on the flight bore little resemblance to the fashion in which the Finns had made the same trip a few days previously. I'm a pretty big guy, but a dwarf in comparison to the two fellows who were sharing my row of seats on a United flight that left a predictable seventy minutes late and had just about enough knee room for a not-too-tall middle schooler.

Well, as a good friend once told me, you're traveling most of the way across the country, it's only going to take a few hours, it's warm and dry, and you're sitting on your butt. By historical human standards, the flight was beyond cushy.

I checked into a government-rate hotel, neither seedy nor elegant. The next morning, I was joined by one of the local agents and we drove out to Finn's place. His Aspen home was considerably more restrained than the Long Island estate, and he answered the door himself. We were invited into the living room, where the views of what would later in the year be ski runs were predictably breathtaking.

"What can I do for you gentlemen?" he asked us after introductions were made.

"We're here about Factor Man," I told him.

"Indeed."

"We think you may know him."

Finn said nothing.

"These conversations are generally simpler if both sides participate," I told him.

"Yes. I expect they are."

Now we all waited.

"I am an investor in the Factor Man enterprise," he eventually said. "I suspect that you somehow already know that, or you wouldn't be here."

"How much did you invest?"

"I invested an amount that I felt to be prudent."

"*Why* did you invest? Did he contact you?"

"He did."

"And how did he convince you to participate?"

"He offered attractive terms."

"That's it?"

"He also told me he could always just take the money without my permission."

"So he threatened you."

"Actually, no. The entire exchange was very amicable. I believe that I could have declined and he would simply have gone elsewhere. Of course," Finn continued, "my investment in him has worked out quite well, as I'm sure you can imagine."

"Why do you think he approached you?"

"I have no way of knowing. I am fairly well known as an investor in small enterprises."

"The Factor Man enterprise can hardly be described as small."

"Not now, no. But back then, I had the impression that he was not a terribly wealthy individual."

"When was that?"

"I'd have to check. As I imagine you know, my initial investment was five million in cash. Perhaps you know the date better than I do."

"Do you know who Factor Man is?"

"I do not."

"Do you believe you know him personally?"

Finn considered. "I have no way of knowing," he eventually responded.

I finally conceded. "Mr. Finn," I said, "We believe that there may be an attempt on Factor Man's life, either at FCOP or before. Is there really nothing you will do to help us find or warn him?"

"I can't help you find him, because I don't know who he is. And if you want to warn him, send him an email. The address is hardly a secret."

And that was basically it. I caught an evening flight back to Los Angeles, warm, dry and cramped as ever.

23

Who Will be at FCOP?
William Burkett, The *New York Times*

FCOP, generally viewed as the party of the century, will be upon us in about a week and a half. But the guest list remains shrouded in mystery.

A little bit is known. Every country except China will have two people in attendance, and those countries have announced the identities of their representatives. They are typically the American ambassador and his or her spouse.

Kate Jackson, of the original *Charlie's Angels*, will be there. So will Robert Downey, Jr. of *Iron Man* fame. What these two actors have in common, no one knows. But Factor Man himself invited them both. Their careers have been examined in minute detail as a commonality has been sought. They appear to have essentially nothing in common beyond fame.

A small number of computer scientists have also been invited, each permitted to bring a few dozen guests. The computer scientists, along with their guests, are being provided with travel by private jet to and from the event. Again, the reason is unknown.

The biggest unknown, of course, is Factor Man himself. And here, the mystery deepens.

Multiple government sources have confirmed that the American government believes that there may be an attempt to prevent Factor Man from attending the event and, presumably, to keep him from releasing the Factor Man technology to the world at large. The government would like to provide Factor Man a safe harbor until the event takes place, but they – like the rest of us – don't know where to look.

Stay tuned. Factor Man showed up a bit over four years ago. Another week and a half isn't that long.

Factor Man
June 30, 2021, ten days to FCOP

I found myself faced with another puzzle of dubious value.

Burkett and I had exchanged a reasonable amount of email on this. For a start, it seemed unlikely that a foreign national already wanted by the FBI could get back into the country to kill me. It wasn't even clear that a potential assassin could *find* me.

In fact, it was clear that he couldn't. If he could, I would presumably be dead. If there were a threat at all.

Revealing my location to the FBI would be a good idea if (a) the Chinese wanted to kill me, (b) they could find me, and (c) the FBI could protect me.

But that was the only case where I was better off revealing my whereabouts. If (a) were false, and the whole thing were just an FBI fabrication, it was presumably designed to smoke me out. Playing into the government's hands would certainly be a mistake, and I was sure there were plenty of folks in the government who would be happier with an effective monopoly on my technology.

If (b) were false, and the Chinese couldn't find me – and I did, after all, only have ten days to go – then revealing my location at best would be neutral and at worst would just tip the Chinese as well, if they had an agent inside the FBI.

And if (c) were false, and the FBI actually couldn't protect me, there was no point in my telling them who I was.

I figured that it was pretty unlikely that all three of the assumptions were true. Each of them might be more likely than not, but that hardly meant that all three of them would be. So I should stay hidden.

There was one other option. I could simply release the code now, which would presumably defuse the whole thing. That seemed like it might well be the best choice. But it, too, had problems.

```
From: tim@apple.com (Tim Cook)
To: factorman0@gmail.com (Factor Man)
Subject: Factor Man code

I saw William Burkett's recent piece, and wonder if you
are considering releasing the Factor Man code early as
a result.

We at Apple hope very much that you don't do that. As I'm
sure you can understand, we are in an extremely competi-
tive industry. Our exclusive license to your code gives us
a significant advantage, and we would like to retain that
advantage for as long as was promised when we originally
licensed the code from you.

I trust you can understand Apple's position here. If there
is anything that you would like us to do to help ensure
your personal safety, please don't hesitate to reach out.

Sincerely,
Tim Cook
```

Outstanding. And here I thought we were buds.

In addition to a possible legal fight with Apple (and don't forget, the stock they were presumably holding on my behalf had now appreciated to the point that it was worth well over $200 billion), there was another reason not to accelerate the timetable.

People had paid hundreds of millions of dollars to watch me reveal my identity and release the code in a week and a half. I'd made a commitment not to do it sooner, and I believe one should honor one's commitments.

So I concluded that I would just follow the plan. William had explained how he had found me, and the email he had used – my private exchanges with Jess MacMurray – was information that no one else had. I was confident I had shaken the tail in Vienna. My life had become quite uneventful over the past year, so I would just hope for another week and a half of the same.

And ask Apple to protect me? I thought not. They had more incentive than pretty much anyone else to keep the code from being released at FCOP.

Hudson
June 30, 2021, ten days to FCOP

Follow the money.

As I returned to Los Angeles, I considered the fact that Finn had been so different from my expectations. I had expected a New York banker of the kind that is perpetually grilled (and embarrassed) on Capitol Hill, demonstrating little more than a lack of understanding about how 99% of the world lives. And that lack of understanding is matched only by an associated lack of compassion.

Finn wasn't like that at all. I found him unassuming, gracious, smart (very smart), and, while careful, forthcoming.

But he was certainly careful. I knew that he had invested at least $5 million in the Factor Man "enterprise," and I also knew that government estimates of his net worth put it at around half a billion. So the investment was enough that he would have thought twice before making it.

I believed him – I think – that he didn't know who Factor Man was. But I also suspected that he knew more than he was letting on about why Factor Man should be a good investment.

All of this was rattling around in my head as I fell asleep on the relatively short flight back to the city of angels.

* * *

I woke with a start as the wheels hit the tarmac. With a start and an idea.

Before anyone had even heard of Factor Man, I had investigated a case of Internet fraud where an "Internet of Things" startup, riding the latest tech bubble, had managed to convince a bunch of venture capitalists to dump about $30 million into a project that was complete "vaporware". In other words, there was no "there" there.

Now, venture capitalists lose their money all the time. It's sort of the point; it's almost as if the goal is to lose on a bunch of investments but make it all up with a single investment in a so-called unicorn, or a company that is worth in excess of $1 billion before it goes public.

But this particular case was special. The Internet of Things was all the rage at the time, and it turned out that the founder of the company in question had actually lifted his business plan straight from a competitor. Cutthroat though the venture world may be, this went beyond the pale. Trade secrets had been involved, along with cyber espionage, and the FBI had been called in.

That involvement had taught me a great deal about the high-tech world in general and the venture world in particular. For example, venture capitalists don't have the easy job everyone thinks they do. They are in fact under enormous pressure to invest their money, which comes from a set of so-called "limited partners".

Each limited partner, or LP, gives money to the venture capitalist (or VC) on the assumption that the VC will find the next unicorn for him. If that money is just sitting on the sidelines because the VC has yet to invest it, then the chances that it's invested in a unicorn are precisely zero. Put somewhat more graciously, the LP gave the VC the money in the expectation that the VC would invest it wisely, and thereby earn the management fee that all VC's charge. If the VC leaves the money in the bank, the LP gets to pay the management fee without the upside of a well-informed investment.

The result is that VCs are always under pressure to invest. But they are also almost stunningly lemming-like in the investments they choose to make. If one VC invests in an Internet of Things company, all the others feel pressured to do the same, lest they miss the Internet of Things boat. So VCs tend to invest in ventures similar to those in which their colleagues are investing.

They also tend to invest in *people* as much as they do in technology. Be the founder of a unicorn, and the VCs will be falling all over themselves to invest in your next venture. Show a profitable exit at all (an "exit" means that the company went public or was acquired by a larger company), and the same thing will happen. So VCs also tend to invest in people who have worked out well for them in the past.

Finn wasn't a VC; he was more what was called an "angel" or a "super-angel". An angel is someone with a lot of money who invests it in fledgling enterprises that seem like good bets. It's sort of like *Shark Tank*, but without all the publicity.

Angels are just like VCs in that they tend to invest in people who have worked out well for them in the past. So while Finn may not have known who Factor Man was specifically, it was a reasonable bet that he believed, for one reason or another, that he had invested in him previously.

Money leaves a trail. When I got back to the LA office, I started pulling bank records, tax returns, everything I could find. I learned that Finn tended not to invest in companies directly (many angels simply write a check), but to do so via one of a variety of shell companies and partnerships.

But that was just an extra layer.

And in the meantime, I chased it from the other end as well. Finn, as a banker with an international profile, would be an attractive investor for any new company. It was likely that the companies in which he had invested would name Finn as an investor on their web site or in other publicity.

This was the kind of problem at which the FBI excels. Find investments made by Finn. Find founders of companies that mention Finn as an investor. See if any of those founders was in Europe when Factor Man visited the safe deposit box.

We're very good at sifting through data like this. And our friends at State and Treasury aren't bad, either.

Liu
July 3, 2021, seven days to FCOP

Our assets: A J-20 within striking distance of Los Angeles. Two front-row tickets to FCOP. A list that contained a scant 536 names. And a week in which to complete our analysis.

Our liabilities: A week was simply not quite long enough. We would find Factor Man only if we were at least somewhat fortunate.

The tickets were in the names of Li Qiang Wu and Ma Yong Feng. Li was in fact a field agent named Lin, but I will refer to him here as Li. And, after considerable discussion, it was decided that I would be Ma.

The most obvious issue here is that Yong Feng is a man's name, and I am not a man. But perhaps that was a blessing in disguise.

Li and I were given diplomatic credentials, which would ensure us freedom of movement within the United States.

As I looked at the photograph in my new passport, the change was profound. My hair had been cut short and my breasts bound uncomfortably tightly. The young man in the photograph was a stranger to me.

Diplomatic credentials or not, the change in my appearance pleased me. Chinese intelligence services had been monitoring the American news media for any mention of the murders, and there had been none. There was thus no reason to believe that the American authorities had realized that the crimes were connected, and no reason to believe that they thought me to have been involved in any way. But, on the chance that they knew more than we expected, I was glad to see a stranger staring back at me from the passport. That the stranger in the passport was a man would provide an additional layer of concealment.

Before departing, Li and I were briefed by General Zhao himself. We were told that we had been authorized to use any means necessary to keep Factor Man from releasing his technology to the world. But all such authorization ceased the moment the technology was public. At that point, China's political future would unfortunately depend on the support of the world community. Such dependence was unprecedented, but China's cause was unlikely to be furthered by the elimination of Factor Man or by any other direct action. To quote Sun Tzu: He will win who knows when to fight and when not to fight.

Weaponry was provided in our diplomatic pouch. We were each supplied two handguns: a Glock 17 and a 3-D printed weapon. The Glocks might well be useful, even though we would not be able to carry them through airport security. The plastic used in the 3-D guns was specifically designed to be invisible to the full-body scanners in use at American airports. Possession of the gun would be a violation of the American Undetectable Firearms Act originally signed by President Reagan, but our diplomatic credentials would presumably protect us from harassment in this regard. I note, incidentally, that the famous "porcelain Glock 7" from American cinema is a myth.

While the 3-D guns were relatively straightforward, bullets were much more challenging. Bullets are generally measured in grains, with one gram being approximately 15.4 grains. A typical bullet weighs some 150 grains, or 10 grams. A modern security screening system can reliably detect triple that amount.

Li and I would each have two bullets, concealed in spare battery packs for our smartphones. Perhaps it was just as well, since the 3-D printed handguns were unlikely to be reliable for more than a small number of shots in any case.

Air China has three direct flights from Beijing to Los Angeles, each an overnight journey. We left six days before FCOP, and arrived five days before. Our first class seats were comfortable, and we arrived in Los Angeles well rested.

457 names remained.

July 8, 2021, two days to FCOP

Two days remained when my colleagues in Beijing emailed me a possible match for Factor Man. It was evening in Los Angeles, midday in China.

The information they sent was essentially a dossier on one of the remaining possibilities. A businessman with a background in computer science, older than our original profile had assumed. If this were Factor Man, it was not surprising that we had initially missed him.

The packet included a photograph, which showed an approximation of the nose I had come to see in my dreams. But it also included video, a local television story on one of the businesses run by the individual in question.

He was walking, which was of little assistance because the man in Vienna had used a cane. But he was talking, and he was gesturing.

I recognized the gestures. I saw him wave his hand, and scratch his nose. There was something about the tilt of his head, something *forward* about it. As if he were always looking for the next thing. I couldn't describe it specifically, but I certainly recognized it.

I pulled up the video of Factor Man in Vienna just to be sure. It was absolutely the same individual.

We had him.

An immediate problem was that he lived in rural Oregon. There was no flight that could get us there before midday the next day, at which point it was reasonable to assume that Factor Man might have left for Pasadena.

I tried chartering a flight, but it was impossible. Every private jet in the country was already committed to bringing one American capitalist or another to FCOP. I called the embassy, and they tried borrowing a jet from one of China's many friends in the United States. That, too, was impossible.

It was a twelve-hour drive from Los Angeles. We would travel through the night, but we would get there an hour or two earlier than if we flew. We would also have a car in Oregon, and be able to return to Pasadena in time for FCOP if Factor Man himself escaped us.

Li drove while I conferred with Beijing. Factor Man was apparently planning on traveling to FCOP via private jet; there was a single flight plan recorded out of the airport nearest to him that left at 10AM the next day. The passenger manifest indicated that there would be twelve people aboard.

We might or might not reach Factor Man's departure airport by 10AM, but Beijing confirmed that we were the closest agents to the scene. A satellite was repositioned to a geostationary orbit over Factor Man's house, a relatively modest dwelling on a large plot of land southwest of Eugene, Oregon. The weather forecast, however, suggested that satellite surveillance might be impossible.

We had three chances. Two of those chances were mine: We might reach Eugene in time to intercept Factor Man before he boarded his charter flight to Pasadena or as a last resort, Li and I would have time for a brief rest in Eugene before returning to California to deal with Factor Man there.

The other chance was the J-20. The aircraft had not been fit to use the catapult on the *Liaoning*, and the nearly vertical takeoff that was required instead would use a great deal of fuel. So a Xian H-6U aerial refueling tanker lifted off from Nanjing, ready to replenish the J-20 on its flight to California.

We had one other advantage, as well. There was no evidence that the American government was going to intercede on Factor Man's behalf, or even that they knew who he was.

24

My phone rang at an ungodly hour, and I was told to get my butt to Edwards Air Force Base. A car and driver would be in front of the hotel in fifteen minutes.

Edwards is located a couple hours' drive north of Los Angeles in the Mojave Desert. Although its primary mission is flight testing, it is the closest place to Los Angeles where one can find fighter aircraft.

Upon my arrival at Edwards, I was whisked through security and shortly found myself in a large control room, rows of desks with computer terminals on them. It looked like NASA during a space mission. I was met by a stone-faced Major General Donald A. Harkin, commander of the Air Force Test Center. In a gravelly voice that sounded straight out of Georgia, Harkin informed me that satellite imagery had shown that at 9 PM the previous night, a Chinese tanker had taken off from Nanjing Air Base on the east coast of China, and headed out over the Pacific.

A variety of satellites had observed the flight intermittently as it traveled toward the Americas. The most recent observation had been within two hundred nautical miles of the Chinese aircraft carrier that had taken position off Los Angeles.

The Chinese carrier was carrying a specially modified stealth fighter called a J-20. The J-20 would need to refuel if it was to reach targets in the continental United States, and everyone's assumption was that the Chinese tanker was planning to help it do just that. And the assumed target was the plane carrying Factor Man to FCOP.

The problem was that we had no way to defend him.

There are five airports that serve the Los Angeles area. There is LAX, of course, along with somewhat smaller locations at Burbank, Long Beach, Santa Ana, and Ontario. Any of these could be the destination for what we assumed would be a charter flight bringing Factor Man to Pasadena.

Beyond that, we knew nothing. We had a guest list with almost 100,000 names on it. About 300 new names – Factor Man's guests – would be provided to us in a few hours. All we really knew was that while a normal day had about 6,000 scheduled landings at the five airports combined, there were 10,000 planned for today. There were going to be delays, and much of the airspace over the LA Basin had already been closed to air traffic other than regularly scheduled commercial flights and flights that could prove they were related to FCOP.

A terse message was sent to the Chinese ambassador, warning him that any violation of American airspace by unauthorized aircraft would be dealt with in the harshest possible fashion. A terse message was sent back, indicating that all Chinese operations were in international airspace and waters, that China also reserved the right to defend its national interests, and that America should basically mind its own damn business.

Tensions rose.

I think I was on my fifth cup of coffee when there was flurry of activity in the control room. There was a rush of typing at a handful of desks, with someone coming up to brief Harkin shortly thereafter. He came to brief me.

"There's a lot of fog this morning, but one of the ships shadowing the Chinese carrier just got a pretty good look at it. The J-20 is no longer on deck. We assume it's airborne and headed toward California. If you're going to help us, Mr. Hudson, the time is now. We can't defend 10,000 civilian flights. Anything you can do, do it. Point of departure. Likely landing spot in California. Expected times. Anything at all."

It was just after nine in the morning.

Factor Man
July 9, 2021, one day to FCOP. 7:00 AM

I don't like flying very much. It doesn't worry me, it's just inconvenient.

I don't live near a hub, so getting pretty much anywhere involves at least two flights, and often three. Add the necessary interval between flights, and it takes a day to get where you're going.

It takes a day to get to Los Angeles. A day to get to New York. A day to get to Minneapolis. A day to get anywhere, and a day to get back.

And that's if you're lucky. I often try to get on the last flight of the day, coming or going, and if I don't miss a connection and spend an extra night somewhere unintended, that's a win.

Finn's $25M hadn't helped, either. I couldn't afford the attention that would come with chartering a plane, and it turns out that first class customers are pretty much as likely to get stuck overnight because of a missed connection as everyone else is.

Flying is also sometimes just plain weird. Here's an example.

I was flying home one day, changing in Salt Lake City. I get on the plane, an aisle seat. In the middle seat next to me is someone that I will simply describe as "Steroid Man." He really is a poster child for the problems with steroid use. Arms like tree trunks, no hair, and an attitude to match. Doing something or other on his iPad, but mostly just cursing at the device.

Well, I don't have to listen. I get out my Kindle and start to read. My eyes are, sadly, not as good as they once were. I refuse to admit that by changing the font on the Kindle. So I turn on the overhead light.

Steroid Man turns it off. Tells me that my Kindle has a backlight (which it does) and that should be good enough (which it isn't).

I try to read without the light, but I just can't do it. So I tell him that my eyes are old, and I'm sorry, but I need the light. I turn it back on.

He smashes his fist into it, turning it off again. "Givin' me a fuckin' headache."

Terrific.

The guy across the aisle from me isn't using his light, so I tell him that my light is bothering my neighbor and ask if he would be willing to switch. He says fine, but he's traveling with his wife, and they'll want me to take their middle seat, so they have the two aisle seats next to one another.

I figure sure. Better to read and leave Steroid Man alone and be in the middle seat. We all switch. I walk up and explain what's going on to the flight attendant, including the reason for the seat shuffle.

So far, so good. The wife of the guy who swapped with me is normal size, and I've got about the same amount of room in my new seat as in my old.

But now the flight attendant shows up. She tells Steroid Man that no, he can't turn off the light of a fellow passenger. The passenger gets to decide whether to turn the light on or not. I have no idea why she did this, but Steroid Man is visibly upset.

I say nothing and just read my book, waiting for the flight to end. I figure I'll let Steroid Man get off first; no reason to interact with him and aggravate him further.

So he gets off the plane, and I follow him. He's walking about a mile and a half an hour, legs all bowed up. I actually feel bad for the guy.

Well, I have a connection to make, so I walk briskly by him.

And he, miraculously, speeds up.

I slow down, he slows down. I speed up, he speeds up.

Really? I mean, really? What is he doing, waiting for me to go into a bathroom so he can assault me?

We pass a couple of cops, and I decide I've had enough. I do a U-turn, tell them what's going on, and ask for help.

Steroid Man walks on, and the cops tell me that they had already singled him out as a risk of some kind. A really angry guy. They decide to walk me to my connecting gate.

So here I am, getting a police escort between gates at Salt Lake City.

We get to the first choice point in the terminal; I need to turn here to get onto the concourse where my next flight will be. And there is Steroid Man, waiting for me in a bookshop. I turn, he puts his magazine down, and starts following us. One of the cops detaches, grabs him (he has to actually put his hands on the guy to get his attention), and they have a chat. I soldier on to the gate, where the cop still accompanying me has the person handling the flight put me on my plane early. I'm confused (and hungry; I was hoping to grab some food), but the cop says that Steroid Man is really mad and I should just get on my flight and they'll put him on his flight to Yakima, not where I'm going at all. The whole thing will be over.

And so it is.

True story. But it sure didn't make me feel any better about air travel.

But today was going to be different, I figured. Direct flight, Eugene to Burbank. Closest airport to the Rose Bowl. Twelve people on the flight: Me and my family, my pastor and his family, and a business colleague and his family. The colleague, David Etherington, had cofounded a research lab and two of my three startups with me. We had moved to Eugene together in 1993 to start the research lab, and David's oldest son, Ian, had been born the next year and been an airplane buff for as long as any of us could remember.

The plane was a Gulfstream G550. Ian told us it could hold up to 19 passengers, although only eight if they had beds. Our particular plane had an even dozen seats, just right for the twelve of us. It was unbelievably luxurious on the inside, at least to my eye. But still nicer private aircraft certainly existed, all the way up to a Boeing 747. Heck, there's even the Aerion AS2, scheduled to come out in a couple of years and capable of carrying twelve passengers at Mach 1.5.

My family and I were slated to leave at ten from the Eugene airport. It was bizarre that we had to get to the airport at, well, at ten.

For a flight at ten.

There would be no security. We could bring our dogs if we wanted to, and they would get to run around the cabin with us.

The airport was half an hour's drive from our place, so we had to leave at 9:30. I guess we probably could even have left at ten and been late.

But we just couldn't do it. We left at 8:30 partly because that's when we would normally leave for a ten o'clock flight, and mostly because we couldn't wait to get started. The dogs (who did not actually get to go, much to their disappointment) would be fine until Laurie, the house sitter, arrived around noon. Laurie knew we were going to FCOP but had no idea quite why.

We arrived at the Eugene airport an hour before flight time, and cooled our heels while we waited for the Gulfstream to show up. Eugene was predictably overcast, but it all seemed sunny to us.

Liu
July 9, 2021, one day to FCOP. 9:00 AM

It was just before nine when we arrived at Factor Man's home, southwest of Eugene. It was a modest house with a stunning view. The long gravel drive appeared to be shared with a neighbor; we had initially gone the wrong way at the fork a few hundred meters back. After correcting for the error, we shortly found ourselves at a house matching the picture Beijing had sent over during the night.

The day was overcast, and the satellite above had not been able to determine if Factor Man were still at home. Finding him there was certainly our first choice; it would be simpler to act effectively at a remote country location than at the airport.

Two dogs barked at us from inside the home. Given the commotion the dogs were causing and the lack of response, it was clear that the house was empty. Breaking in would likely necessitate killing the dogs, which would obviously alert the next visitor to our presence. We decided to simply press on to the airport, half an hour away. We would get there before Factor Man's flight was scheduled to depart for Pasadena, but not by much.

The airport was small, but general aviation and the passenger terminal were still in separate locations. By the time we found the general aviation terminal, it was 9:45. A Gulfstream V was parked on the tarmac. A crowd of about a dozen people was climbing the steps to board. Li allowed the car to idle while I stepped out.

I drew the Glock while running toward the aircraft. The passengers were already filing through the boarding door. I could see Factor Man, second in line and well beyond the effective range of the small pistol. I rushed forward, he walked forward, and he boarded the plane before I could arrive. I was too late by moments.

There were still half a dozen passengers on the steps. I could have shot one of them, but I couldn't see how that would help. The authorities would have been alerted, I would be unlikely to escape their pursuit, and I doubted that Factor Man, hearing the shot, would have decided to graciously reemerge from the aircraft.

I returned to Li. We parked the car at the commercial portion of the airport and left the Glocks in it as we went into the terminal to attempt to buy tickets back to Los Angeles. Not surprisingly, all of the flights were full in every class of travel. We checked into a hotel and attempted to get some sleep in preparation for the drive back south.

One of the three chances was gone.

25

HUDSON

I was on my fifth cup of coffee as Harkin came up. "If you're going to help us, Mr. Hudson, the time is now. We can't defend 10,000 civilian flights."

It was just after nine in the morning, and my cell phone rang.

Karen Myers, one of the agents running down Finn's contacts, was on the other end.

"We think we found him," she told me. "Two of Finn's investments are with companies founded by the same guy. We found one the normal way, through tax returns. The other lists Finn as an investor on its web site."

"Who is it?" I asked.

"Some guy in Oregon. Eugene."

"Anything else?"

"We got a picture. The nose is right. I think this is him, John."

"Send me the picture. Send me a name, profile, anything you've got."

"Sure thing. Two minutes."

I hung up and looked at Harkin. Listening to my side of things, he was waiting patiently. Doing so did not appear to be something that came naturally to him. "I think," I told him, "that you'll only need to defend one."

We checked with the FAA. Factor Man was scheduled to take a private jet from Eugene to Burbank, leaving at 10 AM. Harkin scribbled quickly as he got details. Then he picked up another phone. He didn't dial, just waited for a moment.

"This is Don Harkin. I need four fighters scrambled out of Klamath Falls. They are to escort a Gulfstream 550 traveling southbound from Eugene Echo-Uniform-Golf to Burbank Bravo-Uniform-Romeo. Estimated departure 1700 Zulu. Tail number November 3565 Victor." He paused.

"My authority. Charlie 7 bravo bravo 5. The threat is a Chinese J-20 inbound from the Pacific. Engage upon contact." He paused again.

"And send a couple of F-35's out of Edwards to join them as they cross into California."

He hung up. Then back to the other phone, where he asked whoever answered to have the Eugene, Oregon control tower call him back.

It was 9:32. Harkin told me that the American F-15's based at Klamath Falls would be airborne in fifteen minutes, and it would take them nine more to make the 135 nautical mile flight from Klamath Falls to Eugene. Traveling at Mach 1.2, they should get there before the plane carrying Factor Man even took off.

The phone rang, and Harkin picked it up. "Don Harkin." He listened for a moment and pushed a button that put the call on speaker.

"Good morning, Mr. Massey. I'm General Donald Harkin, commander of the Air Force Test Center at Edwards. You have a flight heading down to Burbank this morning, I believe. Tail number November 3565 Victor."

"Yes, sir. What can we do for you?"

"The powers that be have decided to give that plane an escort, and I've got four F-15s headed your way from K Falls. They should get there before 65 Victor departs, but if not, could you please hold them on the ground for a little bit?"

"Absolutely. Not a problem. Anything specific I should know?"

"The F-15's will be in touch via Cascade Approach shortly. Please also have the Gulfstream turn off its transponder and disable any GPS reporting they're including in their ADS-B."

"Excuse me?"

"You heard me, Mr. Massey. No position reporting for that aircraft other than the usual radio chatter. Our folks will stay with him all the way to Burbank."

"I understand. For that aircraft to disable its transponder is a violation of the Federal Aviation Regulations, though."

"Not today it isn't, Mr. Massey. Not today." He hung up.

Harkin explained it to me. Aircraft, not surprisingly, work quite hard to tell the rest of the world where they are. Collisions at speeds in excess of 500 miles an hour are generally to be avoided.

But in this particular case, if Factor Man's flight told the world where it was, it would be telling the Chinese fighter as well. While the Chinese plane could still locate Factor Man even without the transmissions in question, doing so would involve a radar or other signal being emitted by the J-20. Anything along those lines would give the American aircraft a target.

"So tell me, Agent Hudson. My guess is that we just succeeded in trading an international incident of one kind for an international incident of another kind. But when the aircraft gets to Los Angeles, what then?"

I asked what he meant.

"FCOP is tomorrow evening, right? What happens to Factor Man in the meantime?"

"We have choices?"

"Absolutely. We can land him at Edwards, for a start. Keep him here and bring him to FCOP ourselves tomorrow. Or you can let him fly to Burbank as planned. But how you protect him from there would be up to you."

I considered. Mostly, I thought, this decision should be made by someone about three levels above me. But I suspected that, given the time constraints, I was stuck with it.

I eventually decided to let Factor Man land at Burbank for two reasons. First, better that the FBI take care of him than handing the responsibility to the Air Force. This was a much more typical mission for us than for them. And second, if the Chinese had such a good plan for attacking him in LA, they wouldn't have just made a hole in the deck of their one and only aircraft carrier.

"Let him land in Burbank as planned. I'll have a team there to look after him."

Harkin picked up the phone he didn't have to dial again. "This is Harkin. Please let the escorting aircraft know that the destination is at the discretion of the Gulfstream pilot. They are simply to protect and assist as needed."

He hung up. Not big on social pleasantries, this guy.

Factor Man
July 9, 2021, one day to FCOP. 9:52 AM

There were two flight attendants for the twelve of us. While we taxied out to the runway, we were given drinks of our choice in real glasses. We were served canapés that were delicious. I was told without having to ask that mine were gluten-free.

The pilot came on.

"Good morning, ladies and gentlemen. Welcome aboard. Once we're airborne, the flight down to LA should take us a little more than two hours. Our route of flight has us going directly over Mount Shasta and then following the California Central Valley down to Los Angeles. We should be landing at Burbank around noon.

"We do have something a little unusual this morning, hopefully a treat for you. I've been told that we're going to have an escort from Eugene down to our destination. Four F-15's from the Air Force wing in Klamath Falls. They should be arriving here momentarily, and the Eugene air traffic controllers have asked us to delay our departure until they're here. Shouldn't be more than a couple of minutes."

F-15's as an escort. Somehow I didn't think that all the other planes flying into FCOP were getting similar treatment.

The jig, I figured, was up.

* * *

We did indeed take off a few minutes later, departing to the north and then doing a sweeping turn back southbound. The morning fog had cleared, and I got a great view of our house as we climbed out. That view was shortly replaced by a pair of fighters showing up on each side of us.

The F-15's were smaller than we were, although not by much. They were single seaters, close enough that we could make out the features of each of the four pilots. Three men and one woman. Ian was beside himself with glee at seeing them so close.

For me, however, they posed something of a problem.

My plan had been to spend a random and fairly low-key day in the LA area; it was, after all, likely to be my last normal day for quite a while. But if the government thought for some reason that we needed protection, we would presumably need it on the ground as well. I figured that the government would be looking after us there also, but suspected I could probably help by staying public.

So I walked over to my daughter, her face predictably in her phone. "Hey," I began.

"Hey." Face still in phone.

"I was thinking. We're going to get to LA around noon, right? How about if we spend the day at Disneyland?"

Face out of phone. At twenty-three, she's still one of the biggest Disney fans on the planet. "Yes!" Somehow she turned the word into two syllables.

So I asked the group. "Rachel and I think we should go to Disneyland this afternoon. Who's in?"

Pretty much everyone was in, and I asked the captain if he could change our destination to Orange County. He told me that the LA Basin was a bit busier than usual today, but he'd see what he could do.

Flying by private jet definitely has its virtues.

As all of this was going on, two more planes showed up. Single seat, single engine, a little bit stubbier than the F-15's.

Ian announced that they were F-35s, a fifth-generation stealth fighter, probably based at Edwards in Southern California. We all gawked through the windows.

Everyone was behaving fairly predictably. My kids, social media necessities completed, had put down their phones and were poking around the plane, trying to look casual while they embedded in their brains as many aspects as possible of what they assumed would be a once-in-a-lifetime experience.

Ian was staring so intently out the windows that I imagined he would simply have rematerialized in one of the fighters' cockpits, had that been physically possible.

My pastor and his family were simply relaxed, enjoying the ride. Having fun. Ian's parents looked totally engaged, also trying to soak things up but not having quite as much fun as my pastor's family. I think things were just a little too weird for them.

Denise and I were sitting quietly, holding hands.

And then something odd happened. Four of the planes – the F-35's and two of the F-15's – broke away, flying off to our right somewhere. Their tails lit up, and I didn't need Ian to tell me that they were flying on afterburners.

Wherever they were going, they were going in a hurry. And stranger still, two of them fired missiles.

Well, crap.

I hadn't worried when the fighters showed up. It meant the government knew who I was, which was sort of unfortunate, but it also meant that they were on my side, which was clearly fortunate. Concealing my identity all the way to FCOP had always been a long shot anyway.

So the fighters themselves hadn't bothered me. But it bothered me a *lot* that they seemed to be needed. That meant that someone other than the government had not only found me, but actually tried to kill me.

It was presumably the Chinese. Google wasn't angry enough, and they had a lot to lose if I died. Much as Apple might want to keep the technology to itself, hoping the government would do the same, I couldn't see them doing this.

But it was certainly someone. I stared out the window and thought about the fact that I had jeopardized the lives of the eleven wonderful people on the flight with me. Everything was suddenly much more real than it had been even just a few minutes ago. I was glad we had decided to stay in the public eye and go to Disneyland.

As I was trying to sort it all out in my mind, Denise came over and put her hand on my shoulder. She had figured it out, too. "If you had it to do over again," she asked me quietly, "Would you do it any differently?"

Three decades of marriage will do that. "Probably not," I answered.

She smiled. "So there you go."

The missile contrails vanished as the missiles themselves exploded in the distance, but Denise and I remained as we were, somehow alone on the flight with ten other people.

Hudson
July 9, 2021, one day to FCOP. 10:37 AM

Disneyland? Freakin' *Disneyland*?

In reality, it was probably pretty good news. The 25-agent team currently heading to Burbank would race, sirens blazing, to John Wayne Airport in Orange County. They would arrive in time.

The destination change would make it difficult for anyone else planning on tracking Factor Man to pick him up at John Wayne. For a start, they'd need to learn of the change in plans. And even if they did, they would be hard pressed to switch airports themselves. Google Maps indicated that it currently would take almost two hours to drive the 53 miles between the two locations, and Chinese spies were unlikely to have sirens.

Monitoring someone at Disneyland would be child's play. People everywhere, but the density generally small enough that it was easy to keep someone in sight.

I was still at Edwards as all of this got worked out. I instructed the agents heading to Burbank to turn around and go to Orange County, and let them all know they'd need to hustle because they had to be there by 11:45. Everyone would make it except one pair of agents who had been driving south to Burbank and were just a little too far out. I told them to simply head to Disneyland and await instructions. I canceled the two cars being provided at Orange County airport by the owner of the jet Factor Man was traveling on, and replaced them with two of our own vehicles. We obviously couldn't secure Disneyland as a location in its entirety, but we could make sure that the cars, at least, were ours.

And then General Harkin's phone rang. The one he didn't need to dial. He listened for a minute and said, "Wait one." He pointed to a uniformed officer behind one of the desks, and then pointed to me.

The officer came up to me. "I'm sorry, sir," he said. "We need you to clear this room."

"Excuse me?"

"Military personnel only, sir. My apologies." His hand was on my elbow, pressuring me out.

As soon as we left the control room, he pointed out some chairs, apologized again, and headed back in. I took out my cell phone. As the door closed behind him, I heard cheers.

Burkett
July 9, 2021, one day to FCOP. 11:18 AM Pacific time

My day was off to a truly excellent start.

First, I had scooped the world with an article *Make $200 Billion and It's a Safe Bet Someone Else Will Get Rich*. That described both Brian Finn's investment in Factor Man and the fact that he, as owner of 5% of Factor Man's payment from Apple, would make $10B on the effort. That's billion with a B. Finn was suddenly going to be somewhere around 100th on the Forbes list of the world's richest folks.

Jess MacMurray, meanwhile, would get the $400 million in revenue from ticket sales and broadcast rights, less whatever it cost her to put on the event. A reasonable guess was $2 million for the venue, $15 million for catering, and maybe $5 million for jet travel. But however it came out, Pepper Potts was going to be keeping the vast majority of the $400 million she had to work with.

Of course, the world had mostly been interested in Brian Finn's involvement. He had declined all of the interview requests and was reportedly en route to Pasadena himself. With Finn unavailable, the interview requests had turned to me, and I had accepted a few of them.

The questions were always the same. How did I learn of Finn's involvement? He came to me, I said. Did I think Finn was Factor Man? No, I did not. Did I think Finn knew who Factor Man was? Probably not, but I wasn't sure. Did *I* know who Factor Man was?

That was a bit harder. I smiled as evasively as I could, and said simply that if I did know, I had no intention of ruining the guy's party tomorrow. Of course, that just made the feeding frenzy worse.

I decided, hardly for the first time, that I was happier writing about the news than being the news. But in twenty-four hours, no one would care about me any more and that problem would solve itself. I could go back to being the ace investigative journalist I had become, secure in the knowledge that a ton of people would be reading anything I cared to write.

But far and away the *best* thing about today was that I was on a private jet heading to California with Emma. It was such an absurdly romantic experience that we had even spoken briefly about pushing up the wedding and making this trip the honeymoon. That had proven insurmountably complicated, but we were acting pretty much like honeymooners anyway.

Of course, there are limits to how long you can act that way, and Emma and I had probably pushed them. About halfway through the flight, we took a break to reconnect with the outside world. And it was a different place than it had been when we took off.

Reuters: U.S. fighters apparently win dogfight over central California

Reports are coming in that the aircraft destroyed in what the U.S. Air Force had previously described as a training incident was in fact a Chinese fighter. Numerous parties on the ground are reporting finding pieces of wreckage carrying Chinese writing.

The jet that was destroyed is believed to have been a Chengdu J-20, an F-35 copycat designed using information that the Chinese stole from the United States during a cyber security breach in 2009.

Observers have reported that a group of four fighter aircraft intercepted a single plane at extremely high speed over a relatively unpopulated area of central California near the town of Mendenhall Springs, some 50 miles east of San Jose. Multiple parties on the ground reported sonic booms as part of the engagement.

Neither the American nor the Chinese government has commented on the incident, which is sure to raise the already high tensions between the two nations even further. There are no reports of any pilot ejecting from the aircraft that was shot down, and the Air Force, while confirming that the incident took place, has provided no details other than to state that no American servicemen were killed or injured.

Factor Man
July 9, 2021, one day to FCOP. 11:52 AM

The pilot came on as the four jets returned. "Ladies and gentlemen, we've been able to change our destination to Orange County, and transportation will be there to take all of you to Disneyland. They will have twelve VIP tickets for you.

"I hope you enjoy the rides there. Just not quite as much as this one.

"Meanwhile, I'm afraid we don't know any more than you do about what our escorts have been up to. Sorry about that."

I looked at Denise. "About that up to which our escorts have been?" Never end a sentence with a preposition.

She laughed, and my day got a little bit better. My heart got a little bit warmer.

* * *

The fighters stayed with us until we hit the ground. And I mean literally: three fighters off each wing, airborne, until our wheels touched. They couldn't quite stay with us as we touched, but seemed to be pulling away at maybe ten or twenty miles an hour.

We taxied to a private area of the airport. The steps folded out as the Gulfstream's door opened and we climbed down; two black stretch limos were waiting for us. Not surprisingly, it was decided that the kids would ride in one and the adults in the other. Off to Disneyland we went.

I have no idea what transpired in the other car; kids somehow just keep being kids whatever the circumstances. Although all of ours were somewhere in their twenties, I didn't think they were too old to do that.

Our car, however, definitely had an elephant in the room. We talked, not surprisingly, about the escort we had received on the way down from Eugene, but the conversation still tended to be staccato and fairly awkward. Tim Johnson, my pastor, finally just looked at me and asked. "You're Factor Man, aren't you?"

I felt Denise take my hand.

I looked back. "I am."

"Yes!" Tim exclaimed. "I knew it! I knew it!"

I love this man. He views all news as good news. It's all part of God's plan, whether Tim understands that plan or not. His exuberance is both permanent and infectious.

Amy, his wife, smiled.

"I did," Tim explained. "Ask Amy. I've been saying for months that I thought it was you."

"He has," Amy confirmed.

The Etheringtons said nothing, smiling slightly. I suspected that they might have had their suspicions as well.

"Do you want to talk about it?" Tim asked.

I smiled. "Maybe tomorrow."

And the elephant left the room. The rest of the drive was somewhat more normal. Yes, we talked about the fact that we had gotten to fly in a private jet, and that six fighters had given us cover. But we also just talked about the usual nonsense that friends discuss.

What wasn't normal was the insulation of it all. We had gotten up, flown to Orange County, and gotten in a private limo headed to Disneyland without ever waiting in a line. No line for tickets, or for security, or for anything else. We hadn't even *seen* a line. It was surreal.

I've always envied the rich and famous. Private showings of movies. Private cars with private drivers. Private everything.

I know that I'm a bit of a misanthrope; Denise thought I was crazy to want to be so isolated. When the kids were little, I would come home from work and be delighted to be a quarter mile from the nearest neighbor. Many days, Denise would be stuck at home all day, and would miss the times when she could just walk across the street and have a conversation.

I realized during our limo ride how right she had always been. Other people are what make life worth living. While I wasn't looking forward to the lines at Disneyland, I realized that it couldn't be (or even claim to be) the happiest place on earth without them.

As it turned out, however, we got the best of both worlds. Disneyland has what are called "VIP passes." You get a tour guide (actually, we got two tour guides), and get to go not to the front of all the lines, but to about the wait-for-five-minutes point. (It's like a permanent multi-ride FastPass, if you know what those are.)

It was awesome. A great way to spend what I figured would be the last day of anonymity I would ever have. We stayed until the fireworks at midnight, at which point we found that we had already been checked into our hotels (all different) and the limo drivers had the keys. A third car appeared sort of miraculously, since with three separate hotels, we'd need three separate cars. Jess MacMurray was exceptionally good at her job. Once again, there would be no lines.

The only thing that might be called a distraction was a text from William Burkett that I got in the middle of the afternoon.

WB: Chinese jet that was destroyed – you?
FM: I'm at Disneyland
WB: So?
FM: Totally off the record?
WB: Sure
FM: Thinking

I had no idea how to respond. Finally, I just decided to duck the question.

FM: I'm at Disneyland

And I put my cell phone away.

It appeared that everyone simply knew who I was. Tim and Amy knew. The Etheringtons knew. Wilbur knew. The Air Force knew. I suspected mine was the only plane they protected, but if they didn't know before the flight, they certainly knew now. So the government knew. Even the Chinese knew.

Great.

Twenty-four more hours. And then everyone was *supposed* to know. All I needed to do was not mess up the government's apparent desire to look after me until that happened.

It struck me as odd that the government obviously knew exactly what had transpired with the Chinese, but they weren't telling anyone. Why? I suspected that they were trying to avoid a public outcry against what the Chinese had done; that would make it only harder to ratchet tensions back down again later. Given how dependent the Chinese were on the closed nature of their society, they were about to have a whole lot of trouble in any case, and our adding to those difficulties probably wasn't in anyone's real interests.

Space Mountain awaited.

Liu
July 9, 2021, one day to FCOP. 9:52 AM

Li and I watched the American fighters arrive and escort Factor Man's flight out of Eugene. Not only had our chance escaped us, but it seemed unlikely that the J-20 on the *Liaoning* would fare any better. Given the stakes,

I was confident that the attempt would be made in any case, with the pilot likely dying a hero's death in the skies over California.

We checked into a featureless local hotel and slept for six hours before beginning the drive back to Southern California. On waking, we learned that the Chinese pilot had indeed suffered the anticipated fate. The second chance was gone.

We left Eugene as the Americans were leaving their jobs, but the town was small enough that there was little traffic as we headed south.

* * *

Li and I exchanged driving responsibilities intermittently, and drove far more leisurely than we had in the opposite direction. We returned to our Los Angeles hotel shortly after six in the morning, each having dozed occasionally on the drive down and at least partially rested.

We had plenty of time. We reviewed our plans for FCOP itself and retired to our rooms, to meet again at noon and drive to the Rose Bowl. The event itself was scheduled to begin at six, and traffic was projected to be no worse than it was prior to an American football game or similar event.

26

HUDSON
JULY 10, 2021. 6:30 AM, THE DAY OF FCOP

I woke at the usual time on the day of FCOP, and prepared for what would surely be an eventful – and long – day.

I checked in with the bureau. Factor Man and his family were in their hotel. Their rooms were monitored, and they were all still sleeping soundly. They had been booked into adjacent rooms, with agents watching the elevators and the stairs. Other agents began early, posing as staff on various mundane engineering tasks. No one was stirring.

I checked in with CNN. There was nothing of substance to report on the incident that had generated the cheering at Edwards. Some news agencies were reporting that the Chinese were blaming a rogue pilot; others were realizing that didn't make sense because a rogue pilot wouldn't have anything like the fuel needed to get to California. Tensions between the two countries remained high but did not seem in immediate danger of escalating.

I checked in with the local ASAC. He was awake but had nothing new to report. We agreed that I would leave the hotel shortly after eight and head to the Rose Bowl. I had time for a quick breakfast.

Both the hotel restaurant and the Los Angeles traffic were pretty much the same as they had been every day since I arrived in California, which is to say slower than any reasonable explanation warranted. I arrived at the Rose Bowl shortly before eleven and, getting there far before most of the other attendees, parked in one of the closest of the spots open to mere mortals. The venue itself would open at noon.

Security had been delegated to a combination of the FBI, the Pasadena police, and TSA. No single organization was appropriately equipped to deal with all of it. Full body scanners had been installed at every entrance. All your personal possessions had to fit into a one-quart Ziploc; anything larger could be checked with security but would not be allowed into the stadium itself. No electronics were permitted larger than an iPad. The security staff numbered about three thousand, all told.

The president and first lady would get a pass on the security. But they were the only ones who would. Period.

Inside, things were as expected. In addition to the usual stadium seating, thousands of chairs had been arranged on the field. They were separated by about thirty feet from the stage that would be the center of it all.

Hundreds of portable microphones were lined up around the back of the stadium. Factor Man had requested their availability for the event itself, which he viewed as a press conference of sorts, but it had been decided that the mics would be distributed only after the crowd had settled in.

Burkett
8:00 AM, the day of FCOP

Emma and I woke around eight, 11 AM New York time. We stayed in bed, continuing the honeymoon experience, until eleven, at which point we ordered room service.

The packet we had gotten the previous night from the driver who brought us to the Beverly Wilshire Hotel indicated that our ride to the Rose Bowl would meet us at one-thirty. If you're a fan of old movies, the Wilshire is the hotel where Axel Foley gets a room in *Beverly Hills Cop*.

The packet had also contained room keys, lest we suffer the indignity of actually having to check into the hotel ourselves. It was only after a difficult struggle that we managed to haul our overnight bags up to our room without assistance. Good thing that we hadn't bothered to pack pajamas.

I could get used to this.

We got to the Rose Bowl at about a quarter to four, taking a bit over two hours to travel 24 miles. The driver said it was pretty normal for a big event, and it was a mystery to me why anyone would live here.

Security was like an airport where you weren't even allowed a carry-on. This did not go over well with the rich and famous, who apparently felt that they were simply unable to exist without handbags big enough to hold a complete set of golf clubs. The folks manning the entrances were polite but utterly inflexible. You got a clear little plastic bag and were told you could bring in whatever you wanted as long as it fit. If you put a purse in the bag, that was fine, but the purse would be opened and searched by hand.

I wondered what the president did with the "football" containing the nuclear launch codes, which is supposedly about the size of a large attaché case and weighs about 45 pounds. My guess is that they cut him some slack.

Once we got through security, there was food.

Everywhere.

Not only was the food omnipresent, it had two qualities I have never experienced at a sporting event of any kind.

First, it was free. Even the alcohol was free. Everyone got two drink tickets that were tied to their admissions (no giving unused tickets to your nearly drunk friends!). I never drink Scotch, but the bottles looked old. The margaritas were excellent. Emma had a couple glasses of wine and said it was phenomenal.

Second, and even more surprising, the food was as good as the drinks were. Beyond good, actually. It was fantastic. Giant tables piled with crab and shrimp. Mini quiches. Lettuce cups. Beignets with some kind of Caribbean seafood stuffing.

If you wanted more, there was the usual arena food as well. Pizza. *Hot* pizza. The dogs were made by Hebrew National, and they were charred on the outside like they're supposed to be. There were Reubens, piled high with pastrami. Italian sausages and lobster rolls. There were vegan and vegetarian selections as well, in which I had absolutely no interest.

And dessert. Giant ice cream bars where you made your own sundae with every flavor of ice cream you could think of (and many you probably couldn't think of). Every topping imaginable. Whole tables devoted to chocolate fondue, and the chocolate was the best I've ever had. And I've had a lot.

Once your drink tickets were gone, there were plenty of other beverages. Soft drinks, of course. A wide variety of freshly squeezed juices. And the coffee was awesome. As was the espresso. And the lattes. I needed to stop drinking them.

Jess MacMurray knew how to throw a party.

The press was out in force, with reporters everywhere. Their cameras, not surprisingly, were all small enough to fit into the little plastic bags.

I was recognized. Any time someone from the press saw me, he or she wanted to interview me. Always the same question, did I know who Factor Man was.

I told them all that it wasn't me, and that it wasn't Emma. But I was confident Factor Man was in the crowd, and they should just ask around.

Emma eventually pulled me aside and told me I was being an asshole, telling people to ask around in a crowd of a hundred thousand. After that, I went back to telling them that even if I did know, who was I to spoil a surprise that had been four years in the making?

Emma and I gradually made our way to our seats. They were good but not stellar – about the thirty-yard line and maybe forty rows up. I saw all the chairs on the field and wondered if they would be better or worse. Closer in, but maybe harder to see from. People gradually settled in around us, and we collectively waited for the main event.

Liu
11:00 AM

I got about five hours of sleep, which was sufficient. Preparation for the day was remarkably simple: Shower, dress, eat, and leave the hotel. My plastic gun was strapped to the inside of my thigh. In accordance with the instructions I had received with it, the gun was oriented parallel to my sides. Multiple tests had indicated that in this orientation, there was virtually no chance that the gun would be detected by a metal detector (obviously), full body scanner, or any of the other commercially available scanning systems deployed by the Americans.

If they searched me, it would be discovered. But I doubted that they would frisk everyone entering the Rose Bowl. I carried a small man bag, big enough for my passport, a phone and a spare battery. My two bullets fit snugly into the battery itself and could be removed by releasing a latch hidden in the side.

Li and I took an Uber to the Rose Bowl. We had to agree to a special "peak" rate of fifteen times the normal fare. Capitalism at its finest, I supposed. The driver dropped us and we separated so as to maximize the chance that at least one of us managed to get through security.

Security included full-body scanners, which we had fortunately anticipated, since a body scan would make it clear that I was a woman instead of a man. My small man bag also contained a pair of clip-on earrings and some bright red lipstick. While I waited in line between the scanners and the point where my ticket had been checked against my ID, I carefully put on the earrings and appeared to fix my lipstick. By the time it was my turn to be scanned, no one would doubt that I was a fashionably dressed Asian woman.

I cleared security easily and immediately made my way to the loo. I cleaned off the lipstick and discarded the earrings. I withdrew the bullets from the fake battery and loaded the gun, which I placed in my bag. My phone took its place on my thigh. The spare battery case followed the earrings into the trash.

As I exited the loo and made my way toward my seat on the field, I was disgusted by the display of American lavishness that surrounded me. The food and drink that was on display everywhere would feed a moderately sized Chinese village for a week, and I was confident that a significant percentage of it would simply be discarded when the event was over.

Factor Man
12:00 noon

The Langham Huntington Pasadena Hotel was, at least to our eyes, completely over the top.

For a start, we found ourselves with three rooms when we had checked in the previous night. One for Denise and me, one for our son Navarre, and one for our daughter Rachel. When the kids were little, we had traveled as often as we could and had generally been crammed into a single room with two queen beds. One of the kids would sleep on the floor, or on a sofabed, or they had shared a bed. No problem.

As they got older, we would get two rooms. Denise and I would share one, and Navarre and Rachel would share the other.

But three rooms was unheard-of opulence.

And the rooms themselves were just *nice*. The sheets and duvets were luxurious. The furnishings were a bit more Louis XVI than we were used to, but they, too, were stellar. The facilities were similarly elegant, 23-acre grounds that included everything from tennis courts to a multitude of restaurants.

For the first time in our lives, we used a hotel minibar.

Denise and I had talked quietly after we settled in for the night. She reminded me that I would do it all again. She reminded me that my goal all along had been to release the code with as little societal disruption as possible, and I appeared to be doing that. She reminded me that even if I wanted to change something, it was too late. And she reminded me that there were less than twenty-four hours left, and I should enjoy the ride.

And then she kissed me good night. I slept better than I expected.

After we got up on the day of FCOP, and before we headed down for breakfast, we told the kids. As we had expected, neither was surprised. We talked about the attack the previous day and how we hoped we were no longer in danger. We talked about the morality of science. They both understood.

Arguably the best thing about the Langham Huntington Pasadena, though, was that it was in, well, Pasadena. It was about five miles from the Rose Bowl. We left the hotel at a relaxed 2 PM and joined the mad rush to the stadium. We hadn't seen anyone watching over us at the hotel or as we started the drive, but I suspected they were there.

Security was as tight as I had hoped. Tighter, if anything. You went in with the clothes on your back, maybe a tiny purse, and that was it. Anything else got checked at the gate. The purses were searched by hand and without exception. People went through those circular scanners that you see at the airports, where apparently the people examining the images can basically see you naked. That was all just fine with me.

Once inside, I saw how completely Jess had outdone herself. The food and drink was all phenomenal. I was especially pleased by the fact that Jess had told me that anything left over at the end of the event would be donated to local shelters for either the homeless or battered women.

Perhaps most important, the people all seemed to actually be having fun. They were all talking, often clearly to other folks they had never met. Mostly idle speculation about the Chinese plane that had been shot down, or about the identity of Factor Man.

I participated in some of the speculation, suggesting that Factor Man was Bill Gates, and that the Chinese aircraft had in fact been a cleverly disguised drone sent by a jealous Elon Musk to wipe him out.

Denise eventually pulled me aside and told me I was being an asshole.

As the afternoon wore on, we found our way to our seats. The stage I had requested had been placed in the center of the field, but Jess had actually gone one better. Over the course of the afternoon, a variety of local bands played thirty-minute sets. They were all great, and they were all relatively unknown (until now). I wondered if Jess were paying them, or the other way around.

Hudson
2:17 PM

As far as I could tell, everything was going as smoothly as could be expected.

I was wandering somewhat aimlessly around the perimeter of the Rose Bowl, hoping to notice any lapses in security but also realizing that my effort to do so was probably fruitless. The security system would work or it wouldn't. If it didn't and there were bad actors trying to make their way in, we could only hope that they bumped into the security locations that were functioning properly instead of those that weren't.

It was basically the same principal that the TSA used everywhere. And although there were frightening statistics about how easy it was to get a gun, or a knife, or what have you through airport security, the bottom line was that there hadn't been a terrorist incident aboard a United States-flagged aircraft since 2001.

There were a variety of incidents at security, triggered in general by the fact that the rich and/or famous are all too often unwilling to either play by rules that have been designed for "other folk" or to part with any of their personal possessions for any reason.

The diplomats – and there were many – were more difficult still, and the worst incident I saw involved just such an individual. A Chinese man had initially demanded to be exempted from screening on the grounds that diplomatic immunity provided such an exemption.

The screener, in keeping with his training, told the man in question that while immunity meant that he did not have the right to screen him, that same immunity did not give the man the right to enter the facility, and such entry would be denied. The man then agreed to screening and the screener, in addition to the customary full-body scan, decided to pat the man down as well.

To this, he absolutely refused, taking his ticket back with the apparent intention of simply going elsewhere. At this point, the screener called over police officers and the man was detained. This is in keeping with the Vienna Convention on Diplomatic Relations, which is the general source for regulations involving diplomatic immunity. The Convention states that while a diplomat may not be arrested or detained, "reasonable constraints, however, may be applied in emergency circumstances involving self-defense, public safety, or the prevention of serious criminal acts." The man was required to forfeit his ticket and was then released.

His name was Li Qiang Wu. I touched my ear bud and asked that every other Chinese entrant be subjected to additional screening. After a few moments, I was told that there were 136 additional Chinese guests expected. Scrutinizing every one of them would doubtless make Sino-American tensions worse, but I figured the extra safety was worth it. I instructed that any future Chinese entrants be searched by hand, and only hoped that I had made the decision in time.

* * *

Shortly after four, I still hadn't heard back from any of the other security folks about suspicious Chinese attendees, and it bothered me. Something about the behavior of the Chinese diplomat had simply been wrong. I couldn't place it, but it nagged at me.

I eventually called in and was told that of the 136 Chinese nationals on the guest list, one had been denied entry (the diplomat Li Chiang Wu) and all but one of the rest had already passed through security. The one who hadn't had a relatively poor seat, high up and near one of the end zones. The sun would be at their back for the next couple of hours. Great spot for a sniper, although I couldn't imagine how anyone could get a rifle through security. I asked a few agents to check out the location while I rushed over myself.

The seat was empty. We asked the surrounding seat holders if any of them had seen the occupant of the seat in question, and no one had.

My earpiece chimed, and I was told that the last Chinese guest had just arrived. He had been checked by hand and did not appear to be a threat. It was five o'clock.

Li still nagged at me.

I asked how many of the 136 Chinese had arrived before I asked that the Chinese attendees be searched by hand. No one knew exactly when that request had been made.

I asked how many of them had arrived more than ten minutes after Li had and was told that the information wasn't stored that way. I told them to figure it out.

What seemed like an eternity later, I was told that seven Chinese guests had arrived before the hand searches had begun. Five men and two women. Janet Liu on my mind, I asked where the two women were sitting.

It was a little before six.

27

FACTOR MAN
5:50 PM

The last band finished up at about ten to six. They cleared everything off the stage and reset it with a microphone and the thirteen chairs I had requested. As I had asked, the chairs were arranged on three sides of a square, with the mic at the center of the empty edge.

We waited, as the stadium gradually hushed. After it quieted, I took Denise's hand.

"You ready?" I asked her.

"No," she said.

I released her hand, stood, and walked down the stairs toward the stage.

Burkett
5:50 PM

Emma and I were having too much fun to settle into our seats until shortly before six. Yes, I know there was live music. Yes, I know that every band has since become the hottest ticket in town. But what can I say? I like talking.

And the amazing thing is, you could talk to *anyone*. The president had a bit of a crowd around him, but Warren Buffett didn't. Robert Downey, Jr. didn't.

I'm not sure why. Maybe because such a ridiculous number of well-known people were there that no single one of them really stuck out. Maybe because the event truly wasn't about them; they were there for the same reason as everyone else.

So, for that one afternoon, everyone at FCOP was just that: at FCOP. Nothing more or less. Our troubles were all cast aside. We ate, we drank, and we were merry.

It was totally cool.

Some people found their seats early and listened to the bands. Some didn't. But starting around 5:30, everyone began trickling in to the stadium. There was the usual hubbub, a hundred thousand voices talking amongst each other. People were moving around but gradually settling. Every now and then, the crowd would quiet. Some portion would conclude that Factor Man was actually taking the stage, and their conversation would be reduced to whispers. The whispers would spread.

And then it would just be some guy confused about the shortest way to the bathroom, and the noise would pick back up.

And then, at 6:07, a guy about fifteen rows behind me stood up and started making his way down to the field.

I recognized him.

Game on.

Hudson
5:50 PM

The two Chinese women were sitting on nearly opposite sides of the stadium. I raced to one, who turned out to be an elderly woman accompanying her family. Other agents called me over the earbud to tell me that they had reached the other, an attractive woman traveling alone. I had them take a picture of the guest in question and text it to me.

The crowd suddenly quieted. Halfway around the stadium to my right, someone had stood up and was making his way toward the stage. I recognized him from the pictures I had seen of Factor Man's true identity.

The texted image arrived, and it wasn't anyone I recognized. If Janet Liu was in the audience, we couldn't find her.

I weighed my options.

I could cancel the event. The security team had discussed this in considerable detail before FCOP even began, and identified specific conditions that merited cancellation. None of those conditions had been met. We had agreed that both the risk and the sheer turmoil meant that cancellation would only be a response of last resort.

I could have the president removed to a safe location. That required the identification of a specific threat, and a gut feeling didn't qualify.

I could have agents surround Factor Man and escort him to the stage, but that seemed unlikely to matter. Yes, we had known Factor Man's identity for something over 24 hours. Yes, we had known where he was sitting.

But no one else had. So any threat would likely operate only after he took the stage.

There were two things I could do that seemed likely to be productive. I could find out where the last five Chinese guests were sitting, and I could make my way to the stage. Fastest would be to go around the inside of the stadium, so I began doing that while asking about the locations of the five not-yet-located guests.

Liu
5:50 PM

Li had texted me some three hours previously, indicating that he had failed to gain entry to the stadium. His ticket had been confiscated, but our reservations had been made separately and I had no specific reason to believe that our mission had been compromised. Li's text had come from a burner phone that we had left in our rental car for just this sort of a contingency.

I myself entered the stadium as early as appeared to be practical. I was not among the first guests to do so, but entered not long after the first of the bands began playing. I wandered around the stage area before taking my assigned seat, right in front of the stage as expected. I had little to do but wait.

This was America at its opulent worst. The food. The music. The *waste*.

But it was also, I had to concede, America at its best. This was the nation that had, for better or worse, owned the 20th century and defined the 21st. They had invented the car, the airplane, and the computer. They were unmannered and unrefined, but they were also, as every enemy from Britain to ISIS had discovered, a force to be reckoned with.

I have heard it said that for America, failure is not an option. That is not true. For China, failure is not an option.

For America, failure is not even a *consideration*.

I was surrounded by one hundred thousand people who embodied that view. It was, I must confess, unnerving.

I remained in my seat, looking like a Chinese man simply waiting, through one band performance after another. After the bands were done, I continued waiting as the stadium quieted in fits and starts.

At 6:07, the quiet became substantially more pronounced. About halfway up, a single figure had stood. He was gradually making his way down to the field and, eventually, to the stage.

I recognized him.

It was time.

28

Factor Man
6:07 PM

Everything got quiet as I headed down to the field. First just around me. But fairly quickly, the silence enveloped the whole stadium. Initially whispers, then almost pure silence.

People looked at me as I made my way down the stands and to the field. I would smile, and they would smile back. They would never smile first. Kinda weird.

I was wearing what I always wear. Jeans, sneakers, white socks. I normally wear a button-down shirt so that I have a pocket for my phone, but today, I had left my phone in the hotel room. So I got to wear a T-shirt.

I had my watch on my left wrist, and, of course, my wedding ring. On my right ring finger was the diamond ring I inherited when my father died during my junior year in college. I hoped he would have been proud of me.

I'm 65 but, by some generous twist of genetics, still have 20-20 distance vision. So no glasses.

I finally got to the stage; there was a stone-faced security guard standing at each corner and also one midway along each side. The stage itself had been laid out as I had requested: thirteen chairs arranged in three sides of a square, and a microphone on a stand with a podium at the center of the last side. Pretty Spartan, really.

Three steps led up to the mic. One of the police officers providing security came up to me; I gave him the special ticket I had printed out, and he let me head up the steps.

The mic and podium were arranged so that the U of chairs would be at my back as I spoke. I took the index card out of my pocket on which I had written my notes, which were really just a list of names.

I looked up at the crowd. I wondered who exactly was out there. The president, I knew that. But I didn't see him. Most of Hollywood, I expected. But those people never look the same in real life.

The crowd, meanwhile, looked at me.

As a businessman and as a scientist, I've given my share of presentations. I like talking in public, although this was obviously far and away the largest group I had ever addressed. But I find it hard to *start* talking in public. The key to a successful talk is to somehow connect with the audience, to let them know that you're talking to them. But at the beginning, that connection is missing.

You want it to be there. The audience wants it to be there. But until you start talking, it's just not there. What you say first really matters; it will establish the connection or it won't.

My mind was a blank.

Finally, I said the only thing I could really think of. I leaned over to the mic, and I said, "Hello."

Everyone, amazingly enough, laughed. The tension was broken. The connection was there. I smiled. This was going to be fun.

I leaned over and took the mic out of its stand. I can never talk without walking. A crowd of a hundred thousand in real life, or just one other person on the phone. If I'm talking, I have to be walking.

I stepped out from behind the podium.

"Good evening. Thank you all for coming."

Hudson
6:12 PM

The walkway and interior of the Rose Bowl were eerily deserted as I listened to Factor Man begin speaking. Even the concession stands were unattended; everyone had found a place where they could see the stage and listen. As I raced around the stadium, my earbud chimed.

"I'm sorry," I heard. "The guest list just wasn't stored that way. We found the Chinese guests, and now we've been going through it by hand, crossing out the ones who were frisked when they came in. We've got the five names left, and I can give you the locations."

"Go."

"Section 15, row 37."

"Where is that?"

"Where are you?"

I looked around. "Interior, section 16. I was heading to midfield."

"15 is one behind you. Row 37 is about halfway to the field. Seat 46."

Off I went. Everyone was still in their seats, so it was quick. I told the people in my ear that seat 46 was occupied by a kid who was surrounded by an American family.

"I know. Exchange student. Sorry."

"Nothing to apologize for. Who's next?"

"Family of three, across the stadium from you."

"Have someone else check them out. Fifth name?"

"Hang on. I'm working off a sheet of paper here, and it's smudged."

I made my way back to the interior corridor as I waited, once again heading toward midfield.

Factor Man
6:12 PM

I smiled. "Good evening," I began. "Thank you all for coming."

Everyone applauded. They applauded, and they stood.

I hadn't even really said anything yet. But they got it.

And for the first time, I think, so did I.

The $P=NP$ question had been pure science for me. It had been a puzzle, like every other scientific problem I've worked on. It had turned into other puzzles, like how to ensure that the technology benefited the world without messing up e-commerce and everything else. Like avoiding the Chinese so long ago in Vienna. Like keeping my identity a secret as things unfolded. I hadn't done so great at that. Figuring out how to monetize things so that I could retire or (what I really wanted), go back to Stanford and teach a little more before age overtook me and I really did retire.

But none of that mattered to the people in the Rose Bowl. For them, *P=NP* meant the first federal budget surplus in decades. It meant better drugs, and a more efficient transportation system.

I hadn't seen the forest for the trees. I had known it was there, of course. But the trees, the details, had overwhelmed me.

But these people, all they saw was the forest. All they saw was the good that the technology could do. That it was already doing.

It was good that they applauded for a little while, and gave me a chance to figure all of this out. To catch up with myself, as it were.

I did the "calm down" gesture that speakers sometimes give when they are ready to talk. Everyone sat back down.

"I know why you're here. To my mind, this is really a press conference. You have questions, and I want to answer them. I'll answer them until they turn out the lights. But first, there are some things I'd like to say. Please stay in your seats until I've had a chance to say them."

As I had requested, people began bringing portable microphones down, setting them up in the aisles.

"First, there are a lot of people who made everything I've done possible. And I'm sorry, but before we go on, I really need to introduce them to you.

"Number one is my wife, Denise. She is, quite simply, the finest person I have ever known. She has a transcendent clarity and a profound faith at which I can only marvel. She's smart, and she doesn't end sentences with prepositions. We've been married for over thirty years, and she's been a role model to me every day of those thirty years.

"And not only is she the most beautiful person I know on the inside, which is the most important, she's the most beautiful person I know on the outside which, as her husband, is a bonus.

"Denise, I know you hate the spotlight. But just this once, would you do me a favor and join me on stage?"

I waited and watched her walk down from our seats, as beautiful as the day I had married her. The crowd applauded and stood again. Denise deserved every bit of it. As she came on stage, we exchanged a hug and a kiss (to more embarrassing applause), and she sat down.

"Next, my kids, Navarre and Rachel.

"Thank you for putting up with such an imperfect parent. I expect that there are no perfect parents, try though we all may. But I have often thought that my flaws ran deeper than most, and thank you, thank you for tolerating them.

"I want you to know how proud I am of both of you. How amazed I am at the man and woman that you have become. You're both awesome.

"And, as I'm sure you realize, today is the best Mr. Gizmo story ever.

"Please. Come and join me."

I waited and the crowd applauded as my two wonderful kids came up to the stage.

"I also want to introduce some people that you know. The first of them is William Burkett.

"Most all of you know who he is, I expect. He's a journalist working for the *New York Times* and, when I realized what my future was likely to hold, he was the first person I reached out to in an attempt to manage it.

"Not only is Wilbur a journalist, he's a good journalist. And not only is he a good journalist, he's a good journalist whom I trust.

"Wilbur, thanks for your help. Please come up and take a seat.

As the applause died down, I continued. Wilbur arrived on stage a few minutes later.

"Next, Jess MacMurray.

"If you've had a good time today, Jess gets the credit. As I expect you all know, she arranged today's event. She arranged the food, and the bands, and picked the venue, and basically took care of everything. She helped me figure out a way to come anonymously, and took care of that. Every detail, from cars to planes to hotels to everything else. She's amazing.

"And you need to stop calling her Pepper Potts.

"Pepper – I'm sorry, Jess – would you be good enough to join us?"

She came up, gave me a hug, and sat down. It was the first time that the two of us had ever met, or even spoken.

"Lastly, I have a lawyer. It's America, so everyone has a lawyer. I can tell you without qualification that mine is fantastic. Because of Bob's ability to convert my wishes into a contract, about two hundred billion dollars' worth of securities are about to transfer into my name. And because of Bob, I haven't owed a nickel in taxes. Until now.

"I also have friends. Two are business partners as well, and I am truly blessed that these two guys have been willing to share their professional lives with me.

"David Etherington has founded two companies and a research lab with me. David, I hope you've enjoyed the last twenty-five or so years as much as I have. Come on up.

"And Dennis Capovilla. You make my job fun and interesting, every day. You keep your eye on the ball (and on the women), every day. You make coming to work a delight. Please, join us.

"Tim Johnson, my pastor and my friend …"

Burkett
6:15 PM

Factor Man reached the stage and began talking. I recognized him, of course, and Emma and I listened in amusement first, and amazement second.

"I also want to introduce some people that you know, people who have made all of this possible. The first of them is William Burkett."

I wondered if there was another William Burkett in the house. Emma grabbed my shoulder and grinned while Factor Man continued.

"Wilbur, thanks for your help. Please come up and take a seat."

And so I did.

I followed the same path Factor Man and his family had taken to the stage, and Factor Man himself and I exchanged a high five and a quick hug. And then I had certainly not the most momentous, but definitely the most public decision of my life. There were ten seats left.

If I picked one next to Factor Man's family (who had sat as close to Factor Man as possible), I would look like a sheep following the herd. If I picked one across the stage from them, I would look like an angry individualistic reporter.

And if I continued standing there thinking, I would look like a dork.

I eventually compromised, sitting on the bar that was the base of the U, facing Factor Man and the audience behind him.

One of them, an Asian man with arguably the best seat in the house, looked familiar. But I couldn't place him.

Factor Man continued.

"And Dennis Capovilla. You make my job fun and interesting, every day. You keep your eye on the ball (and on the women) …"

That was it. The Chinese man across the stage from me wasn't a man at all. It was a woman. In fact, it was Janet Liu, the woman from the coffee shop in Austin. I would recognize those cheekbones anywhere.

I had no idea what to do.

I could make a scene. I could jump up and explain that the guy across the stage from me was in fact a Chinese woman wanted by the FBI, although I had no idea what for.

I didn't know how that would work out, but I suspected that it was probably not my best option.

Or, I could call John Hudson.

That seemed like it was probably better.

A hundred thousand people had paid a ton of money each to watch Factor Man say what he was currently saying. Those hundred thousand people were also watching the seven of us now on stage.

Every single one of them would see me take my cell phone out of my pocket and make a call.

Emma, who already gave me plenty of grief about the extent to which I was welded to my phone, would also see me make a call. Justified or otherwise, she would ride me about it for the rest of our days.

I took out the phone and dialed.

Factor Man
6:18 PM

As Dennis made his way to the stage, I continued.

"Tim Johnson, my pastor and my friend. Also the most flagrantly optimistic man I have ever known. A man whose goal in life is to run a church that truly welcomes everyone. From the most upstanding citizen – not me, I point out – to the street bum. A church that discriminates against no one, judges no one, and truly is what God intended. Tim, come on up.

"Brian Finn. I've started four businesses in my life, including this Factor Man stuff, and you've actually invested in all of them. I think it's fair to say that you are one of the kindest, wisest people I know. I've turned to you many times over the years for counsel and advice, and you have never disappointed.

"There are three more people who have contributed profoundly to who I am, even though I've never met any of them.

"Mark Cuban. Of my four ventures, Mark has been involved with two. Once he decides you aren't an idiot, he's helpful, and he's very smart. Until he decides you aren't an idiot, not quite so much. I'm glad he thinks well of me, although not well enough to accept any of my various suggestions that we get together for a drink. Mark, I hope you're here, and maybe that drink will work out now after all.

"Kate Jackson. In 1976, Kate was one of the original Charlie's Angels, and I was a graduate student in physics at Cal Tech. I was absolutely miserable, and I wrote her a fan letter.

"She wrote back.

"Kate, that letter saved my life. I can't tell you how many times your note was, for me, the light of Eärendil, a light in dark places when all other lights had gone out. It really did. It saved my life, and I still have it. Thank you.

"One more. Robert Downey, Jr. Iron Man. You showed the world that a mad scientist could have a soul, make a difference, and have a blast doing it. Your portrayal of Iron Man was, in many ways, the genesis of the project that became Factor Man.

"I have no idea if you're here, but I hope you are, and I hope you'll join the rest of us on stage."

Downey was indeed in attendance. We exchanged a hug and he waved to the crowd before taking the last chair.

"That's all of my stuff. I know you've got a lot of questions, and I'm here to answer them. Two of your questions I already know.

"First …"

And then the strangest thing happened. William Burkett attacked me.

29

My cell phone buzzed, and I looked at the display. My pal William Burkett, to my great surprise. I answered it as I hustled around the stadium to find the quickest way to the stage. "Hudson."

"John. It's William Burkett."

I hadn't seen the stage in the past few minutes, but I knew Burkett had been called up. "William? Are you kidding me?"

"John, listen. No, I'm not kidding you. Janet Liu is in the first row of the audience."

Things began to make sense. I asked Burkett if he was sure, but I already knew the answer.

"Sure sure? No. But there's a guy in the front row who absolutely shares her facial features."

I told him I was on my way down and asked that he try not to do anything stupid. Then my earbud chimed, and I disconnected to listen.

"We found him, sir. Ma Yong Feng. Section F-19, row 1."

"Where is that exactly?"

"I'm looking at a seating map, sir. There is no section F-19."

I thought for a moment. "It's the field. The F stands for field. Where is section 19?"

"It's on the side you're on. Right in the middle."

"Did Feng pass through security?"

"Yes, sir. We aren't allowed to keep the images, but I'm seeing it as a clean scan."

I breathed a little easier. That meant no weapon. Assuming that Feng was in fact Janet Liu, there was no way she could have gotten anything through security. And given the pre-event scrutiny the Rose Bowl had seen, I couldn't imagine that she could have retrieved a cached weapon after arriving.

"Okay," I finally said. "First, call the service. Let them know that I believe we have a Chinese operative in the front row facing the stage." I didn't think there was any possible threat to the president, but the Secret Service still needed to be alerted.

The stage was already surrounded by agents who had been trained for exactly this sort of eventuality. "Assuming the scan was clean," I continued, "I think we're ok. Let's try not to create a scene involving the FBI and a Chinese citizen on international television. I'm on my way down there now."

Liu
6:18 PM

I had watched the terrorist who called himself Factor Man take the stage.

"Terrorist" is the only correct word. China has existed for millennia. It predates Christ. And in that time, it has led the world in arts, in science, in culture. Its people have prospered. The structured nature of our society has been the root of all of those accomplishments.

Factor Man's technology puts that structure in jeopardy. It puts our very way of life in jeopardy. And Factor Man does this essentially by force, against our wishes and without consulting us.

He is a terrorist.

I listened to his prepared remarks. I heard the crowd laugh at his apparent jokes.

And I waited.

I recognized him. I recognized him from Vienna, and from the video that had confirmed his identity before the two previous attempts to disrupt his plans.

Grey hair. Looking younger than his reported age. Taking the steps onto the stage two at a time, standing straight. Happy and excited.

Terrorists usually are.

I withdrew the gun from my bag and placed it on my lap, covered by the bag itself. I had two shots.

Security at the event had been better than I expected. Eight armed officers surrounded the stage from which Factor Man was speaking. I watched the eyes of the eight, and they never stopped moving. They were all well-trained and attentive.

I was in a front row seat on one side of the stage, and we had anticipated that Li would be seated across from me, armed with his own version of the 3-D gun that I now held. If one of us had drawn a weapon, the distraction would have helped the other. But Li had been caught up in security.

I waited as Factor Man droned on. All I needed to do was to ensure that I stopped him before he made whatever announcement he intended. He seemed far too busy talking about himself for such an announcement to be imminent.

So I waited.

And then, an opportunity presented itself. One of the workers setting up the microphones to be used by the audience around the stage stumbled. He was slightly to my right, and all of the security guards who could see me were momentarily distracted.

I moved the man bag, stood as I raised my gun, and fired my two shots.

30

BURKETT
6:21 PM

When I was a freshman in high school, I was small and I was slow. The fast kids in high school could outrun me *running backwards*.

So I joined the football team.

I know now that this made no sense. But if you think about it, not many of the decisions you make in high school do make sense. This particular choice was neither the best nor the worst of my high school years.

If you're small and fast, you can be either a running back or a pass receiver. Sort of depends on whether you've got good hands. I had lousy hands, to match the rest of my physical abilities. But the freshman coach, ever the optimist, tried me in both positions, and it was a disaster.

If you're slow but large, they make you a lineman. Coach Kramer tried that, too.

The results were marginally better. I was the defensive lineman who was supposed to follow the play and do something useful.

Most of the time, "useful" turned out to mean getting knocked on my butt by a much larger offensive lineman. But every once in a while, the offensive linemen would take the apparently prudent course of ignoring me in favor of my larger counterparts, and it turned out, to everyone's surprise, that I could actually make a pretty good hit.

By the time I graduated to JV in my sophomore year, the running backs were bigger and even that possibility deserted me. I gave up football and joined the journalism club. You know where that led.

I'll get back to all of this in a moment.

Hudson told me not to do anything stupid, and hung up. I figured that was good advice.

The stage gradually filled up. Last on Factor Man's list of special guests was Robert Downey, Jr., which I thought was a cute touch.

The more I watched the person I suspected of being Janet Liu, the more convinced I became. She – assuming, of course, that it actually was a she – was too still. Hands in lap, one on top of a small man bag and one underneath it. Never moving. I glanced around at some of the other front row audience members; they were generally still but certainly fidgeting about the amount you'd expect. Repositioning in their chairs, what have you. Liu never budged.

The staff was setting up mics all around the stadium so that people could ask their questions. Hundreds of them. I ignored them, just watching the unmoving Liu.

Then, all of a sudden, she was moving. Time stopped.

I listened backward, you know how you can do that, and realized that there had been a little bit of a commotion off to Liu's right, my left.

Liu's man bag moved. Under it, her other hand was holding what looked – no way – like a gun of some sort.

Factor Man kept talking. "I know you've got a lot of questions …" His wandering around the stage had brought him to just a few feet in front of me.

Liu stood. The hand with gun began to come up.

And I did what I had been trained to do.

I tackled Factor Man.

Hudson
6:21 PM

I continued racing toward the stage, my only weapon a government-issued Glock 23. Absolutely not the weapon of choice in a crowded stadium, I realized.

As I was passing one of the guys bringing a couple of mics down, I stopped him. I showed him my badge. "FBI," I said. "I need the mics." Puzzled, he shrugged and gave them to me, then headed back up to get a couple more.

I carried the mics toward the stage, still far too distant for my liking. People kept getting invited up as the chairs filled. Mark Cuban. Kate Jackson, an elderly but stately woman who took a while to make it up to the stage.

Two seats left. I was close enough to pick out Burkett among the people seated on stage.

Robert Downey, Jr. He was just sitting down as I came up the center aisle.

Yes, there was a Chinese national in the front row. An individual with short hair, definitely dressed as a man.

It was easier to picture Liu with short hair than the other way around. Yes, that was what she would look like.

The Chinese man was also just *wrong*. If you're an agent for long enough, you get a feel for it. He was too still, somehow waiting.

I dropped one of the two mics I was carrying, trying to distract him. He glanced at me, but no more.

It seemed unnatural. All of the other nearby audience members had turned to look at me. The security guards around the stage had turned to look at me. Assuming that the Chinese "man" was indeed Liu, she had done nothing more than glance.

I began moving toward her more quickly. The mic and stand that I was still carrying would be reasonably effective, but the Glock would be faster and obviously had more stopping power. It would also magnify the risk for the crowd exponentially, and my guess was that the mic stand would be plenty against whatever Liu had managed to get through security – presumably a knife or other hand weapon.

So I left my Glock in its holster, and I brought the mic and stand to my side to extend my reach. Factor Man was speaking with his back to both of us, facing Burkett and with Liu behind him. He didn't even appear to be aware of what was going on.

Then, to my dismay, Liu stood and raised what appeared to be a gun. Burkett leaped from his chair and tackled Factor Man to the ground. I swung the mic as Liu took two shots.

Factor Man
6:27 PM

I said, "That's all of my stuff. I know you've got a lot of questions, and I'm here to answer them. Two of your questions I already know.

"First …"

And then William Burkett knocked me to the ground as I heard what appeared to be two gunshots behind me.

I had no idea what had happened. If Denise had been shot, or the kids.

An eternity passed until Burkett got off me and I scrambled somewhat awkwardly to my feet behind him. He held up his hands in a sort of "peace" gesture, and said, "Sorry."

I didn't care. I pushed Wilbur aside and ran to my family, touching each of them and confirming that they were all ok. They looked at me fairly incredulously as security agents jumped onto the stage and asked everyone to stay in their seats. A man who appeared to have been wielding one of the microphone stands as a weapon produced FBI credentials and security backed away from him. He spoke into one of those earpiece headphones like the Secret Service wears, saying, "No, I think we're good. I deflected the shots into the ground. It appears to have been a sole actor. No casualties on the stage."

Security handcuffed a Chinese man. I remembered him; he had been in the front row, sitting very still. He produced a diplomatic passport, but the FBI agent simply took it, looked at it and handed it to an associate. "This passport is for a man, Ms. Liu. How embarrassing would you like this to be?" The objections stopped and the Chinese man (woman?) was led away, wrists behind his or her back.

The agent came up to me and shook my hand. He introduced himself. "Special Agent John Hudson, FBI."

I started to return the introduction, but caught myself and smiled. "Factor Man," I responded.

Hudson put his hand on my shoulder reassuringly as he looked at the agents surrounding everyone else on stage. They nodded at each other. "Do me a favor," he said. "We've got this. We do. The biggest thing you can do to help is pick up right where you left off. Let's keep this whole thing as contained as possible."

I looked around. Hudson was right. The crowd had leaped to their collective feet when Burkett had tackled me onstage, and they were now growing increasingly restless.

I asked Burkett to return to his seat, and he did. I told Hudson, "In a minute," and checked in with my family. Rachel nodded at me; she was fine. Navarre just shrugged. Denise, my rock, smiled and said that the show had to go on.

I turned back to the crowd and picked up the microphone as they quieted and slowly sat down. "OK," I said. "Maybe I know *three* of your questions. Don't worry; there'll be time for all the ones I don't know, too.

"First, I have no idea what that was about. We'll presumably find out together in tomorrow's paper.

"Second. The Apple CEO's password is 'Rainbeau.' Capital-R, a, i, n, b, e, a, u. It's kind of sweet, really. You can use that to decrypt the code I posted back in March. It'll be in exactly the same form as what I gave to Apple and to the government. With great power comes great responsibility, so use it well.

"And one last thing.

"My name is Montgomery Grimes, and I am Factor Man."

Epilogue

BURKETT

In the end, some things came out like everyone had expected and some didn't.

E-commerce turned out to be just fine. The credit card companies arranged for every transaction to use a different card number, and when you sent that number to an e-tailer, they could decode the number faster than Factor Man's code could factor the public key. So the transaction went through and the card number could never be used again.

Secrets, however, did become something of a thing of the past. There were no more anonymous bloggers. No anonymous comments on other people's blogs. The world seemed a better place for it. If you wanted to keep a message a secret, you had to just write it down on a piece of paper and send it.

China remained China, her people and institutions far more stable than even her leadership had realized.

Having $200 billion changes your life, but apparently much less than you'd imagine. Factor Man was interviewed often, and commented that he still couldn't buy happiness, but with Denise at his side, that was a purchase he really didn't need to make. He was more interested in buying youth, but that didn't turn out to be for sale, either. Most of the money just went to charity.

He got that faculty job at Stanford.

As far as the technology itself, the most important use turned out to be nanotech. Not unlike drug design, nanotech involved a limited number of basic operations that could be used to make microscopic objects in a variety of shapes. Given a target shape, the Factor Man technology could be used to identify the steps needed to produce it. Computers became smaller; no one needed anything bigger than a cell phone any more. Nanoparticles delivered drugs to tumors, and it was clear that cancer would soon be a thing of the past. It turned out that Factor Man had been right in that very first blog post: People were healthier, the poorest among us were significantly less poor, and the efficiencies offered by his technology touched the lives of each of us.

Emma and I got married on schedule, long enough after FCOP that the press pretty much left us alone. We added Factor Man to the guest list but he passed, saying he was afraid his presence would make the wedding more about him than about us.

And then he showed up anyway. It turns out privacy is one of the few things money actually can buy. He and Denise simply appeared in the back of the congregation as the ceremony was beginning. Their wedding gift was a framed copy of "Take Me Out to the Ballgame," along with a pair of tickets to the 1908 Cubs game where the song was introduced.

Emma and I kept our jobs, because the world continued to need investigative reporters.

And literary agents.

Fiction and non-fiction, together forever.

Acknowledgments

William Burkett and Emma Hardaway are made up, but pretty much everyone else in this book is real. Well, the good people are real. The bad guys are pretty much made up, too.

To these folks who have been kind enough to let me use their names and likenesses, my thanks. I've tried to paint each of you as you really are, so please forgive me if I've gotten something wrong.

Some folks didn't make the editorial cut; as my readers kept telling me, FCOP was not the Academy Awards. Stuart Meyer, Larry Gordon, Mike Genesereth, Ethan Coven and Dana Delany: I think the world of all of you. But there were already arguably too many chairs on the Factor Man stage.

Scott Aaronson and Steven Rudich: I am pleased that this book has strengthened my relationship with each of you. I've done my best throughout to keep the science accurate. I know that there are compromises here and there, but they are infrequent and should not detract from the overall impression a reader will get of complexity theory, computer science, and the P vs. NP question generally.

For roughly the reasons given by Montgomery Grimes at the beginning of the book, I really do believe that $P=NP$. Montgomery Grimes itself was an alias I used for a mystery radio show during my undergraduate days at Wesleyan University.

John Hudson is modeled after an FBI agent whom I've known for many years but who asked that I not use his real last name. John, thanks for reading an early version of *Factor Man* and for giving me your insightful comments.

Amy Rogers's name appears only here in the acknowledgments, but she has touched every page. Amy, many thanks to both you and to ScienceThrillers Media. Julian Green also provided many useful editorial suggestions.

Some people who do appear are given somewhat short shrift. Dennis Capovilla has complained incessantly about the fact that he doesn't have a larger part; I guess that triggering the chain of events that saves the world isn't good enough.

As I explained from the Rose Bowl stage, my children are awesome. My daughter Skyelar asked that I not use her real name, and I obliged. My son asked that I not use his real name, either, saying that he preferred to be called "Megatron: Destroyer of Worlds." That was not a request that I felt I could honor. Sorry about that, Navarre.

The things I say about my wife do not even scratch the surface of who she is. Every page could be filled with her, and it would not be remotely enough. Pamela, thank you for being who you are, for inspiring me to do so many things, and for putting up with me as I try to do them.

Finally, my thanks to you, the reader. It turns out that writing is fun, so thank you for letting me do it! And if you've managed to enjoy the result, and perhaps learned a little bit of computer science along the way, so much the better.

Matt Ginsberg
July, 2017

About the Author

Matt Ginsberg got a doctorate in astrophysics from Oxford when he was 24. He quickly came to his senses, however, switching to artificial intelligence and teaching at Stanford for a decade. He's been on the front page of the *New York Times* and, surprisingly, was happy about it. He's been a political columnist and published playwright, and constructs crosswords for the *Times*. He has written about a hundred technical papers. And one novel.

MattGinsberg.com